BADD BUSINESS

A BADD BROTHERS NOVEL

Jasinda Wilder

BADD
BUSINESS

ONE

Remington

HOLY MOTHER OF SHIT.

I didn't dare let go of her, or she'd hit the ground. My reflexes had kicked into gear before I even realized what was going on, and in a matter of a few seconds my world got turned upside down. We had accidentally bumped into each other in a hospital hallway and she went flying. It might have been the best bit of serendipity I've ever experienced.

Oh, man. Now that I had my hands on this girl, there was no way I was letting go. I was not giving up the juicy handful of her soft, squishy ass, or the up close and personal look at her big, wide, soulful, startled brown eyes. And no way was I walking away from that cleavage spilling out of her top.

She was just staring up at me, her big brown eyes fixed on mine, staring into me, through me. It was almost as if she couldn't believe I was real, and that this was happening.

But trust me, honey, I'm real, and this *is* happening.

"Hi…" Her voice was low and musical. "Thanks," she breathed softly, "I'm Juneau." And with that she regained her balance and stood up in the middle of the hospital corridor.

Juneau?

Yet her name fit her perfectly. She was clearly Native American…or Native Alaskan, more accurately. I knew enough about northern cultures to know there were several different ethnic groups, but I couldn't even begin to guess whether she was Eskimo, Inuit, or Aleut. I didn't understand the differences between these groups—I just knew enough to know that I knew nothing.

The point was, this girl was a vision of exotic sensuality. As she stood before me I could see that her flawless skin was a dark olive, and her hair was a glossy black, and thick and braided down her back. She was almost a full foot shorter than me, standing maybe five feet four and she had absolutely stunning curves.

Eye-popping, mouth-watering, cock-hardening curves.

She was something else.

God, what was wrong with me? I was still standing there, staring at her like a love-struck teenager.

I laughed at myself, a rumble of amusement at my idiotic inability to stop drooling over this chick. I had to take control.

But all I could manage was, "Hi, I'm Remington."

She just stared up at me, those liquid chocolate eyes blinking at me, her mouth open in an absolutely adorable little O. Gahh...that lower lip. Pouty. Full. Kissable. Biteable.

I moved aside before I actually did bite and kiss the lower lip of a random stranger in a hospital hallway. People tend to frown on that.

Although, the way she was still staring at me had me wondering if maybe she wouldn't mind all that much.

"Remington," she breathed, not taking her eyes off me. "Hi, Remington. I'm Juneau."

I laughed again. "Yeah, I know—you just told me."

Considering her olive complexion it was hard to tell, but I had a feeling she was blushing. "Oh. You're right. Yeah. Sorry."

"Don't be sorry," I told her. "With a cool-ass

name like Juneau, I'd be saying it a lot too."

Could I sound any more idiotic? I think my IQ just dropped to room temperature.

"Remington is a cool name, too."

Guess I wasn't the only one fumbling for something to say.

Juneau and I seemed to be at the end of our conversational repartee when we both heard someone break our reverie.

"Wow," said a female voice, amused and mocking. "You two…are not cool. Like, not at all."

I glanced at the speaker, and was immediately reminded of what my brother, Roman, said the first day we walked into Badd's Bar and Grill in Ketchikan and saw all the beautiful women: *Seriously, what the FUCK is in the water up here?*

A good question.

There had to be something in the air or the water up here, because the women were fucking ridiculously gorgeous. And this girl, this sassy redhead who was mouthing us off was no exception. She was, in a word, stunning. I couldn't believe I had two gorgeous women standing in front of me. If I weren't already halfway to the altar with Juneau, I'd be salivating over this goddess; she was tall—five-seven or -eight—with strawberry blonde hair and creamy, freckled skin to go with it. I took in her mammoth tits, tight waist, and popping booty. Her green eyes sparkled with fire, telling me she knew that she had it going on, and I knew getting this girl into bed would be taking a tiger by the tail.

Juneau spoke up, shooting the redhead an eye roll, "Be nice, Izzy."

"I *am* being nice. It's just that you two are so adorably lame as hell."

I narrowed my eyes at the redhead—Izzy. "First, let me introduce myself. I'm Remington. I'm gonna have to agree with Juneau, here. You should be nice."

Her eyes raked me over blatantly. "Uh-huh. I'll be nice if you take off your shirt."

"You first," I said.

"Wouldn't you like that?" she said, flipping her long, wavy copper hair over her shoulder.

I shrugged. "I mean, if we're taking off our shirts, I'd rather *you* start," I said to Juneau with a grin.

"No one is taking off their shirt," Juneau said with a sigh that spoke of long-suffering familiarity with Izzy's antics. "Not Izzy, not you, and certainly not me."

"Hell, if it gets me a gander at his abs, I'll take my top off in a New York minute," Izzy said.

Juneau groaned. "You know, sadly, I think you'd actually do it."

Izzy just smirked. "You know it, babe." She eyed

me. "So. Do we have a deal?"

How the hell had I gotten myself into this? As much as I'd appreciate seeing anyone's tits—because tits are the best—I'd much rather see Juneau's.

Izzy's were definitely on display, framed by an expensive-looking white silk shirt with a plunging neckline, hints of a white lace bra peeking out—intentionally, I assumed.

Juneau wasn't going out of her way to display her assets and, in a way, that was way sexier to me. There was just something about Juneau that kept pulling my gaze to her.

She was wearing a black ankle-length skirt that hugged her hips and ass and thighs before loosening to drift airily around her feet, a black T-shirt underneath an open-front green, white, and black zigzag patterned sweater. The T-shirt clung to and emphasized her plump, perky, round breasts while hardly revealing any skin at all. Her black braid hung over her left shoulder, and she reached up to twist the end of it as she and I once more locked stares.

She tugged the edges of her sweater closer together, and then crossed her arms over her breasts.

Was I staring? Yes.

Definitely staring.

But then, she was staring back—at my arms.

Which, I admit, were pretty nicely showcased by

the tight, plain white T-shirt I was wearing.

"Well, this is a riveting conversation," Izzy said, her tone dripping sarcasm, pulling both my gaze and Juneau's back to her. "Remington, since you are not going to answer my questions, could you please tell Kitty we're here to see her?"

"Kitty?" I asked, momentarily blanking.

"Yeah, Kitty. 'bout my height, light brown hair, big boobs, dating your brother?" She looked at me as if I was a mouth-breathing caveman, which to be fair, I *was* kind of acting like. "Our best friend and roommate?"

"Oh, right. Kitty." I shook my head. "Kitty— yeah. She's in there." I jerked my thumb at the closed hospital door behind me.

Izzy closed her eyes and sighed, and then spoke as if dealing with someone particularly slow on the uptake. "I *know*, Remington. That's why we're here. Juneau and I flew down from Ketchikan to support her. We just arrived here in Seattle and we want *you* to go in *there* and tell *Kitty* we're out *here*."

"Why?" I was not normally this slow or stupid but, for some reason, Juneau seemed to have turned me into a moron.

"Because she's our friend and we want to see her?" Izzy replied, enunciating each word slowly and clearly.

The message finally arrived. I blinked at her for a moment, and then turned around, opened the door, and said to the assembled visitors: "Kitty! Your friends are here." I leaned against the doorframe. "This is Juneau, the nice one, and this is Isabel, the mouthy one."

"I'm not mouthy, I'm opinionated," Izzy said, primly. "And my name is Isadora, not Isabel."

"Right, Isabel," I said, getting it wrong just to annoy her.

She clearly wasn't going to be baited. She just snorted, rolling her eyes and shaking her head. "You can have this one, Juneau. He's a little dense for my taste. I like my men to be able to talk *and* breathe at the same time."

"Fine by me," I shot back. "Because I like my women without inflatable boobs."

She cupped the body parts in question and shook them at me; they jiggled in such a way that made it clear they were all natural. "Does it look like they're inflatable, you big dumb moose?"

"They look one hundred percent real to me," I heard Ramsey say from just inside the room. "You're welcome to bring them in here and shake them at me if you want…Isadora."

She stuck her tongue out at me. "I think I will, thank you. At least *someone* around here has manners."

I heard my brother Roman bark a laugh from inside the hospital room. "If you think Ramsey has manners, you're in for a rude surprise, sweetheart. He makes the rest of us look civilized."

"Izzy, seriously, do have to cause trouble literally everywhere you go?" That was Kitty, chastising her friend with a sigh.

"Yes, I do. It's my trademark." And with that Izzy flounced into the hospital room, shooting daggers at me over her shoulder.

"God, Izzy, you're such a problem," Juneau said, but I could tell it was meant with love.

Juneau shot me a look and said quietly, "She's sensitive about her boobs. People think they're fake all the time, and it pisses her off."

I let my gaze wander down Juneau's chest. "I bet you get the same thing."

She ducked her head with a sharp laugh. "Yeah… not so much."

"No?"

"Ha—nice try, Remington, but I'm not buying your backhanded flattery. If you're trying to impress me, that's not the way to go about it."

"Sorry. But, honestly, I'm basically telling you your tits are perfect. I mean, that's why women get implants, right? To try and make their boobs look as close to perfect as possible?"

She tilted her head and eyed me with a puzzled frown. "Um, I guess I can see where you are coming from, but it only works if my boobs actually look like they could be fake. Izzy's do. Mine? Not so much."

I shrugged. "I don't know—I think they do. They're big, they're round, they're perky."

She frowned. "Um. Thanks? But why are we talking about my breasts?"

I grinned. "Because they're beautiful. Just like the rest of you."

Again, I had the feeling she was blushing, but before I could say anything more, she turned toward the door.

"Thanks," she murmured, "well, um…I'm going to say hi to Kitty and Mr. Badd."

A nurse bustled between us and entered the room at that moment. "Excuse me, there are *way* too many people in this room," she said, making a shooing motion with her hands. "Immediate family only. Mr. Badd has just suffered a terrible car accident. He's injured, and he needs his rest."

"Kitty *is* family," I heard Roman growl. "She's staying with me and my brothers."

I could see the nurse going pale at the warning tone in Roman's voice. "Um. I'm sorry, but your father really needs his rest. I must insist you all come back during visiting hours."

As everyone said their goodbyes and slowly exited the room I turned to Juneau. "Well, there goes that plan," I said. "Wanna go get a cup of shitty hospital coffee with me?"

"Mmmm, shitty coffee," she said, faking enthusiasm. "You really know the way to a girl's heart."

"Maybe it's not your heart I'm trying to get into." Jesus, why did I say that? That's a line Roman would use and I'm usually not as uncouth as he is. What's wrong with me all of a sudden?

Juneau just rolled her eyes at me—it's actually kind of amazing how many different kinds of expression she could pack into one look; so far, she'd given an irritated eye roll, a frustrated eye roll, an amused eye roll, and now this one—a bit of all three, along with a dash of…I don't know. Thinly disguised attraction? There's something there, I can tell. She was irritated at my admittedly inappropriate innuendo, but she didn't slap me, or walk away.

Yet.

Give it time, and she might. In my experience, women have three ways of dealing with us Badd boys when we're being dicks: we either get slapped, or they walk away, or we fuck.

And sometimes, all three.

Please god, all three. Or just the third.

"Well, regardless of where else you may be trying

to get, shitty coffee isn't going to open the door." She patted me on the shoulder. "Just a word of unsolicited advice."

I laughed. "Yeah, probably not." I leaned closer so I was towering over her, smirking down at her; I was giving her my best smirk, the one that always drops the panties. "How about I promise you shitty coffee now, and really great coffee in the morning?"

She frowned at me. "In the morning?"

I lifted an eyebrow suggestively. "Yeah. I make a mean pot of coffee."

She closed her eyes as she arrived at the realization of what I was suggesting. "Oh. Ahh…Yeah. I see." She moved past me, walking away down the hallway. "That's gonna be a no. But thanks for the oh-so-romantic offer…I think."

"I wasn't trying to be romantic, Juneau," I said, catching up.

"Was that your idea of a pickup line?"

"Which part?"

She waved behind us. "The whole thing. Flirting with me. Offering to make me coffee in the morning, suggesting I spend the night the night with you. Admitting you're not trying to be romantic. Shall I go on?"

"I dunno," I said. "I guess it's only a pickup line if it works." I grinned at her. "So, seeing as you haven't told me to fuck off yet, I guess I'd say…yeah, it's my idea of a pickup line."

"Would you listen if I did tell you to go away?"

"Not right away. Like your friend with the attitude said, I'm a little slow on the uptake."

"Don't mind Izzy. Her bark is worse than her bite."

"She bites?" I asked.

She shrugged. "God, I don't know. Probably? There's not much she won't do, from what I understand."

I laughed. "Good to know. I'll let Ramsey figure that one out on his own. He's into that kind of thing too."

"You're not?"

I shook my head, and I wasn't grinning, now. "No, not really. My tastes are…a little more straightforward."

She cleared her throat and picked up her pace. "I see. Thanks for sharing, but I'm not sure I needed to know that."

"Sure you did. It's handy information to have." I quirked an eyebrow at her. "You know. For later."

She just shook her head. "Awfully confident of yourself, aren't you?"

"Yeah, I guess I am."

She eyed me steadily as we got on the elevator

together. "They say confidence is attractive but, you know, arrogance really isn't." She quirked an eyebrow back at me. "Nor is blatant sexual innuendo with someone you've literally just met."

"Are you offended?" I asked.

She shrugged. "Not offended, no. I'm more just curious to know if this approach actually works for you."

"Honestly?"

She nodded. "Yeah, honestly."

I laughed, somewhat sheepishly, and raked my hand through my hair. "Yeah, it usually does work."

"Really?"

I nodded. "Yeah. I'd say…eighty percent of the time."

"And the other twenty percent of the time?"

I grinned at her. "Well…the other twenty percent of the time is evenly split between being slapped, or being told to fuck off."

"Is it worth it?"

"What, getting slapped, or told to fuck off?"

"Yeah, usually."

"Usually? That means sometimes it's not worth it?" She exited the elevator and glanced at the signs on the wall opposite. "Have you been to the cafeteria here? I thought it was on this floor."

I laughed, indicating she should turn right. "Yeah,

it's down this way. Not very well marked, is it?"

"No," she said, following my direction. "Ugh. I hate hospitals. I don't trust them."

"Same."

We soon found ourselves in the cafeteria, pouring no-so-great coffee into paper cups, Juneau adding cream and sugar to hers. I drank mine black, out of long habit. She also grabbed a pastry from the case, while I stuck to just the coffee. We headed, in unspoken unison, to the register. Before Juneau could dig her wallet out of her purse, I handed a ten to the cashier.

"I've got this," I said to the cashier.

Juneau eyed me warily. "Thanks?"

I took my change from the cashier and shoved it into my pocket. "You're welcome?" I replied, mimicking her questioning tone of voice. "Why is it a question?"

"You buying me my coffee and a donut doesn't make this a date."

I snorted. "Of course not."

"Glad we're on the same page," she said, heading to an empty booth along one wall.

"It's a pre-date," I said.

She slid into the booth and, instead of sitting opposite her like she was obviously expecting, I sat down beside her.

"Um. Hi?" she said, inching away. "What are you doing over here on my side?"

"This is more fun."

"More fun, huh?" She inched away a bit further. "So. What's a pre-date?"

I grinned at her and pinched off a bit of her donut, popping it into my mouth. "It's where you decide if you like me, and want to go on an actual date with me."

"Oh." She cleared her throat, moving her donut away from me. "If you want a donut, get your own. This is mine, even though it was bought with your money."

I laughed. "I don't want a whole one, I just want some of yours."

She narrowed her eyes at me. "So what's next? We fight over our food, or where to eat?"

"Something like that. I'll ask you where you want to go, and you'll say wherever, you don't care, and then I'll suggest a place, and then you'll shoot it down."

"And we do that until we've started fighting, and neither of us want to be on a date anymore."

"And then we'll finally agree on somewhere but, because we got off to a bad start, when we finally go on the date everything is super tense, so we spend half the date in a tense, awkward silence."

She laughed. "The awkward, tense silence is only made worse by the fact that you can't seem to hold my gaze and you being totally focused on my chest isn't helping your case any. And because we've been fighting, there's precisely zero chance of sex later."

I burst out laughing, because she'd caught me doing exactly that a couple minutes ago. "So I try to keep my eyes on yours, but your cleavage is so spectacular I just can't help myself. It becomes this oddly funny thing, and you end up laughing at me, because I'm so helplessly attracted to you that you can't help but be endeared by it."

Her eyes narrowed. "That's not where I saw this going."

"No?"

"No. Staring at my breasts, or anyone's breasts for that matter, is never sexy, nor is having zero control over your own eyes or attention."

"If it's of any consolation, Juneau, this behavior is totally involuntary," I said with a shrug. "I'm like a moth drawn to a light. I know it's going to get me zapped, but I can't help it."

"Helplessly attracted?" she asked, with a quirked eyebrow.

"Completely and utterly helpless."

"To me, or my breasts?"

"To you, of course, and especially to your breasts

which do not, in any way, resemble implants." I hesitated for effect. "They are obviously all natural, and could never in a million years be mistaken as fakes."

"You're an expert, I'm guessing?"

I affected a posh British accent. "Obviously I am one of the world's foremost experts on human female mammary glands."

She quirked an eyebrow at me. "Well, good to know. Is that on your resume?"

"Obviously."

"Listen, Remington, we literally just met about thirty minutes ago. You're talking as if you have already fantasized about me."

"To be honest, I have."

"What? You have? Really?" she asked.

I nodded seriously. "I have. Really."

"I just know I'm going to regret this, but...do tell," she said.

I quirked an eyebrow back at her. "Are you sure you want to know?"

"Absolutely. Hit me with it."

I covered my grin with a hand. "All right, Juneau. But remember—you asked for it, so you don't get to call me a pervert for it."

TWO

Juneau

"OH, I'LL PROBABLY CALL YOU A PERVERT FOR IT anyway but honestly, I'm honestly curious. So, go ahead—do your worst." I had a feeling I'd regret asking him, but curiosity was one of my greatest downfalls.

A tendril of blond hair fell across his left eye, and Remington swept it back over his scalp with a casual swipe of his hand. God, that move was sexy.

"Okay, well, here you go, then." His gaze, once again, swept downward, hesitated, and then he met my eyes. His voice dropped low, and I had to strain to hear him over the din in the cafeteria. "You'd be wearing...well, not much. A scrap of lace here, a bit of silk there..."

"Not naked?" I asked, pretending my heartbeat wasn't pounding, or that my palms weren't sweaty.

"Nope. See, maybe I'm weird, but I've always maintained that a woman is sexier when she's mostly naked instead of all naked. Stripping a woman to her skin is half the fun of sex, for one thing. And for another, having certain things hidden and obscured is just...sexy."

"Thus the skimpy lingerie," I said. "Not all that weird."

"Exactly." He filled the booth beside me, trapping me against the wall, and his heat and muscle were sucking all the oxygen out of my lungs. His eyes bored into mine, and it took all of my faculties to pretend I was just conducting research and not a red-blooded female completely affected by him.

"Okay, so I'm wearing lingerie..." I prompted, proud of how casual I sounded

His eyes raked over me yet again and this time, for some reason, I'm not offended but aroused. Usually when a guy ogles me so openly, I find it offensive. But this time it must be because I'm unable to take my eyes off him. I can't stop staring at his rippling arms that stretch the sleeves of his shirt, or his chest bulging against the fabric...or the fold in his jeans that's far too thick and bulging to be anything other than what I think it is.

"You're dancing for me," he continued. "Moving, twisting, gyrating. And those big sexy tits of yours bounce and sway and jiggle all over the place, until they fall out of the lingerie."

I rolled my eyes at him. "Wow. Super original."

He shrugged. "I didn't say it was original, and remember, you asked." He hesitated a long moment. "Plus, that's the PG-13 version of the fantasy. I don't think you really want to hear the X-rated version."

I swallowed hard. "You don't think so, huh?"

"No."

"Try me." I wanted to slap myself, or pinch myself. What was I doing? Why am I goading him? Why am I sitting in this booth with him, having this conversation?

Because it's safe, that's why—it's just talk.

I have no intention of letting this go beyond a pretend, silly, ridiculous conversation. Not with anyone, but especially not with him.

"You're sure about that, Juneau?" he murmured in my ear. "You really want to hear the X-rated version?"

"I'm sure," I whispered back.

He hesitated. Looked around. Sighed. "Not here."

I frowned at him. "Not here? Why? There's no

one within earshot. And aren't I the one who's supposed to be unwilling to talk about this kind of thing in public?"

He shrugged. "I don't know, are you? We just met, after all. You could be an exhibitionist for all I know."

I stared at him. "Really? You *really* think so?"

He shrugged again. "Well, it's possible. I mean, the majority of this conversation has been about your boobs, and it hasn't exactly been low-key. Talking about my X-rated fantasy isn't that crazy in comparison."

"I can guarantee you I'm not an exhibitionist," I replied. "This entire conversation with you has been surreal. I never do stuff like this."

"Like what?"

"Have an R-rated conversation with a basic stranger."

"I'm not a stranger," he reminded me. "I'm your roommate Kitty's boyfriend's identical triplet brother."

"That's quite a mouthful, but you're still a stranger to me. In fact, having this conversation with a random stranger would be less weird, honestly. I don't know what's gotten into me." I pinched the bridge of my nose. "I should be under medical supervision."

Remington rumbled a laugh. "I'd like to think it's

less about you being crazy, and more about me being irresistible."

I laughed. "Yeah, whatever. You just keep thinking that."

They say the best place to hide something is in plain sight so, logically, the best way to keep him from suspecting the truth about how I'm feeling right now is to admit it, but make it sound super sarcastic.

And I think it's working.

"*Any*way. Back to the topic at hand, why not here?" I asked, glancing around the cafeteria.

He kept his voice low. "Because I need to walk out of here in a second, and if I tell you, I'll get a hard-on, and there's no way in fuck I'm walking through this hospital with monster wood."

I felt myself blushing and I'm thankful, not for the first time since I ran into Remington in the hallway, that my complexion doesn't show it. "Oh. It's that X-rated?"

He leaned against me, and his lips brushed my ear. "Let's just say in this particular fantasy, you *are* totally naked."

"I see," I murmured.

"And you're bouncing…"

"Yeah—mmm-hmm. I'm still waiting for the X-rated part." God, who am I, right now? Not shy, quiet Juneau Isaac, that's for sure. This was some daring, brazen version of Juneau that I'd never met before.

"You really want me to say it?" He wrapped an arm around my waist and pulled me up against his side, and I felt my breast being crushed against his chest. His voice dropped to a whisper. "Fine. I'll say it."

Oh, man. I didn't think this through. Why am I goading him? From what Kitty has told Izzy and me about Roman, these guys are not men to trifle with. "You don't have to, you know."

"You want to know," he murmured. "You're not wimping out on me now, are you?"

"I'm just saying, you don't have to say it if you don't want to."

His fingers danced along my ribcage, and then traipsed slowly upward until his knuckles brushed the underside of my breast. "Now I *have* to say it. And you know you're curious."

"I can probably guess what you're going to say."

"Oh yeah? Go for it."

I shook my head and laughed. "Not a chance. This is your fantasy."

"Chicken?" he said, and now he's intentionally caressing the underside of my left breast with the knuckle of his index finger.

I glared sideways at him, angling away from his touch, but I was pinned in the booth and there was nowhere to go. But part of me liked this, and I didn't want him to stop. "I'm not chicken."

"Then tell me what I was going to say."

"We're having sex," I blurted in a whisper. "And I'm…bouncing."

His lips touched the outer shell of my ear, and his breath tickled, hot and close. "You're bouncing on my cock," he whispered. "That's what I'm fantasizing about. You—sitting up in my bed, facing me, your arms around my neck, your thighs around my waist. You're on my lap, and I'm fucking you as hard as I can, and those big, beautiful tits of yours are bouncing so hard…"

"*Remington!*" I hissed.

His ice blue eyes bored into mine. "You asked. I *told* you it was X-rated."

I pushed at him. "Let me out of here."

Suddenly I couldn't breathe—I had to get air.

He didn't move. "Oh, come on. You asked!"

I pushed harder. "Please. Let me out."

Reluctantly, he slid out of the booth. "See? I knew you couldn't handle it."

I didn't answer. I didn't even look at him. Instead, I bolted from the cafeteria as quickly as I could without actually running.

I found the elevator, ran inside, and then stabbed the button for the floor Remington's dad was on. As I ascended, I leaned against the corner of the elevator, fighting for breath.

Seriously—what the *hell* was wrong with me?

That entire conversation was so far out character for me it wasn't even funny.

I'm more like Kitty—reserved, conservative. Unlikely to talk about sex even with my best friends, much less…whatever *that* conversation was.

Filthy, inappropriate, ridiculous, and embarrassing—that's what it was.

I found the correct room, and entered to find Izzy and Kitty sharing a chair, listening to Remington's father tell a story. An inappropriate one, from the sound of it. Apparently, the nurse's orders to vacate the room so that Mr. Badd could rest had been ignored.

"…Well, there I was, innocent as could be, mindin' my own business, chattin' at the bar with some drinking buddies. And this lady comes up to me, bold as you please, and suggests I buy her a drink. Now, I wasn't plannin' on buyin' no drinks for no ladies—to be totally honest, I's plannin' on tyin' on a hell of a hangover. It'd been a long as fuck week, and I'd barely had time to even think, and I needed to de-stress a little, you know? And, in the name of honesty, hookin' up with a lady ain't a great way to de-stress. Got it's place in life, and I won't even pretend I ain't done my share of it—baby-makin' is a lot of things, but relaxin' ain't one of 'em." He shifted on the bed, wincing, his grizzled features betraying pain. "Anyway, bold as you please, she asks me to buy her a drink. Not bein' one to look a gift horse in the mouth, I went along with it. I bought her a drink. Ain't much I regret, but I regret buyin' that bitch a beer. She was the goddamn craziest little slut I ever met, and I'm sorry if that offends you, but it's nothin' but the gospel truth."

Izzy laughed. "Why? What'd she do?"

"What'd she do? What *didn't* she do? First, you gotta know somethin' about me: I may be a cranky, ornery, difficult old drunk, and I definitely ain't on any list of folks gettin' sainted anytime soon, but I ain't ever intentionally, knowingly been the *other* guy, you know? I got *some* standards."

"She had a boyfriend?" Kitty asked.

He laughed. "Boyfriend? She was married and had four kids! Wasn't wearing a ring, wasn't no tan line neither, and I looked." He sighed, scrubbing the silver stubble on his jaw with a gnarled finger. "I bought her a drink, and she convinced me to walk her home. And, as you can prolly guess, one thing led to another, and I found myself balls-deep in a fine slice of lady."

"Dad!" Roman shouted.

The elder Badd just shrugged. "Just tellin' the story, son. And neither of these fine ladies seem too offended."

Kitty hid her face in Roman's arm. "I'm not offended, but I'm not sure I needed to hear it quite that explicitly."

Izzy, predictably, was cackling hysterically. "Oh boy. This sounds promising. What happened then?"

"What happened then was her husband came home." Lucas indicated his left bicep, where a thin white scar sliced across the outside of his arm. "He shot at me. Thank god he was blind drunk, because he was point blank and still missed. Nicked me here, and left another scar across my ass cheek, which I won't show you, but I was inches from having two ass cracks."

Kitty sighed. "And you learned your lesson, I'm guessing?"

He chuckled ruefully. "Can't say I did. Never been the brightest bulb in the room."

I turned to Izzy. "These Badd men are all alike," I whispered, disgusted. "Always thinking about one thing."

Izzy frowned at me. "To be fair, it's not just Badd men, it's all men."

I shook my head with a sigh. "True." I fidgeted with my handbag. "Look, I need to get back to Ketchikan. I've got work tomorrow and I'm supposed to be preparing for my bar ads."

"The hell you do," Mr. Badd said, obviously

having heard us. "We ain't even met yet and you're trying to skedaddle on me?"

"No, I just—"

"Unless you ain't even here for poor ol' me," he said, glancing behind me with a mischievous twinkle in his deep-set brown eyes. "Think I may be a mite old and a touch out of shape for a cute little thing like you."

"Dad, quit flirting," I heard a deep, rumbling voice from behind me say.

I knew that voice. I shivered at the proximity of him.

Mr. Badd just waved a hand in dismissal. "Oh, go fly a kite, you big dumb humbug. I'll flirt all I want. It's about all I got left, especially being all but hogtied in this damn hospital bed." He winked at me before continuing to address Remington. "Plus, I can't help it—a pretty girl walks in, I'm gonna flirt with her. Too damn old and set in my ways to change now."

I stood beside Mr. Badd and shook his hand. "It's nice to meet you, Mr. Badd. My name is Juneau. I really do hope you feel better soon."

"Juneau, huh? Pretty name for a damned lovely girl." He hesitated, scratching at his silver stubble. "Which one of my lunkheaded boys pissed you off?"

I frowned at him. "What? How did you—?"

He chuckled. "Pretty girl walks into my hospital

room—a pretty girl I ain't met before, and she's got a bug up her ass about somethin'—well, stands to reason one of my idiot sons did somethin' dumb to piss her off. I know it ain't Rome, 'cause I been workin' on gettin' li'l miss Kitty here to leave him for me. And judgin' by the way Izzy is avoiding looking at Ram like he's got the damn plague, it ain't him." He stabbed a finger at Remington. "Which means it's you, Rem. What'd you do? Came on too strong, most likely."

Remington was silent a long moment. "What do you know, you dirty old coot?" he snarled.

Mr. Badd wasn't fazed. "Less than most, but a damn sight more'n others."

I turned to assess Remington's response to this not-so-thinly veiled insult.

Remington just rolled his eyes and shook his head. It seemed as if this was a familiar dance for this group of men. "Oh, fuck off."

"Come a little closer and I'll teach you some respect," Mr. Badd growled, sounding for all the world like an irritated bear. "Even with a busted leg and arm I can still whup you."

"You wish," Remington said. "You ain't been able to whup any of us since we was teenagers." He winced at the twang in his voice, which I hadn't heard before. "Dammit, old man. Two minutes in a room with you and I'm talking country all over all again."

"Ashamed of your upbringing, are you?" Mr. Badd asked.

"Our height and looks already leave people assuming the worst about us," Remington answered. "Sounding like a country bumpkin only makes it worse. So yeah, I worked hard to leave the accent behind when we left."

"Bein' as dumb as you are big, and as much an asshole as you are good-lookin'—that's what has people assuming the worst."

Remington flipped him the bird. "Yeah, well... everything I know, I learned from you. So what's that say about you?"

Roman—normally clean-shaven, his jaw now heavily stubbled, his hair short and gelled into spikes, still wearing the trousers and button-down shirt from a suit—shot a hard look at Remington. "Dude, what crawled up your ass and died?"

Mr. Badd chuckled. "Rem is as even-keeled as any Badd will ever get, so if something has him acting a fool, I guaran-damn-tee you it's a woman." His eyes went to mine. "Don't take it personally, darlin'. My boys are clueless about women."

I shifted uncomfortably. "It has nothing to do with me, I'm sure," I lied.

Mr. Badd just laughed again. "Honey, you can't sell bullshit to a bullshit artist."

I patted his hand. "It was a pleasure to meet you, Mr. Badd. I hope you recover quickly." I glanced at Izzy and then Kitty. "I'm gonna head back to Ketchikan. My boss has a case he needs help preparing for." I waved at the room in general, but specifically, intentionally, and somewhat blatantly ignoring Remington. "Goodbye, everyone."

Izzy and Kitty exchanged glances, and then followed me out as I hustled toward the elevators.

"Whoa, whoa, whoa, Juneau, wait," Izzy called after me.

I didn't wait, but instead walked even faster. I had no intention of waiting around for the Izzy Inquisition, or for Kitty's quiet, well-meaning, and often effective questioning.

Of course, short of running, there was no way I was going to outpace them, and they both caught up to me as I reached the elevator bank.

"Juneau, what the hell?" Izzy demanded, standing in front of the elevator, preventing me from calling it. "You're acting weird."

"I am not," I protested. "I just have to get back to Ketchikan."

"Juneau, it's *us*," Kitty said, the good cop, as always. "What's going on with you? There is something wrong."

"Nothing!" I all but shouted.

Which was a mistake, because me raising my voice was a dead giveaway that something *is* wrong.

"Well, I was almost buying the 'have to get back for work' excuse," Izzy said. "But I *know* something is wrong."

I groaned, tilting my head backward. "Okay, you know what? Fine. Remington Badd is a disgusting, arrogant, crude, foul-mouthed barbarian."

Kitty burst out laughing. "Well…yeah. He's a *Badd*. Have you met Roman?" She shook her head, amused at me. "For that matter, have you met any of my eight bosses? Who are, may I remind you, all Badds, and they have their questionable moments just like Remington, Ramsey, and Roman do."

"Hearing you talk about Roman being that way, or hearing about a few crude jokes from Bast or Zane is one thing," I huffed, "but having it directed *at* you is different."

"No joke," Izzy said, fanning her face. "I didn't think anyone could make me blush, but Ramsey? Hooooo-*boy*, that man is *dirty*."

Kitty and I exchanged glances. "Wait, what?" I asked. "When did you meet him? I thought you'd never seen him before."

Izzy faked a ditzy, demure shrug. "I have my ways."

"Izzy." Kitty stared hard at our best friend. "You

haven't had sex with him already, have you?"

She shook her head. "No...not exactly."

"Izzy." Kitty's tone demanded details.

She just grinned. "We're not talking about me. We're talking about Juneau, and how Remington clearly said or did something that has her acting like she has sand in her vag."

"Izzy!" Kitty and I scolded in unison.

"What? It's true!"

I huffed in irritation. "You are so nasty sometimes, Isadora."

"I just calls 'em like I sees 'em," Izzy drawled, cackling. "And you know how much I love getting your goat."

I reached past them and jabbed the call button. "I'm going home. I'm heading back to Ketchikan as soon as I can change my flight."

Kitty just patted me on the shoulder. "You're in for a long day then, because I think the last nonstop leaves in, like, twenty minutes."

I sighed. "I'll figure something out. I just see no point in hanging around in the hospital with a bunch of crude, vulgar, arrogant men...whom I have no desire to know any further."

Kitty's expression hardened a little. "That's not fair, Juneau. Roman may be all those things, but he has a really good heart. He's actually very sweet, it's just buried under a pretty thick layer of—"

"Macho assholery?" I suggested.

Kitty laughed, nodding. "Yeah, pretty much. But once you see that the whole macho asshole thing is just a big front, you start seeing a lot more beneath it."

"That's just the sex talking," I muttered.

Kitty's eyebrow lifted. "Oh? You think so?" She poked me in the shoulder. "You and I are a lot alike, and we both know it. You really think I'd be this blinded by sex? Even world-class, earthshaking, unforgettable sex? Do you *really* think I'd let myself be sucked into a relationship with someone like Roman Badd unless I genuinely believed there's something valuable and worthwhile in it for me? Beyond sex, I mean."

I eyed her levelly. "World class, earthshaking, *and* unforgettable?"

Her grin was...lascivious, really the only way I could describe it. "Juneau, you have *no* idea."

I glanced at Izzy. "You have anything to add?"

She just shrugged. "Nope!" she sang. "Not a thing."

"*Izzy*," I snapped. "I know you have something to say. You always do."

She gave me an uncharacteristically opaque stare. "I'll have something to say on the subject eventually, but not yet."

"Okay, well I *do* have something to say," Kitty said. "I don't think you're giving Remington a fair chance."

"I just met the man. He's not my type, and I'm not interested." I shrugged, acting as matter-of-fact and nonchalant as I could. "I don't need to know anything else."

Finally, after what seemed like an eternity of waiting, the elevator arrived, the doors sliding open; I stepped on and put my back to the farthest corner. "I'll see you guys back at home."

I watched Kitty and Izzy exchange significant glances, the kind which told me they'd be having a conversation about me as soon as the doors closed.

Fine, let them talk.

I knew all I needed to know about Remington Badd, and I knew I wasn't interested.

THREE

Remington

"GOD, YOU ASSHATS DON'T HAVE A SINGLE GODDAMN clue about what the fuck you're doing here, do you?" This was my cousin, Sebastian, whom we've taken to calling Bast like everyone else.

He was standing in the stockroom of our bar, sorting through our inventory. He had on a pair of cut-off khaki shorts which hung past his knees, battered red cross trainers, and a heather-gray Badd's Bar and Grill pullover hoodie, the sleeves tugged up to his elbows, revealing his tattooed forearms. He had a clipboard in one hand, a pen in the other, a bar towel folded in thirds and tucked into his back right pocket. A tattered, well-worn Seattle Seahawks hat, worn backward, covered his black hair.

Ramsey and Roman were standing on either side of me, outside the stockroom, wearing expressions which mirrored my own—equal parts pissed off and embarrassed.

"It's a bar—you sell booze." Roman toyed with a purple velvet bag, the kind that came with bottles of Crown Royal.

"So you figured it couldn't be that hard," Bast interpreted. "Newsflash—it's fuckin' hard. Any monkey with half a brain can pour beer and take money for it. That's the easy part. Everything else that leads up to that, and comes after it, is the hard part. Inventory, POS, loss percentages, overhead, paper stock, breakage, food sales, food inventory, food prep, employee hours, salaries, register balances, cash deposits…"

He tapped his clipboard, and the stack of paper on it. "I've been running Badd's pretty much on my own since I was seventeen. I took over inventory, and then I took over the deposits, and then I took over the rest of the management duties so Dad could just tend bar—and drink himself to death, it turns out. I make it look easy because I've been in the bar business my whole life—it's literally the only thing I've ever known. You three numbskulls—" He shook his head, huffing a laugh.

"Cousin or not, I can still break your teeth,"

Roman growled.

"You're acting like a teenager. Swing at me and I'll leave you to figure this out on your own."

Roman groaned in aggravation, raking his scalp with his fingernails. "Fuck! Fine. What about us three numbskulls?"

"Well, you picked a hell of a good location for your bar—I've actually been eying this property for a few months—I've been thinking about expanding." He left the stockroom and led us back into the main bar area, gesturing with his clipboard at the work we'd done so far. "You did a hell of a good job with the renovation. Not what I'd have done, but it works. It really works."

It was good to know from Bast that we had done something right. We started out thinking we'd do a minimal renovation, but once we started yanking shit out one thing led to another, until finally the place was down to the studs. And then Roman, in a stroke of blind luck, came across a guy who had torn down a century-old barn and farmhouse and was selling the wood for cheap. Rome bought it, rented a flatbed, brought it here, and we used it for the floors and walls. We combined that weathered look with more reclaimed and recycled pieces of steel, tin, and copper for the trim and light fixtures.

And suddenly the whole place took on a…shit, I

don't know the right term. Industrial? Factory sort of look? That's not totally right, though. We found some old batwing doors for the kitchen and bathrooms, and we stripped, sanded, and restained the bar that had been in here. Then we repurposed a bunch of mismatched stools, and we had ourselves a bar that sort of felt like a modern interpretation of an Old West saloon.

We put up all sorts of eclectic artwork—pages from pinup calendars from the forties and fifties, classic movie posters, some old revolvers with their barrels crossed, and a gun belt hung above them, even a junked-out old antique motorcycle that had taken us an entire day to hang on the wall.

I'd even convinced Roman to let us alter the name just a bit: it was now called *Badd Kitty Saloon*.

All in all, I was proud of the work we'd done in here, making the place look cool and professional, and I was relieved that Bast saw the quality in what we'd accomplished.

In a way, that was the easy part of opening this bar.

It's the rest of my concerns about the whole "opening and running a bar" that I was reluctant to share with my brothers.

Fortunately, I think we can depend on Bast to give us a reality check.

Still on his tour of our saloon, Bast said, "Great feel in here. Super masculine. Since our place is sort of designed to attract the women, hopefully this place will attract more of the men." He indicated the bar. "You don't have a POS, do you?"

Roman frowned. "POS? You mean piece of shit?"

Bast barked a laugh. "No—point of sale. A cash register. The computer where you ring up orders and take money."

Rome folded the velvet bag in half and in half again. "Oh. Um—no. I wasn't sure where to get one, or what to look for. I did some research on it, but there's a bunch of different types and different operating systems, so I just said fuck it, I'll use Square."

Bast nodded. "Actually, that's not a bad idea. I've been thinking of switching to a system like that myself. Hell of a lot easier to learn to use." He clapped Roman on the shoulder. "You were planning on opening…when?"

Roman shrugged. "I dunno. ASAP, I guess."

"Well, good news is, your interior is good to go, for the most part. You need soap dispensers, and either a hand towel dispenser or an air dryer of some kind in the washrooms." He idly tapped his pen against the clipboard. "You're missing a bunch of shit, though— basically all that stuff I was talking about back in the storeroom."

"Well, you're the expert," Roman said. "What's the best plan?"

Bast spun the pen around his thumb in a fancy flicking maneuver. "Well, it's more complicated than me just outlining you a plan which, honestly, probably sounds a lot easier than it would actually end up being. I can't just say do this, this, and this, and then let you go and do it—even if you managed to follow my directions exactly, you'd still miss shit and end up getting shut down, if not sued."

"Sued?"

"Well, in order to run any business that serves food or beverages, you need a Food Serve certification, on top of a health department inspection. Have you done either of those?" Bast was answered by Roman's glare and shuffling feet. "Didn't think so. You try to run without that shit, yeah, you'll get shut down so fast your head will spin, and there'll likely be fines of some kind along with it."

"Fuck."

"Did you do any electrical or plumbing work?" Bast asked.

"Nope. All we did was update the fixtures. But we did have an inspector come out and look at it. We have a properly marked and functioning emergency exit, fire extinguishers, all that." Roman sounded inordinately proud of himself for being able to provide that answer.

"Well, that's one thing off the list," Bast said. "Listen, getting this place up to speed so it can run smoothly will be...a *shitload* of work."

Roman's scowl was an ugly one. "Yeah, I'm gathering that."

"Plus, you're gonna need more than just the three of you, unless you each plan on working eighteen-hour days." He paused. "And, in order to get up to speed, you're gonna need expertise that none of you have." Bast was clearly thinking about something.

"Out with it, Bast," I said. "What are you getting at?"

Bast took a seat on a nearby stool, set his clipboard down, and fiddled with the pen, eyeing the three of us. "How committed to this place are you?"

"I can't answer for these bozos," Roman said. "But I'm all in. With Dad still recovering and obviously being prone to relapse, I just don't see myself going back to fighting fires anytime soon. Plus, I like this town. And, despite myself, I'm starting to like you assholes and your women. And I *really* like Kitty. So...I'm committed to it. A hundred percent. I'll do whatever it takes to make it work."

"You really want to learn how to run a bar?" Bast asked, his eyes sharp, his tone sharper.

"I'm not stupid, okay? I know I bit off way more

than I could chew when I jumped on this bar idea—and then dragged these two yokels with me. But I've had fun so far. And I see the way you guys run your place, and I like it. So, yeah, I do want to learn."

Bast nodded, and then glanced at Ram and then me. "What about you two?"

Ram eyed me, and I eyed him back—we'd both always been skeptical about this plan, but we support Rome no matter what. Plus, we didn't really have any better ideas at the time, so…here we were.

I don't know about Ram, but I didn't love the bar scene quite as much as Rome. When it comes to drinking, I've always preferred to do mine on my own, with some buddies, out in the woods, or at home. The only reason I'd ever go to a bar is to pick up some company for the night; Ram is even less about the bar scene than I am, being the most outdoorsy of the three of us; he hates being inside for any length of time, so I can't imagine him being cool stuck in a bar eighteen-plus hours a day.

"I'm still trying to figure out a better plan for myself," Ram says. "So I'm in, for now. But it's provisional. You know I'm down to support whatever you guys want to do—three musketeers and all that shit, right? But, eventually, I know I'm going to get sick of playing bartender."

Rome toyed with a pair of beverage straws. "I

feel you. That's all I can ask for." He eyed me. "What about you, Rem?"

I sighed, flipping my hand through my hair. "You know, I've never been super excited about opening a bar. Bars have always been your thing, not mine, and certainly not Ram's."

"Yeah, I know that," Rome said. "You two assholes aren't as sociable as I am."

Bast's eyebrows shot up. "*You're* the sociable one?"

"Believe it or not, yeah, I am," Rome said, laughing. His laugh died as he glanced at me. "So, Rem. You're in for now? Provisionally, like Ram?"

I nodded. "Yeah."

Bast nodded, stabbing the pen's clicker against the clipboard repeatedly. "Okay, we've got one of you all in, a hundred percent, and the other two of you are provisional. I can work with that, I guess." He flipped pages on the clipboard, bringing it to a blank page. "Let's talk business."

"Business?" Rome asked, sounding skeptical. "What kind of business?"

Bast laughed. "Expertise don't come free, Rome, even for cousins." He wrote some figures on the paper. "You need my help—in fact, you need me and my brothers. We've been batting around the idea of expanding for months now—we've hired some outsiders to staff Badd's, and Kitty is shaping up to be a kick-ass manager, which means Zane and I can start spending time over here getting this place up and running and making us all some money."

"What are you proposing?" Rome asked.

"Well, I know what you paid for the place, and I can guess roughly what you've put into it so far, which gives me a decent estimate of your total stake so far. Which is…not a small amount. You've actually gambled pretty heavily that this place will work."

Rome nodded. "We all had some cash saved, which was enough for a down payment on a loan to buy the place, and some extra to start it up." He eyed Bast. "So you're proposing a partnership—a percentage of ownership?"

Bast nodded. "That's exactly what I'm talking about. Twenty or thirty percent. We'd stake you some cash to bring in everything you need—which is a pretty sizable amount when you start factoring in back stock and food inventory, and the new kitchen equipment you'll need."

"We weren't thinking we'd serve much food," Rome said. "That's a whole different ballgame and I know it, so I was gonna focus on the alcohol."

"Nah, nah, nah," Bast said, waving a hand. "Food's where it's at. You just gotta do it right—serve till you close, and make it comfort food, easy to make, easy to eat, easy to clean up after, with a decent mark-up value. The more you feed 'em, the more they'll drink. When we started serving food right up to closing time a couple years ago our alcohol sales went through the roof. Late-night food is a moneymaker. Believe that."

"Which means we'll need new equipment in the kitchen, is what you're saying, because the stuff in there is old and shitty."

Bast nodded. "You got it in one. Clean out the whole kitchen—scrap it to the studs and start fresh. It'll be pricey, but worth it. The vibe you have going on in here actually makes me feel like you'll get a lot of afternoon and evening customers if your menu is right. This kind of atmosphere, you serve sandwiches, burgers, prime rib, maybe even some steak and seafood. You'll need actual, experienced line cooks, though, not just short-order cooks, but it'd be worth it." Bast slapped the bar with his palm. "I'm telling you, I have a good feeling about this place."

Rome perked up. "Really?"

Bast nodded. "Absolutely. You're on the right track with the renovations, it's the finer details of actually running the business where you're lost." He tapped his chin. "And actually, if you're serving that kind of food, you'll want to find a kitchen manager. I can get you up to speed as the front of house manager, but you'll want someone knowledgeable in the kitchen if you're serving pricier menu items. You want to do it right." He scanned the interior again. "Come to think of it, you're gonna need more tables. The booths along the wall are great, but the middle area is lost space. Put a bunch of four-tops in here and you can almost quadruple the number of people you can seat."

"I was leaving it open for people to mill around," Rome said.

Bast nodded, shrugging. "And I get what you were going for, but giving people a place to sit down will be better overall. People sit, eat, drink, and then leave, and someone else takes their spot—or they camp out and keep drinking; either way, you win. If you've got a bunch of open space and nowhere to sit down because the bar is full, and the booths are full, they're just gonna leave and go somewhere that has a table or two." He indicated the front window, which ran the width of the storefront. "And you'll want a bar over there with more stools. Give people places to put their asses, and you'll gain customers who will spend more."

"I guess that makes sense."

"So, what I'm saying is that I'm thinking of a little bit of a rebrand from where you saw yourself going." Bast gestured around again. "To me, this says somewhere to sit and eat and have some good stiff drinks, maybe listen to some live music, just sort of chill, hang out. Our place is the rowdy sort of bar, where things get wild. You're gonna come here for a less rowdy atmosphere."

"I like things rowdy, though," Rome said.

Bast chuckled. "I could have guessed that. And your late-night crowd will get you that. Trust me— shit is gonna get rowdy. But you need a theme or focus that fits your atmosphere, and I'm just telling you what I see when I sit in here."

Rome nodded. "No, you're right." He glanced at Ramsey and me. "What do you guys think?"

Ram shrugged. "Honestly, bro, this is your place. Do what feels right to you. We're here to support you." He hesitated. "I want it to be successful, because I did stake most of my savings on this."

"Same here," I said. "I think Bast is right, and I think he knows this shit better than we do, so it only makes sense to listen to him—it's why you called him over here in the first place."

Rome nodded again, thoughtful. "And what do you guys think about selling him a percentage?"

"I think we're sunk without it, Rome," I said. "We're in over our heads. I can learn how to pour beer and whiskey and mix drinks and use a register. But I don't know the first goddamn thing about running a business. Bast does. He's been doing it successfully for a long time. We'd be morons not to stake him in when he's got the know-how and we don't."

"Look, guys. I won't mince words, okay?" Bast hesitated a moment, then fired away. "You won't last another month without help. You're hemorrhaging cash and you're flailing around like a monkey with its balls stuck in a vise. Stake us in, let us take over and show you the ropes, and I guarantee you'll see profits faster than you'll believe."

"So, hold on, though," Ram cut in. "Stake *us* in? Who's us?"

Bast tilted his head to one side. "I dunno exactly, yet. Zane for sure. Brock is likely to want in, and Bax might, too. The others? Probably not so much. But between Zane, Brock, Bax, and me, we'll be able to scrounge up enough cash to renovate the kitchen, get your inventory squared away, and do whatever else needs doing. While the kitchen is being worked on, we'll start looking for a B-O-H manager."

"B-O-H?" Rome asked.

"Back of house, meaning the kitchen. F-O-H is the front of the house, meaning the bar and restaurant area."

"Oh. Right."

"So, percentages…" Bast tapped the sheet with the figures he'd been working on while he talked, occasionally doing math on the calculator on his phone. "I'll have to talk to my brothers and see who's interested in joining me on this, and then I'll come back to you with more specific figures as to what kind of a percentage will make sense for everyone involved."

"Sounds good to me," Rome said.

Bast stood up. "So you're in? We're in business?"

Rome stuck out his hand and the two men shook. "Yeah, we are. Family business, oddly enough."

Bast laughed at that. "I'd never have thought this was even possible. Then you crazy assholes come waltzing into my bar, and now here we are getting ready to buy into a business together."

"Wasn't on my radar when I first tossed out the idea of moving up here and opening a bar," Rome said. "But it makes sense."

"All right, well, after I talk to my brothers I'll get back to you. We'll work up a contract and get the ball rolling." He paused halfway out the front door. "You know, I'm actually getting excited about this the more I think about it. I've been getting a little bored at the bar lately—it's so routine now that there's no challenge or excitement anymore. This? This is new, something I've never done before, and it's gonna be fun."

"Now that you're on board, I think I can get

excited again," Rome said. "I was getting a little over-whelmed and worried, I don't mind admitting."

Bast laughed. "It's still gonna be a lot of work. Don't think I'm gonna come in and do everything for you. You're gonna have to work your ass to the bone if you want this place to take off and run smoothly."

"Hey, I got no problem working hard," Rome said. "We've been working since we were eleven. Our first job was collecting scrap metal for Old Man Harney, remember that, guys?"

Ram laughed. "Old Man Harney. Wow, haven't thought about that ornery old cuss in years." He shook his head, tugging at his beard. "He was a real dick, as I remember."

"Yeah, he was a dick," I said. "But he was a dick who paid decent cash for scrap metal, and had a bad habit of leaving half-finished forties on his back porch."

"Which we'd steal regularly," Rome added. "I think he did that on purpose. Looking back, he ough-ta be shot for enabling our underage drinking habit, but at the time I thought it was the best thing ever."

Bast laughed. "We're gonna have to get drunk and trade stories sometime. I gotta go, though. I'm taking my wife to lunch."

We exchanged fist bumps and goodbyes, and then Bast was gone and it was just the three of us standing in our bar.

Rome sat at the bar, lost in thought. When Ram plopped down beside him, Rome eyed our brother. "So how long before you think you're gonna bail on me, Ram?"

Ram frowned. "I wouldn't call it bailing, Rome. I'll never bail on you. If you need me, I'll be here. But you know I need to be outside. Hunting, hiking, fishing, riding, roping. This city shit ain't my scene, and you know it. I'm all for a change in scenery and, to be honest, I was getting to the point with the smoke-jumping that it was starting to feel like it was time to let the younger cats get at it. Not that thirty-two is old, but for something that physically demanding? It was getting dangerous. And with the increase in forest fires lately, it was nonstop work." He rapped the bar with his knuckle. "It was a matter of *when* one of us got hurt or killed, not *if*. So, changing things up makes sense to me. Plus, it will be good to be available if Pops needs us."

"But?" Rome prompted.

"But, I want to be out there," Ram said, gesturing at the walls, meaning the wilderness beyond Ketchikan. "Alaska is one of the last truly wild frontiers on the planet, and I want to get lost in it." He laughed. "Not literally lost, but you know what I mean."

Rome nodded. "Yeah, I got you." He glanced at me. "Rem?"

I shifted in my seat, less willing to air out my inner thoughts just yet. "I'm all in, for now. You know I've never loved the idea of running a bar, so I guess just count on me finding something else at some point. What or when, I don't know. But like Ram said, I support you guys no matter what, so if you need me, I'm here."

"You've got deeper thoughts than that, Rem," Roman said. "Don't bullshit me."

I sighed. "I'm not bullshitting you, I'm just...still thinking."

"About what?" Rome asked. "That girl? Kitty's friend, Juneau?"

"That girl was one hell of a fine piece of Alaskan hotness," Ramsey said. "Can't believe you let her walk away like that."

"It's not about her," I snapped. "That was one stupid conversation over shitty hospital coffee, and that was it."

Rome and Ram exchanged glances, and then they both burst out laughing.

"Oh, man," Ram said, once he stopped laughing. "That's just great."

I frowned. "What? What are you talking about?"

Rome bumped his knuckles against Ram's.

"You," he said, with another laugh. "You're in deep shit, bro."

I shot off my stool. "The fuck are you talking about?"

Ram shook his head. "Nope, not saying anything. Not going there. You'll have to figure this one out on your own."

Rome nodded. "Totally agree."

I shot them both daggers. "If I never see her again, it'll be too soon. She was annoying."

"And sexy as fuck," Ram said. "That curvy little body? That's all you, buddy. You're saying you don't want to take a bite out of that juicy ass of hers?"

I answered by giving both of them my middle fingers as I left the bar.

I could hear them laughing as the door slammed shut.

FOUR

Juneau

"AFTER LOOKING AT PREVIOUS CASE FILES, I THINK there's a clear precedent for what we're trying to prove. We need not only the previous cases which establish precedent, but the laws they used to win those cases..." my boss, Daniel Ulujuk, was essentially talking to himself.

He had a brilliant legal mind, and was ferociously dedicated to cases affecting Native Alaskans, often taking on the cases pro bono. But he was...eccentric. He liked to walk through his cases verbally, well in advance of the actual judgment, and my job was to take dictation for each new argument. Then, after he'd listened to himself, as well as read through my transcripts, he'd rip apart his own arguments as if he were the opposing counsel. I would turn those dictations into readable transcripts, and then make my own notes and thoughts on his arguments, identifying areas where he may need to shore up his reasoning, or provide more evidence for a particular item.

It was boring as hell ninety-nine percent of the time. But it was all part of articling and getting ready to write the bar ads and then becoming a lawyer myself.

He found it all endlessly exciting, and while I enjoyed the actual trials, the actual work to get to trial was mind-numbing drudgery. I was good at taking dictation so I could do it on autopilot while the rest of my mind wandered. Normally, I daydreamed about the random detritus that fills your mind—my last workout, what I'm going to have for lunch, what to wear that night when going out with Izzy and Kitty, the podcast I'd listened to on my lunch break yesterday…

Today, my thoughts were focused on something else entirely.

On a certain male.

An obnoxious, arrogant, filthy-minded, dirty-talking male with piercing, mesmerizing, violently blue eyes. And golden blond hair that had a tendency to fall in front of his left eye, which he would then brush aside with a casual sexiness that could utterly destroy my ability to think straight. And that's not all. He had arms the size of my thighs, shoulders so broad and hard and thick you could stand on them, and a jawline that was rugged and craggy. One minute, his lips begged to be kissed, and the next they could twist in a sarcastic grin, or transform into a heated, sensual grin dripping with sexual promise.

Gah, Juneau. Stop thinking about Remington Badd. Just stop. He's annoying. Worse—he's infuriating.

I want nothing to do with him.

I do *NOT* want to know what it would feel like for his X-rated fantasy to come true.

I do *NOT*, in any way, shape, or form, want to feel his cock inside me, thrusting with feral, pounding force into my tight channel, bouncing me on his thighs so hard my tits ache from jouncing against him.

"Juneau?" A sharp, irritated voice cut through my lustful reverie.

"Wha—? What?" I blinked, cleared my throat, and shifted with awkward arousal in my swivel chair. "What was that? Sorry, Daniel."

I must be losing my mind.

Daniel—late fifties, black hair in a short, neat, classic side part, wearing rimless glasses—had little patience for nonsense. "I asked you to read back the last minute or two."

I glanced down at my handwritten dictation—my usual shorthand notes had morphed into...err...a sketch of my thoughts:

Remington. Head down, just his jawline visible—and a thick, muscled chest, and rippling abs...and his thick, veiny cock. And the lower half of a female body, a very curvy female body, facing away, a section of back and serpentine spine, her round ass spread out, his cock an instant from being buried inside her, one strong hand greedily clutching at her hips, his fingers dimpling her flesh, the other gripping himself.

Good grief. I *am* losing it.

I hurriedly covered the graphic sketch with a scrap of paper so Daniel wouldn't accidentally see it, and read back the last few lines of notation.

"You lost at least three minutes of dictation, Juneau," Daniel said, a note of displeasure in his voice. "I have court in an hour, so we have to focus."

"Sorry, Daniel. I was..."

His eyebrow lifted. "You were what?"

I felt myself blushing. "Nothing. I wasn't paying attention, and I'm sorry. It won't happen again."

"Okay, let's get back to it." He cleared his throat, stared at the ceiling, whispering the last few lines I'd read back to him as he tried to recall his mental train of thought. "Ah, yes. The truth of such matters, then, far too infrequently penetrates our global consciousness. Our people are lost in time, all but forgotten, and this man's case is an example of why we must right this wrong…"

I forced myself to focus entirely on Daniel's words, refusing to allow my thoughts to wander back to Remington. I couldn't afford to daydream like that again. Thank god no one would see my notes but me, and I would be sure to destroy them as soon as Daniel left for court.

We had just enough time to hurry to the courthouse for the preliminary hearing, and that process—thankfully—required all of my attention. Once that was finished, we would have a quick working lunch, and Daniel would spend most of it outlining his strategies and tactics for the case. And then I would transcribe the morning's dictations.

Typically, the morning was all pretty boring, for the most part, until I got to my notes and the page containing my sketch. I ripped that piece of paper free from the notepad and set it aside, continuing to work my way to the end of the dictation, packaged it up for Daniel, and brought it to him to look over. Normally, this was when I destroyed my old notes, so there was no chance of previous dictations getting mixed up with the most recent version.

Folded the single offending sheet of paper into a tiny square, I stuffed it into my bra, peeking around to make sure no one saw me do it, and then I put everything else into the paper shredder.

All through the day, that piece of paper seemed to burn inside my bra, as if it were on fire. The corners poked into my skin when I moved and sat and stood and leaned over; it shifted further and further down inside my bra until a corner of it was poking into my nipple, a sharp pain that was also somehow arousing.

It shouldn't have been, but it was.

My nipples stood on end, and stayed that way, achingly hard.

Unfortunately, there was no opportunity all afternoon to reach in and adjust it. Daniel had me busy taking dictations, working on transcriptions, attending a meeting at the courthouse and a thousand and one other things.

By the time I was able to collect my things and leave for the day, I was a miserable mess of knotted-up, pent-up, tangled-up arousal and frustration. Normally, I walked home with Izzy—she worked at fashion boutique just down the street from my law firm's office—and the apartment we shared with Kitty was just a few blocks away, so we walked home as often as we could.

Today, though, Izzy had a meeting with the owner of the boutique and wouldn't be home until later, and Kitty was currently training with Sebastian and Zane Badd to take over as general manager of Badd's, which meant she wouldn't be home until super late herself.

All of which left me with a rare evening to myself.

Strictly speaking, most of the time I'm so busy that I don't get up to much in terms of my own devices. Most of my waking hours are consumed with work, and what little time is left I usually spend with Kitty and Izzy. There is one thing I'd like to spend more time on, but it's the one thing I'm not allowed to pursue.

I've indulged it, in secret, over the years. It's stupid, because there's absolutely nothing weird or illicit about my secret passion. But considering how I was raised, and what my mom does for a living, it's something I've always kept to myself. Circumstances being what they are, and my parents being who they are, it's not worth risking my relationship with them to pursue it openly.

So, instead of heading for my apartment, I start walking in the opposite direction, away from the wharves and docks and tourist shops and restaurants and bars. The long walk would do me good, and a visit with my cousin was long overdue.

When I arrived, nearly an hour later, I stood outside his building and exhaled a deep breath. Just standing there, outside in the fresh air, made me feel like I was shedding a false skin. It was like taking a weight off and setting it aside. It also represented a slippery slope from which I was teetering dangerously close.

I was still wearing my conservative legal assistant clothing: a black skirt, a white button-down shirt, and a pale gray cardigan. None of it was tight or revealing or the least bit sexy. Considering where I was, my attire couldn't be more out of place.

I was standing at the front entrance of Yup'ik Tattoo.

The glass door of the shop was decorated with an intricate work of art—done with a Sharpie—all Native Alaskan tattoo designs: arrows and triangles and lines and quasi-abstract representations of animals and the natural world. The design filled the entire rectangle of the glass door, and continued across to the plate glass window beside it, where the design was still a work in progress. The work was done by my cousin and owner of this tattoo parlor—Ink Isaac.

Ink is my cousin, and the closest thing to a brother I have. I have plenty of sisters—five. But brothers? None. Ink has been my best friend since before we could walk. We discovered tattooing together—his first tattoo was done by me, and my first was done by him. We come from very strictly traditional Yup'ik families, but we're both engaged in nontraditional vocations. The difference is, Ink chased his dream and his passion, and I didn't. And, deep down, I harbor a lot of resentment for that—but not against Ink. He followed our dream, and did the thing we talked about under the tundra stars from the time we were ten years old and did fake tattoos on each other with colored pens. My resentment is against myself, and my parents. But mostly, I'm angry at myself for chickening out and not following my dreams.

I smiled to myself as "Killing In The Name" by Rage Against The Machine smashes against me in a palpable wall of sound as I open the door. The only thing Ink takes as seriously as tattooing is music. Before he even put in his tattoo chairs, or put up art on the walls of this shop, he installed a stupidly expensive surround sound system, which he always has turned up to an ear-splitting volume if there's nobody in the shop.

The second the bell on the door jangles, the volume is immediately lowered to a tolerable level.

"With you in a second," I heard Ink say, in his *I'm not looking at you because I'm concentrating* voice.

"Just me, Ink."

"June-bug!" His low, powerful voice envelops me, filling me with the pure warmth that is totally Ink.

He is a bear of a man. When you hear that phrase, people usually just mean a large person—in stature and in weight. Ink is more than that. He seems to physically embody a Kodiak bear in human form. Six feet seven, weighing…well, who knows?—he is a man of mind-boggling amounts of muscle with a solid layer of what he calls "insulation" over it. Darker skinned than me, he's often mistaken for someone from India or Polynesia. Almost every inch of his skin is covered in tattoos, most of which he did himself. If he could reach it, he'd ink it—and I did everything else. Even his face—where there's no beard—is covered in traditional Inuit tattoos, although not all of Ink's ink is traditional Inuit tribal markings—there's a lot of other imagery as well, in a wide variety of styles, some in grayscale, some in full color, and some a mixture of both.

The funny thing is, Uncle Andrew named him Ink when he was just a baby, yet Ink seemed to naturally gravitate to skin marking as if his father's choice of name had predetermined his future. It was as if he'd been inexorably drawn to the ancient art. From the time Ink was able to grab things with his pudgy little hands, he was marking his skin somehow—scratching himself with his fingernails, coloring on himself with pens, pencils, lipstick, soot, wax, food, whatever he could find to make his skin look different. Eventually this turned into making designs, which turned into even more elaborate works of art on his skin—temporary at first—with a pen. And then, at the age of eleven, we actually tattooed each other, but that's a story for another time.

I waited a few minutes and then he lumbered to his feet, setting aside his tattoo gun—he was working on a piece on his ankle. He towered over me, standing a full fifteen inches taller, and his monstrous arms wrapped around me, lifting me easily into the air, and he swung me in a circle, rumbling in laughter.

"You been gone too long, June-bug." He set me down, deep brown eyes scrutinizing me, assessing me, searching out my secrets. "I had nobody to tattoo me, and I got empty spaces I can't reach."

"I'm sorry," I said, wrapping my arms around his broad waist. "Work can get so busy, you know? Sometimes it's hard to get away."

"Have you come to tell me you're quittin' that nonsense job of yours?" His voice was hopeful.

I frowned as I stepped away from him. "You know I can't do that, Ink."

As always, Ink was bare from the waist up, wearing a pair of blue gym shorts that hung to his knees, and he was barefoot—this was how Ink dressed pretty much all the time. Even in the winter, he might stuff his bare feet into a pair of winter boots and throw a coat on if it was *really* cold outside, but for the most part, Ink hated wearing more clothes than necessary. He lived behind the shop in a modular tiny home he built himself, so he rarely left this particular stretch of Ketchikan, especially since there was a little market a few doors down where he could get food and anything else he needed.

Ink shook his beard at me—his beard was a thing of beauty, hanging down to his chest, always combed and clean and trimmed into a neat oval, it was thick and bushy and amazing. He tended to shift his jaw around when he was thinking really hard, and it made his beard waggle—so, if his beard did that little dance, I knew I was about to get an earful.

"Bullshit," he grumbled.

I blinked at him. "Ink, come on. I just came over for a visit...can we not have this conversation right off the bat?"

"It ain't conversation. You tell me you can't quit that mess, I tell you you have to. You're goin' to—you just don't know it yet. Ain't no lawyers or no courts that need you. That's work for somebody else. Art needs you. Skin needs you." He's always had a distinctive way of speaking—almost spiritual—and I'm used to it, but it takes some people time to figure him out.

I wiped my face with both hands. "You know I'd love nothing more than to quit the firm and come work for you, Ink. But you know what Mom and Dad will say."

His expression darkened. "They think they're doin' you a favor, pushin' you into that fancy law job. You're an *artist*, June-bug. And you always have been. The sooner they get that through their thick skulls, the better."

"They mean well, Ink."

He slumped heavily back into his tattoo chair, propped up his foot, twisted it awkwardly to one side, and pulled on a fresh pair of black rubber gloves. He resumed work.

He was doing what I loved best in the world. I'm a tattoo artist. No one but Ink knows, not even Izzy or Kitty, and especially not my parents. The only people I've ever tattooed are Ink and myself and I would give anything to do what Ink does.

We spent some time in companionable silence as he finished the outline of his newest ankle piece. He set his gun aside, stripped off the gloves, and shot me a glance.

"You here to do one or get one?" he asked.

I shrugged, smiling. "Both?"

He nodded. "Best answer." He gestured to the chair. "I'll finish coloring the piece on your shoulder blade, and then you can do more on my hip."

I grinned at him, shrugging out of my cardigan,

folding it and setting it aside. I faced away from Ink as I unbuttoned my shirt, flipped it around so I was wearing it backward, and then straddled the tattoo chair to give Ink access to my shoulder.

He playfully snapped my bra strap as he settled on his rolling stool. "Gotta undo this, June-bug. Need to get around it."

I reached around behind my back and unfastened the bra strap, shrugging the straps down around my arms; I had to adjust the bra cups to stay tight against my chest, and as I did so, the folded piece of paper fell out and onto my lap. I picked it up, fiddling with it as Ink ran his fingertips along the outline of a mother bear with her two cubs. The meaning of this tattoo was very personal to me and Ink—the mother bear was art, and the two cubs were Ink and myself.

Ink rumbled an amused laugh. "You're weird, you know that, June-Bug?"

I rested my cheek against the cold leather of the chair. "Well, maybe. But why do you say that?"

"You are the most modest lady I've ever met. You never show off all this sexy ink of yours. You never wear nothin' Meemaw Isaac wouldn't wear. We two are cousins. We took baths together as kids, went skinny-dipping in the channel up till we were teenagers. You know that as a tattoo artist I view the human body as a canvas, and you know I've seen plenty of women naked in a professional capacity, and that if you was sittin' there in that chair without nothing coverin' you, it wouldn't be weird. You know that, and I know you know, but you still cover up like you got somethin' secret from me hidden under that shirt."

I sighed as the gun started buzzing—I loved that sound more than anything else. "Yes, Ink, I know. And if I were to decide I wanted a tattoo on one of my breasts, I'd be fine having you do it. When I get in the chair, it stops being weird to be naked, because you're my best friend and my family, and you're a professional. I know all this." I pulled my braid over my shoulder to get it out of the way as he rested his hands on my back, and then I felt the sharp buzzing sting of the needle as he set to work. "It's just how I am. I'm not…comfortable being exposed. I don't know why. I just like being clothed."

He was quiet a few moments as he settled into the rhythm of inking me. "You know, people tend to look at us tattoo artists as shrinks."

"Yes, I know."

"I've always been a good listener. So, you know I hear some shit you ain't sayin', yeah?"

I secretly relished the sting of the needle, the dragging ache of it. I wouldn't consider myself a masochist, but I did somehow love the pain of getting a tattoo. "Yes, Ink, I know—you don't need to say it."

"Tough titty, I'm gonna say it anyway."

"Of course you are. And you don't have to use vulgar phrases like that. It's not cute."

He snorted. "I say what I say, June-bug. You ain't my mama." He paused, wiped the excess ink away, and brought the needle back to my skin. "You keep covered up 'cause you're ashamed of your ink."

"I am not!"

"I don't mean ashamed of your ink, meanin' me. I mean your tats."

"I'm not ashamed of you *or* my tattoos."

"Then why do you cover 'em up even when you're not playin' fancy lawyer lady?"

I sighed. "I'm not a lawyer, I'm a legal assistant. And I cover them up because…" I trailed off, not sure how to answer.

"You can't find the words, 'cause I already said 'em."

"It's not shame, it's…fear."

"What you scared of?"

"Mom and Dad." I paused. "Mom, mostly."

"They don't know you got tats?"

"You know they don't."

"I thought maybe it was a thing you just didn't talk about."

I shook my head. "No, they don't know. I keep

them covered up. Not even Kitty or Izzy know about them."

Ink stopped tattooing—I felt his incredulous stare. "They are your best friends, your roommates. Three ladies, you all sharin' *one* bathroom, and they don't know you got tats all over?"

"I keep them covered up. I wear a towel coming out of or going into the shower. I dress in my room. They know I'm modest and that I don't like being naked around other people. They just accept it as part of the weirdness that is me."

"What about dudes?" he asked.

"What about them?"

"You keep 'em covered when you're...you know...doin' the nasty?"

I blushed hard. "We are *not* talking about my sex life, Ink Isaac."

"I'm just curious if you hide 'em even from guys you hook up with." I couldn't answer, and for someone who knew me as well as Ink did, it was all the answer he needed. "You do! You're so scared and so ashamed, you don't let no one but me know you got all this beautiful ink?"

"It's not their business," I told him. "Just because we're sharing a few minutes of mutual pleasure doesn't mean they get to know everything about me. And you know damn well how personal my ink is, and you know *why* it's personal. I keep the lights off, and I let them think it's because I'm insecure about being..." I shrugged, hating to say it, knowing he would pounce on it and get mad at me for it, "...bigger," I finished, lamely.

He didn't just pull the gun away; he turned it off and spun the chair around so I had to look him in the eye. "The *fuck* you just say?"

I remained as I was, lying forward against the tattoo chair, twisting and flipping the folded piece of paper in my fingers. I eyed him steadily. "I'm not a dainty girl, Ink."

He stood up to his full, imposing height, and I was reminded that while I'm comfortable with him, and I know him as a big, sweet teddy bear, he can get up close and personal. "Juneau Isaac, you take that back right now or we'll be fightin' for real."

"It's just the truth. I know I'm not, like, fat or anything, but I'm not a skinny girl either."

He continued to glare at me. "You see me?" He pounded both fists against his chest like an angry gorilla. "You take a good look at this, June-bug."

"I see you, Ink."

He shook his head. "Naw, you don't. Six feet seven inches. Three hundred pounds. My whole life I've been told I'm not just fat, but obese. They don't see the muscle I got under this," he said, and pinched his belly roll. "Me? *I'm* big. I coulda been an NFL football player. Strong, fast, tough. But I ain't that, I ain't no athlete. I only ever wanted one thing—this." He gestured at his shop. "I own this, free and clear, all paid up and all *mine*. I paid for it doin' tattoos from the time I was legally allowed to. I paid for it with my art. I know I'm big, June-bug. But I also know I got somethin' to offer. I know some ladies like the way I look, and I know some don't. I may not be a sexy celebrity with them wash pan abs. But I know I got my own way of lookin' good, and I don't take no shit about it from nobody—'specially not my own self."

"Ink—" I protested.

"No. I can hear what you're saying. I know you, and I know you know you're sexy as anything. But giving off this insecure vibe—this feeling that you are too big, or whatever, when you have no reason to feel that way means, deep down, you *do* have some shit you need to deal with. And it ain't just about bein' afraid of Uncle Simon and Aunt Judy findin' out you *got* tats and want to *do* tats."

I blinked hard. "Ink—dammit."

He sank back down on his stool, and it protested under his weight, the casters rattling as he pivoted me around and picked up the gun again. "You gotta figure this shit out, cuz. You won't never quit that stupid law firm if you don't."

"Ink, listen—"

He cut me off. "No more listening. I heard every-thing you got to say. The rest is work you got to do inside. There's nothing I can say to fix it, and there's nothin' you can say to me that'll make it less true."

"Shut up, you big stupid bear," I muttered, an old insult between us.

"I *told* you, I'm a tattoo chair shrink. Ain't no lie in that, June-bug."

I sighed and let the silence grow between us; he was right, at least, in that there wasn't any more val-ue in talking about it, because he'd said his piece and nothing I could say would change his mind. Once he saw what he considered to be the truth, there was no changing his mind.

Was he right, though?

Maybe a little bit. I did have a tiny bit of insecu-rity about my figure. About my weight, and the size on the tags of my dresses, blouses, and skirts. But, like Ink, I do know my value, and I know I'm a good person no matter what I look like. I also know a lot of men like the way I'm shaped, and they like my curves and my softness; not everyone likes skinny women.

So, really, if I'm being honest with myself, the insecurity thing is a front. And… it's complicated.

The silence was broken only by the buzzing of the tattoo gun, and the low music from the speakers, and after about an hour and a half he wiped the excess ink away, and turned off the gun and set it aside. He dabbed and wiped around the tattoo until my skin was clean and dry, and then he spun the chair around and handed me a wide mirror with a long handle.

"There. I think that piece is done."

I examined the tattoo in the mirror. It was brightly colored, almost photorealistic, and absolutely beautiful. The cubs follow their mother across the plane of my back and shoulder, and the mama bear's muzzle angles down over my shoulder and onto the upper portion of my arm. The cubs are spread from just under the base of my neck to just behind my underarm. Warm brown fur, white and brown eyes, black claws on their paws, pink tongues, all against the dark olive-brown of my skin.

"Ink...god, I love it."

He touched the cub nearer the base of my neck. "This one's me. Because I got your back."

I teared up. "I know you do."

He made a gruff huffing sound in his throat and turned away to strip off his gloves; he's always had a soft spot for me. "My turn. I want some dots and triangles on my hip, and maybe some of those half-circle cross things."

I nodded, knowing what he meant. "I'll sketch

out a design while you clean the gun."

I found his sketch pad and a charcoal pencil, and went to work designing his tattoo, thinking about what I know of our tribe's history of ritual tattoos, what he already has, and what will look best with the ink around it.

I left my shirt on backward, but I buttoned the bottom couple of buttons, just so it would stay in place. I also kept my bra unhooked, letting the straps dangle, just so the angry skin around my tattoo could breathe.

I showed Ink my design, and he gave it an approving nod. "Looks great." He eyed me with sarcastic amusement. "You gonna barf when I pull my shorts down?"

"Do you have underwear on?" I asked as I finished copying the design onto tracing paper.

He tugged the waistband of his shorts away, glancing down. "Nope. Forgot them."

"Then yes, probably."

He rolled his eyes. "Like you never saw a johnson before."

I faked a gag as I slipped on the tattooing gloves. "Of course I have. But you're my cousin and I don't want to see yours." I glared at him. "And it's more about your butt than your ding-dong."

He snorted in laughter. "Did you really just call

it that?" After adjusting the angle of the chair, Ink worked his shorts down around his left hip and lay against the reclined chair, partially on his side. "And who even cares about butts? A butt is a butt is a butt. No big deal."

I laid the tracing paper with the design on it against his hip, finding the perfect placement for it before I began tracing the design onto his skin with a tattoo marker.

For the next twenty minutes or so, I let myself get utterly lost in the process of tracing the design on his skin, making sure each line and circle and dot was absolutely perfect. Then, finally, I picked up the gun and placed the ink he'd chosen on the tray, turned the gun on, and dipped it into the ink. The gun hummed reassuringly in my hand, and I began permanently inking the tattoo onto my cousin's skin.

Halfway through the first series of dots and tri-angles, the bell over the door jangled.

"Be with you in a while," Ink yelled. "Sorta busy at the moment."

My shirt was on backward, held against my body with two little buttons, my bra was undone and hanging from my shoulders, leaving my entire back bare.

My bare back...with the fresh tattoo of the mama Kodiak and her cubs, around them the salmon in vivid pink leaping out of a raging river in churning blues and whites. My left shoulder depicted a narrow fjord angling diagonally away from my shoulder with the towering pines reflected in the mirror-still waters, a setting sun in violent oranges and pinks and reds on the round of my shoulder, and the stylized wolf tracks in deep dark black ink trailing from high on my left ribcage down around my lower back where they disappeared under the hem of my skirt, merging with the tribal circles, dots, triangles, V- and Y- shapes on my right hip.

Each tattoo had a very specific story and meaning, and they were deeply and intensely personal to me. I only allowed myself to be vulnerable here in Ink's shop because it was so far out of the way from anywhere my family or friends might go that there's no chance they'd ever see me here. Because he worked by appointment only—due to the insane and ever-growing demand for his skills—walk-ins were rare.

"Juneau?" a familiar bass voice rumbled. "That you?"

Something inside me lurched. A prickling of the fine hairs on my skin, a tightening in my belly, a heating further south, a shortness of breath. I froze.

No way.

NO.

Gingerly, carefully, I pulled the gun away from Ink's skin and turned it off. I tried to close the edges of my shirt together—which was impossible and futile. He'd already seen my tattoos…

I turned around. "Remington…hi."

FIVE

Remington

I STARED, STANDING IN MUTE, STUNNED SILENCE, MY JAW ON the floor.

Juneau was the last person I expected to see when I walked in the front door of Ketchikan's most famous tattoo parlor.

She had tattoos.

A *lot* of them.

Big, elaborate, full-color pieces done by someone with an obvious love for and dedication to the art. They were done by someone with incredible talent.

Her back was thrilling to look at; alluring, sexy, and spiritual all at the same time.

The curve of it, the hint of breast on one side,

plus all that incredible, beautiful ink…I was in serious danger of springing a hard-on right here, just from a quick glimpse of her back.

But now she was staring at me as if terrified, mortified, and angry all at the same time. It seemed she was mad that I was here, that I'd dared…I don't quite know how to pinpoint it—that I'd dared see her in this environment.

"Juneau," I said, only barely managing to stammer out her name. "What are you…you're…what are—"

So much for not stammering like a quibbling fuckhead.

"She's in the middle of a tattoo, my man," the massive man in the chair said. "Take a seat and I'll be with you in a minute."

"Remington, I…" Her mouth worked, but nothing else came out.

"June-bug." His voice was hard, and full of meaning she clearly understood. "Finish the tat."

"Ink. He—I—"

"No place for drama in the tattoo chair, June-bug. You know the rules."

"If the gun's on, the drama's off. The ink is sacred." She repeated the well-known phrases, her tone and expression fully imparting their ritual importance.

"Go sit, Remington. There's a rack of design

books by the coffee maker. Help yourself." Her voice was cold and distant and professional.

I didn't do well with being told what to do, and her words were an order, no mistaking that.

Instead of heading for the waiting area like I was told, I wandered over to where Juneau was leaning over the giant man in the tattoo chair. She'd dismissed me, and had expected me to listen, or she was doing a good job of ignoring me as I stood a few feet away, examining the tattoo in progress with intense interest.

She flicked the gun back on after a moment, let out a short, sharp breath, and then bent over the man, whose name, if she was to be believed, was Ink. She dragged the gun with exaggerated care over the design drawn on his skin in black marker, following the lines and circles and dots across the plane of his hip. She was very good, I could tell that much. I could also tell, from the style of the other tattoos on the man's thigh and across his back that she'd done quite a lot of his work, if not most of it.

"You're distracting me," Juneau said, not looking up. "I told you to go sit."

"I don't do orders, babe. I'm just watching." I inched a little closer. "You do good work."

"Hey, my man." Ink's voice was low and threatening, and I felt even my stomach flip a little at the prospect of making this mammoth bruiser of a man angry. "Come here."

I circled wide around Juneau and stopped where I could see his face. "What's up?"

"Hold on a sec, June-bug," he said, and the buzzing stopped immediately. Then, he extended his hand to me; I took it, shook, and was careful to not give away the pain of his crushing grip. "I'm Ink. I own this place. And she's my cousin. So if you won't take orders from her, you'll take orders from me." He looked me over. "You're plenty big, but I'm guessin' I can still toss you out on your ass if you want to make this a thing."

I backed up, holding my hands up. "I'm just curious. Call it...professional curiosity."

His eyebrow shot up. "You do ink?" he glanced at me, catching the hints of tattoos peeking out from the sleeves of my T-shirt.

I bobbled my head side to side. "Sort of."

Juneau frowned. "According to Kitty, you and your brothers were wildfire fighters. And now you own a bar. Since when do you do tattoos?"

"It's a long story and not one I'm telling now," I said. "You want to be precise, call my curiosity quasi-professional, or...hopefully professional."

"Well, it's my ass that's hanging out of my shorts, so unless you got a damn good and specific reason you're sniffing around after my cousin, you can go fuck off till this tat is done. Got me?"

"I'm not sniffing around after anyone. I came to look at getting a tattoo." I glanced at Juneau, taking in her backward shirt and the way she was desperately trying to pretend she wasn't aware of me. "I didn't know she was here. Honestly, this is the last place on earth I'd expect to find her."

"Yeah, you and everyone else, and that's how she likes it." Ink jutted his chin at the waiting area. "Go sit, or no tattoo."

Unwilling to piss off the owner of this kick-ass tattoo studio, I complied and took a seat, but I made sure to position myself in such a way that I could steal glances at Juneau's back.

I wanted to see those tats up close and personal. I wanted to flick open those two stupid little buttons near the small of her back and push aside those straps and bare the rest of her skin, and take my time perusing the ink I now knew she had been hiding under those conservative clothes.

After a while, Juneau's voice broke the relative silence. "Quit staring at me, Remington."

"I'm not. I'm just looking." I stood up to pour myself a cup of coffee. "Your ink is beautiful."

"Thank you." Her voice was small and hesitant. "Ink did it."

"Is that really your name?" I asked.

"Yep. Or so it says on my birth certificate."

"You did all those tattoos on her back?" I asked, unable to help myself from taking my Styrofoam cup of coffee across the shop to stand close enough that I could see her ink more closely.

"Yep."

"Damn, dude. You're really good." I laughed. "I guess that's why you're named Ink, huh?"

He rumbled a laugh. "Got it backward, actually. I was named Ink because my dad thought it was a cool name. I took to tattoos because of my name rather than the other way around."

I was close enough now, having been inching back over, that I could see the tattoos on her back in full detail. I only barely restrained myself from running my fingers over the brilliant colors and vivid images on her soft, perfect skin.

She pulled the gun away from Ink and twisted on the stool to glare up at me, holding on to her shirt with her free hand, keeping the ink-smeared glove away. "You're making me nervous, standing there staring at my back."

"I'm sorry, I just...I love tattoos, and yours are beautiful."

"Thank you, but you need to go sit. You're making me nervous, and if I'm nervous, I'm liable to mess up, and that would be—"

"That would be your ass on a silver platter, my friend," Ink rumbled.

"All right, all right," I said, holding up both hands.

I headed back to the waiting area and snagged a design book from the rack. It was a three-ring binder with sketches of tattoo design ideas enclosed in plastic sleeves. Along with the usual stuff—cursive lettering, birds, trees, flowers, and clocks—there were examples of more elaborate landscapes, and animals-in-action scenes, both of which were featured in dramatic fashion on Juneau's back.

Ink was clearly a master of those styles, because there were several pages of photographs, each one beautifully and lovingly illustrated on human flesh. A few things were noticeably absent from his portfolio of designs: the fake so-called "tribal" stuff, Asian calligraphy, and impersonal, ubiquitous crap like barbed wire and hearts with arrows. He also had a whole book dedicated to Inuit tattoos, but at the front of this book, he had a disclaimer done in pencil-and-ink lettering: *These designs are samples only, as each tattoo must be designed specifically for each person, based on meaning and personal history. I will not do these tattoos on someone who is not Native Alaskan or from some other Inuit tribe, so don't ask. If you don't know what these mean, you don't get them. No exceptions. I can do poke tattoos and I can use needle and thread, but I use tattoo ink, for health inspection reasons.*

"All right, Ink. I think you're done." I heard Juneau's voice break the silence after another hour or so, during which I perused the native designs book, just out of curiosity.

"Damn girl, that looks better than I'd hoped," I heard Ink tell Juneau.

She laughed. "You thought I'd let him mess me up?"

"No, but it's been more than a month since you been back here," he said. "Figured you may be out of practice."

"I'll come back sooner next time, I promise."

"Wouldn't have to be a next time if you'd just—"

"Ink." Her voice was sharp as she cut him off. "Don't."

"I'm just sayin'."

"We've already talked this to death. Enough."

"Chicken."

She laughed. "Shut up, you big dumb bear."

I glanced over to see her putting a wrap on Ink's hip.

"I'm going to the market," he said, after she finished. "You want anything?"

She shrugged. "Whatever is fine. I'm hungry, so I'll eat anything."

Ink glanced at me, and then at Juneau. "You good here for a few minutes?"

She understood what he was getting at, and then simply nodded. "Yeah, I'm good."

His eyes narrowed. "You're uncomfortable with him around, June-bug. I can see it."

She shook her head, smiling reassuringly. "It's fine, I promise."

"You gonna tattoo him?"

Her eyes widened at the suggestion. "No, I am not. You know me better than that."

Ink jutted his chin at me. "I'll be back soon, and we can go over your design."

I waved a hand. "No rush." I glanced at Juneau. "I'm good here with her."

Ink's expression hardened. "Yeah, well…you better *be* good, know what I mean, pretty boy?"

I laughed. "Crystal clear."

Barefoot, shirtless, with his shorts still tugged low under his left hip to bare his new tattoo—and a fair chunk of his left buttock—he lumbered on deceptively light feet out the door, his long black ponytail swaying, his thick, chest-length beard fluttering in the wind.

And then I was alone in the tattoo shop with Juneau.

She was capping the tattoo ink bottles, sanitizing the gun, and wiping down the chair. Facing away from me, she studiously ignored me.

I approached her quietly, and I don't think she noticed me at first.

I was standing behind her and I itched to touch those tattoos, itched to feel that satin-soft skin.

Finally, I knew she felt my presence—she stiffened, but didn't turn around. "What are you doing, Remington?" she asked, pausing in the act of stripping off her gloves.

"Just looking at your tattoos."

"Ink is really talented, isn't he?" she said, her head ducked down, her braid over one shoulder. She twisted her head to one side, glancing at me with a sidelong glance over her shoulder. "Why are you here? Did you know I'd be here?"

I felt my hands drifting up, and I knew she saw their movement—already stiff, she tensed further as my hands fluttered like birds alighting on a thin branch. "Scout's honor, Juneau. I had no idea you'd be here. I came to look at tattoos, and his place had the best rating on Google."

"You were a Boy Scout?"

I snorted. "Hell, yes, I was. Eagle Scout, babe. All three of us were. It was one of the few things that wasn't military school or sports we could do that would keep us out of trouble."

"You weren't into sports? I'd have thought you and your brothers were three letter varsity sort of guys."

I laughed again. "Think again. We don't play well with others, Juneau. We tried flag football in third grade, but we got kicked off because we kept tackling the other kids. We tried out in high school, but during the tryouts Ram tackled the star quarterback wrong and broke his collarbone, and that was that. We grew up in Fuck-Everything-Ville, Oklahoma, where there wasn't shit to do except sports, Boy Scouts, and D-F-F-ing."

"D-F-F-ing?" she asked.

"Drinking, fighting, and fucking."

She went back to cleaning up the workstation, but it seemed to me, in my admittedly limited experience, that the station was pretty clean already.

"Juneau, I—" I trailed off, not sure what I intended to say.

"What?"

That was a lie—I knew what I wanted to say, and I also knew how she'd react. "Your tattoos are gorgeous."

Her laugh was soft, and not unkind. "You've said that already. Thanks."

"Show me the rest."

She stiffened again. "I don't think so. You weren't even supposed to see these."

"Why not? They're amazing?"

She shrugged, and glanced at me in the mirror

that took up the entire wall behind the tattoo station. "You just weren't. Like you said, it's a long story and not one I want to tell. Not to you—not now, and probably not ever."

"Even if I ask really nicely?" I said, meeting her gaze.

She watched my hands drift up again—I'd restrained them once, but now they had a mind of their own. They lifted, drifted, settling lightly on her shoulders, on the shirt. Her eyes widened, and her lips parted—her tongue peeked out and ran along her lower lip, that plump, pink curve. She watched in the mirror, her dark eyes unreadable and intense, as I slid my fingers onto her skin. Soft—so soft—softer than I'd even imagined it to be. I brushed the fine cotton of her shirt across her shoulders, to the edges.

"Remington—" she whispered.

I watched her eyes, held her gaze, and swept the shirt off her shoulders entirely; her breath caught in a sharp gasp as the garment sagged against her elbows. Her back was entirely bared, now...except—

I slipped the two buttons free of the buttonholes, and the shirt draped forward, falling off, held in place now only by one of her hands. Her bra straps were dangling around her elbows as well, and I could see hints of the cups, white lace, innocent and sensual. A swell of breast, and the curve of her spine, and the alluring, exotic dark caramel of her dark skin, and the colorful sweep of her tattoos.

I caressed a palm across her shoulders, careful to avoid the fresh tattoo, and then followed down her arm, and her ribs, and then her back, fingertips tracing the wolf paw tracks as they danced in single file. Then up, rubbing a thumb across the curved beaks of the salmons' mouths, and the deep rippling blue hues of the fjord waters and the blushing fiery sun setting on her shoulder...

"What do they mean?" I asked, my voice a low whisper. "I know they have meaning."

"The new one—the mama bear is art, the art of tattooing, specifically. The cubs are Ink and me." She reached up and tapped the wolf tracks. "Those are my sisters. The salmon jumping upriver is my father. The fjord and the sunset is my mother." Her voice dropped to a whisper. "I don't know why I told you any of that."

I lifted my shirt to show her the left side of my ribcage; there was a doorframe, partly closed, just a hint of a woman's high heel vanishing through it. "That's my mother." I tapped the heel. "She left when we were seven."

"Oh. I—I'm sorry."

"I only tell you that to share my personal story so we're even." I ran my palms over her back, exploring now, testing her limits, feeling the swelling thrill of touching her glorious skin with its delicate softness and vivid illustrations.

I dragged my fingers up her sides—she wasn't ticklish, but she did shudder. For a different reason, I'd like to think.

"Remington…" She curled away from my touch, and then twisted away.

Only, in her haste to retreat from my touch, she seemed to have forgotten that her shirt wasn't fastened in any way, and the movement as she twisted away sent the garment tumbling to the ground, her bra with it. She lurched down, snatching the shirt and clasping it desperately against her front.

She stood in front of me, trembling, eyes locked on mine, shirt knotted in her fists, pressed hard against her chest. Keeping my eyes on hers, I bent, retrieved her bra, and gestured to her with it.

"Move your hands," I murmured.

She shook her head.

"Trust me."

She shot me a disgusted eye roll. "You just want to see my boobs."

"Absolutely." When she started to protest, I cut over her. "I absolutely, desperately want to see you bare, all over. I already told you that. But I only want that when you show me yourself voluntarily."

"I won't," she whispered. "Not ever."

I just smirked. "Don't be so sure."

"Remington, you don't understand—"

I held the bra cups in one hand, and clasped her wrists in the other. "I'm gonna put it on you." I tugged them away. "Trust me, Juneau."

"Why would I?" she asked, resisting.

"Why wouldn't you?" I countered, letting her keep the shirt pressed against herself.

"The last time we talked, you told me you wanted to—"

"I remember. And I also remember telling you you probably didn't want to know." I leaned closer to her, until I could smell the faint tang of her perfume. "I want that. I fantasize about that, Juneau. And you want to know something else?" I asked, applying pressure, testing her resistance.

"What?" she whispered, gradually letting me pull the shirt away from her body, my eyes locked on hers.

This is a funny situation: I'm trying to put her clothing on her, and she's resisting.

I kept our gazes locked, kept my eyes on hers. "I think you fantasize about that, too."

Her eyes flicked away, to a tiny square of much-folded yellow, lined notebook paper sitting on the counter of the tattoo station.

Interesting.

"I do not," she muttered, the lie obvious in her eyes, her voice.

"Such a bad liar, Juneau," I said, smirking at her.

"I am not."

I decided, in that moment, to give in to the asshole inside me—in this case, the asshole was fed by equal parts lust and curiosity.

I reached forward and snatched the square of paper.

"Give me that!" Juneau snapped. "That's mine."

I just smirked, holding up the bra in one hand and the square of paper in the other. "Choose."

I knew she couldn't put the shirt on without letting me see, and we both knew there was zero chance I was turning away to give her privacy.

"You're such a bastard."

"Yeah, well, you already knew that about me, didn't you?"

She bit her lip hard, and then huffed in anger. "Give them to me, Remington."

"Not a chance." I stared down at her. "Make you a deal. Trust me—let me help you get dressed, and I'll give you your little note back without reading it."

"Go to hell. Just give me the bra and the...note. Don't be a dick!"

"Oooh, a swear word!" I backed up a step. "Getting feisty."

She glared at me. "You think because you're so damn sexy and good-looking you can just do what you want, is that it?" she said, her eyes sparking fire. "You can go to hell."

She set her jaw, lifted her chin, and I knew she'd made some kind of decision. She unclenched her fists, letting the shirt—knotted in her fists—drape loose in front of her. Sucking in a deep breath, keeping her eyes locked defiantly on mine, she shook it out, oriented it, and slipped her right hand through the correct sleeve, swinging the button-down around behind her.

And, just like that, she was bare for me, her entire front exposed. Heavy, round breasts with wide, dark areolae that took up almost the entire front of each breast, her thick dark nipples standing out on end. Her skin was decorated across her breastbone and shoulders above her cleavage with lines and triangles and various rune-like shapes—things I recognized from Ink's sample book as being culturally significant for her—and then across her stomach and ribcage and down both sides, vanishing under her skirt's waistband—more tribal markings and animals and a jumble of images.

And then I stepped forward, covering her breasts with the bra; I had to cover them, or I'd lose what little control I had left. The vision of her lasted barely a moment—only an instant, and it was a glance I knew would haunt me forever. I pressed the cups against her dusky flesh, guiding her arms through the straps, and then helping her with her shirt. I leaned close enough to smell her hair and her perfume and her skin and her breath—and reached around behind her with both hands, hooking the eyelets together behind her back, and then set to work buttoning the shirt from the bottom up, my eyes on hers the entire time. I was careful not to get too close, not to let my painful erection press against her.

Her gaze was troubled, confused, angry—and aroused. "Happy now?"

"Happy?" I snorted derisively. "No, not even close. That was like giving a man dying of thirst two little drops of water on his tongue."

Her eyes rolled. "So dramatic." Her gaze shot to the piece of paper still gripped in one of my hands. "Will you please give me that?"

"What's it worth to you?" I asked, grinning at her.

She narrowed her eyes at me. "If you were anything like honorable or a gentleman, you'd just give it back."

"If I was anything like honorable or a gentleman, I wouldn't have taken it in the first place," I said. "And one my greatest failings is that I'm insatiably curious."

"If you don't give me that back, I'll never speak to you again, Remington."

I laughed. "I was under the impression that was already the plan. What with the way you left Seattle and all…" I shrugged, flipping the square of folded notebook paper between my fingers. "Yet…here we are."

"You are SUCH an asshole, Remington Badd," she snapped. "For real."

I just grinned all the harder. "You know it. All my life, baby, and I ain't plannin' on changing anytime soon."

"Give…it…*back*," she snarled. "Now." Her eyes met mine, shifted to desperate pleading. "Please?"

I frowned. "It's really that important to you?"

"I'm a very private person, Remington," she whispered. "You've already invaded my privacy in ways you'll never understand."

"Invaded your privacy?" I echoed in disbelief. "What, by one little peek at your tits? Come on, Juneau—they're just boobs, at the end of the day. And I didn't really see all that much or for that long, except that you've got more seriously killer tats covered up under there."

She shook her head. "It's not about that. I mean, yeah, that was mortifying. I never let anyone see me like that, not ever. Just like I never have these conversations, but yet with you, this crap is happening again." She closed her eyes.

"Me just being here, in this tattoo parlor, with you, is an invasion of your privacy?" I asked, still not quite following. "And what do you mean, you never let anyone see you like that?"

She shook her head. "You wouldn't get it." She gestured at her torso, now once again modestly covered. "I don't show people my tattoos. Ink is literally the only human being alive who even knows I have them. And now…you."

I blinked in shock. "So what, you're a virgin? No guy has ever seen you naked?"

"No, I'm not a virgin, thank you very much," she snapped. The ire quickly faded, however, morphing into…insecurity, or something similar to it. "There are ways of…hiding them."

I stepped back, turning in a circle, running my hands through my hair. "Well then I'm just confused to hell and gone," I said. "Because while I had you pegged for modest and reserved and all that, and probably more on the innocent side of things, sexually, I didn't have you pegged as insecure."

"I'm not insecure!" she snapped. "I told you, you wouldn't understand."

I stepped up close to her and stared down into her deep, warm, conflicted brown eyes. "No, I don't.

But I *could*, and I'd sure as fuck like the opportunity to try."

She shook her head. "No, no." She backed away. "You say that, but…you don't, not really. You just want to lure me into sleeping with you."

"You're underestimating me in a big way," I said, my voice low and quiet. "I'm not gonna lie—yes, I have every intention of seducing you into sleeping with me. But I'm capable of a hell of a lot more than just that."

I cupped her cheek in one hand, and she blinked, and then her eyes went wide and her eyebrows crinkled and her teeth caught at her lower lip, and her face tilted up to mine.

"You just have to give me a chance, Juneau."

SIX

Juneau

HIS HAND WAS WARM AND HARD AND ROUGH, YET somehow gentle.

He was a man of contradictions. He asked me to trust him, yet he snatched the note like a troublemaking eighth grader; he refused to give me my clothes, manipulating me into exposing myself to him, and then he immediately covered me, gently, almost lovingly dressing me when he could have drawn out the moment to get an eyeful of my breasts; he flat out told me he planned on seducing me, but in the same breath, he asked me to just give him a chance.

How do I reconcile all that?

His deep-set, vividly blue eyes pierced me. His

lips were parted, his chest rising and falling deeply, swiftly, as if fighting for breath...or control. He still had my sketch. It was, honestly, safer to call it a "note," because if I called it a sketch, he'd be even more curious.

I wanted to kiss him.

I wanted to know what his mouth felt like against mine. I wanted his arms around me, blocking out the world, his chest against mine in a solid wall of male muscle; I wanted his body against mine. I wanted to feel the evidence of his arousal against my belly.

I wanted his hands to wander my curves.

I *wanted* him.

I wanted *him*.

The bell tinkled, and I staggered backward, out of his touch.

"Hey, hey, I got some good stuff, cuz! We're gonna eat *good*!" Ink said as the front bell tinkled. "Ol' Joe just dropped off some salmon candy, and I got us some lunch meat, some sliced cheese, a big ol' salad, some chips and salsa, beer..."

"I have to go, Ink." I snatched my purse off the floor where I'd deposited it near the tattoo station. "I'm sorry."

Ink's brown eyes reflected hurt and puzzlement. "But I just bought all this food for the two of us." He slowly set the bags down on the floor at his feet.

I didn't want to go, but I couldn't stay here with Remington any longer; I'd do or say something monumentally stupid, something I'd regret. "I'm sorry, Ink. I—I have to go."

Ink's eyes cut to Remington, who was standing with my note between his fingers, watching me very closely. "Good job, asshole. I don't know what you said to her, but you just ruined my day."

"I'll come back, Ink," I said. "Soon. I promise."

"Yeah. Like, a month or two. Whatever." He snatched the bags up. "Go. I'll see you later."

Remington sprang into action, then, heading for the door. "Juneau, you stay here."

"I really have to go," I said, lying through my teeth. "It's not about you."

He smirked down at me as he paused beside me. "Like my dad says—never bullshit a bullshit artist, honey. You're just trying to escape the fact that you were about to kiss me." He touched a finger to his lips, and then to mine. "Soon. For now, you stay here with your cousin."

And then he was out the door, and gone. I was dumbfounded.

I sprinted to the door and half fell out of it onto the sidewalk, shouting after him. "HEY! My note!"

He was swaggering away, hands swinging at his sides, powerful legs driving him swiftly, tight hard ass cupped in faded blue denim, oblivious to the chill in the air with his skin-tight T-shirt. He spun around without slowing his pace, walking backward, flipping the note between his fingers in a dramatic flourish.

"Consider it insurance that I'll see you again!"

I stomped a foot and cursed, huffing, knowing it was futile. "You better not open it!"

He stopped walking and stood facing me about twenty feet away, stuffed the note into his back pocket, and then lifted his fingers in the Scout's Honor salute. "You have my word of honor as an Eagle Scout, and as a smokejumper, that I won't look at it...for three days. If I don't see you by the end of the third day, I'm opening it."

"That's not fair!"

He just smirked. "That's the deal." He pointed at me. "Seventy-two hours, Juneau."

I watched him reach a pickup truck that had seen better days: rust had eaten away at the wheel wells, the tailgate was fastened in place with a combination of duct tape and bungee cords, there was a sizable dent in the front right quarter panel, and there was a crack in the windshield running from one side to the other. He hopped in, slamming the door closed, and the engine started right away with a powerful rumble that said while the outside may have been in rough shape, the motor had been well-maintained. He drove away, and I stood outside watching until he was out of sight.

Back in the tattoo parlor, Ink was laying squares of cheddar cheese and circles of sliced turkey together on a plate in neatly overlapping layers. He had blue corn chips dumped into a big bowl, and the salsa poured into another smaller bowl, and the salad mixed up in a third bowl. There was a six-pack of locally brewed beer, as well, the bottles sweating with fresh condensation, as well as half of an apple pie—which Ink was famous for within our extended family. In the center of the spread was a bowl of sweet, smoked Salmon candy. This stuff was like crack to me, and I put Remington out of my mind while I helped myself.

"You stayin', then, June-bug?" he asked, glancing up at me as he finished layering the meat and cheese.

I sank in the tattoo chair with a heavy sigh. "Yeah, I'm staying."

He only just barely suppressed a grin. "So the *cheechako* was right, huh?"

I glared at my cousin. "No."

"You say that like our little cousin John John tells his mama he didn't steal the cookies."

"Shut up, Ink."

"Ain't like you to get all petulant, June-bug. Sassin' me like this tells me I'm more right than I'm figurin'."

I lurched out of the chair and drew up one of the waiting chairs over to the low coffee table where Ink had our dinner spread out. I took a bit more salmon and then dipped a chip into the salsa, and then washed it all down with a freshly cracked beer.

"Not answering."

He nodded, and plucked a chip from the bag. "I see how it is. Can't trust your own cousin with the truth. Ain't like I haven't known you since we was pissin' our diapers or nothin'."

"It's complicated, okay?"

"You keep saying that. What's complicated about it?" Ink lifted an eyebrow at me. "He wants your mukluks by his door. Seems simple to me."

I rolled my eyes at him as I chewed and swallowed. "By his door…and then gone by morning, you mean."

"So? You lookin' for your mate and I just didn't know?"

I took another roll of meat and cheese. "No, but that doesn't mean I want a one-and-done hookup either." I kept my eyes on the table instead of on Ink. "And with a guy like Remington? I'm not sure either one is a smart idea."

"How do you know him, anyways?" Ink asked, dipping meat and cheese into the salsa.

"He's a triplet, and one of his brothers is dating Kitty."

"I didn't think Kitty did dating any more than you do."

"It didn't start as dating, I guess."

"And he's an asshole who can't be trusted like your boy Remington?"

"We all thought so," I said with a sigh. "He's… well…I guess he's turning out to be different than we thought. Even to his own surprise, I think."

Ink brushed crumbs out of his beard. "So there's two more identical to him?" Ink shook his head in disbelief. "Don't seem right."

"Exactly."

"Want to know what I think?" Ink asked, his gaze intense on mine.

I met it steadily, afraid of the way his beard waggled as he considered his words. "Always."

"I think you want a mate *and* you want a one-and-done, you just can't decide which you want him for more. And you're scared of both."

"I've never had a one-night stand, Ink, and I don't plan to start now."

"Yeah, and you never had a mate. Unless I'm wrong you don't plan on startin' that either?"

I sighed. "No, I don't. I have to focus on my career."

He blew a raspberry, waving his hand at me as if to wave away a putrid smell. "That mess you call a job ain't a career, it's a distraction. It's you pacifyin' Uncle Simon and Aunt Judy."

"Ink, please."

"Okay, okay." He eyed me curiously. "I feel a truth, and I'm gonna tell it to you, now, like it or not."

I sighed again, taking a swig of beer. "Oh god, here we go."

"You're gonna tat that man. You're gonna put your mark on him, and he's gonna put his mark on you." He met my eyes for a long moment, and then shrugged as he looked away. "What that means, I dunno. It just feels like truth in my belly."

I rolled my eyes and sighed. "Okay, mister shaman."

He waved at me with a partially eaten meat-and-cheese roll. "Hey, I ever been wrong when I tell a belly-truth?"

I didn't answer, because the answer worried me more than I was willing to admit.

"Thought so." He patted me on the shoulder with a heavy hand. "Deny it all you want, June-bug, but you know I'm right."

"That's what I'm afraid of," I admitted.

He chuckled. "Eat up, cuz—I got a late-night client in fifteen." He glanced at me. "I gotta put a wrap on that tat before you go. You shouldn't even have that shirt on without it, and you know it. Bad girl."

"Extenuating circumstances," I mumbled.

"Sure, sure." He gestured at me as he washed his hands and got the supplies to cover my new tattoo. "Get that shirt off for me again. And don't worry, I won't peek."

I shucked my shirt, holding it against my chest as he put ointment on the tattoo, covered it with Saniderm, and then patted my other shoulder.

"Thanks," I said.

He just smirked, his beard not quite hiding it. "When you gonna show him the rest of your tats? He seemed to like the piece on your chest."

"I'll slap that smirk off your big dumb face, Ink, and don't think I'm kidding," I snapped as I put my shirt back on.

Ink just chortled a rumbling laugh. "You never hurt a fly in your whole damn life, June-bug."

"I'll make an exception for you if you don't lay off the subject."

Ink raised his hands palms out in surrender. "Okay, okay. You know I just mess with you because I love you, yeah?"

Finished eating, I washed my hands and dried them, and then wrapped my cousin up in a tight hug, my arms around his middle, my head against his thick, warm chest. "Yes, Ink, I know. I love you too."

"Of course you love me. I'm awesome." He

shoved me gently toward the door. "You can go now. I gotta get ready for my client."

"It's late anyway."

"Hey—how you getting home?" Ink asked. "You don't have a car. For that matter, how you even get here in the first place?"

"I...walked. Same way I always get here."

He frowned. "Ain't safe. I been saying that for years."

"And I keep telling you, I'll be fine."

"Yeah...till you ain't."

Ink moved behind the counter where the cash register was, withdrew an old rotary phone, dialed a number, and spoke in Yup'ik, which I spoke, but not as fluently as Ink did. I followed the conversation enough to know he was asking whoever was on the other end to come pick me up and take me home.

"Who are you pawning me off on, Ink?" I asked, as he hung up.

"Just a friend. You can trust him."

"Him?" I asked, skeptical.

"His name's Jasper Fox. I did some tattoos for him, and he keeps me supplied in fresh game, since you know I don't hunt no more. He's good people."

"Why don't you drive me home?" I asked. "I don't want to go with a random stranger."

"I don't have a car anymore—my old Jetta died

months ago. Plus, my client is gonna be here soon." He looked out the window and indicated a pickup even older than the one Remington had driven off in, as it sidled noisily up to the curb outside the parlor. "That's him. Just call him Fox."

"I don't know, Ink."

"June-bug. You trust me?"

"Of course."

"Then trust him. You're fine."

I let out a breath. "Okay, okay. Bye, Ink. I love you."

"You better come back here sooner next time, yeah?"

"I will."

The pickup was probably older than me, just this side of being an actual classic, but it was lovingly maintained, with not a scrap of rust on it anywhere, the engine idling with a rattling grumble. The man standing outside the truck, leaning a hip on the hood, was Yup'ik, of course—tall, thin, with jet-black hair cut short and left messy, as if he wore a hat more often than not and didn't care what it looked like. He wore loose blue jeans over scuffed, aged work boots, and a denim vest lined with fluffy white fleece, his chest and arms bare beneath it. He had an enormous knife strapped to his belt at his right hip, and there was a rifle in a rack on the back window of the cab.

His eyes were so dark they were almost black, glittering as they watched me approach, his clean-shaven jaw shifting. He said nothing.

"Jasper Fox?"

"Just Fox," he muttered.

"Okay. Fox, then."

He indicated the passenger door. "Get in."

Okay, then. I climbed in and buckled up; the inside of the truck smelled like old cigarettes, engine grease, and skinned animal carcass—the latter because there was a killed, cleaned, and skinned hare lying directly on the cracked leather bench seat between me and the driver's seat.

Fox climbed in, buckled up, put the truck in gear, and drove away. After a moment, he glanced at the carcass, and then reached down, snagged a leather game bag off the floorboard, and shoved the hare into it. "Sorry. Dinner."

I laughed. "If you know Ink, then you probably have heard some of the stories about my dad."

Fox nodded, a ghost of a grin on his face. "Drivin' around with out-of-season deer carcasses in the front seat of his truck."

"Still does it, too," I said. "A little old bunny doesn't bother me."

He seemed to know where he was going, as I remember hearing Ink mention my street address on the phone to Fox. The rest of the drive was silent, and oddly, not uncomfortable at all.

When we pulled up to my apartment building, he parked, jutted his chin at me, and that seemed to be his version of goodbye. It should have been weird that a man I didn't know, and had spoken less fifty words to knew where I lived, and had driven me home, but it wasn't. For some reason, Fox felt similar to Ink, in that familial, platonic sort of way.

I opened the door and stepped out of the truck. "Thank you for the ride, Fox."

He nodded once. "Welcome."

And then, as soon as I shut the door, he was gone in a cloud of blue-gray exhaust.

"Well," I said to no one. "That was weird."

"Who was that?" I heard Kitty say from behind me, startling me so badly I screamed and jumped a foot in the air.

I spun around, clapping my hand over my heart. "Holy crap, Kitty. You scared the bejesus out of me."

She was standing in the entryway to our building, dressed in her comfy lounging outfit—meaning her tiny green cotton shorts and a see-through white V-neck T-shirt, which she was wearing braless. "Sorry." She indicated the direction Fox had gone. "Who was he?"

"A friend of…a friend." I was being evasive, but

I wasn't ready to answer questions about Ink, or why I'd kept my tattoos secret from my best friends and roommates.

Kitty shook her head. "You are so mysterious, Juneau. A friend of a friend." She widened her eyes at me dramatically. "He had a rifle in the cab."

"This is Alaska, Kitty. You should be used to that by now."

"Out in the bush, maybe. This is downtown Ketchikan."

"You're acting like a *cheechako*," I muttered.

"A what?"

"An outsider. Someone not from Alaska."

Kitty blinked at me in surprise: I rarely gave away clues to my deeply traditional Yup'ik background—my great-grandmother was one of the last generations to get the traditional face tattoos as a girl, and it was from her I'd learned to appreciate the beauty of marking one's skin. My father was a hunting and hiking guide in the deep bush, and my mother made native art, which she sold to tourists as they got off the cruise ships. My sisters—all five of them—were married and had several children each, and kept homes; their husbands offset the family food budget through hunting year-round, using their subsistence licenses. I was the only one in the family to ever move away from our traditional Yup'ik territory: I went to the

University of Alaska in Anchorage to study law, and even though I moved back after I got my degree, I'm still Yup'ik, and always will be.

She frowned at me. "So, if you're getting rides from 'a friend of a friend,'" she put air quotes around the phrase, "Does that mean you're not seeing Remington?"

I closed my eyes and sighed. "Why does it have to be an either-or situation? I'm not *seeing* Remington, and Fox was, like I said, a friend of a friend who gave me a lift home since it was getting late."

Kitty's eyes narrowed. Right then a cold wind blew and Kitty shivered, wrapping her arms around her middle. "Get your evasive ass in here, Juneau. I'm getting cold standing here in the open doorway."

I pushed past her. "You *are* wearing your slutty jammies."

She whacked me on the butt as I trotted up the stairs in front of her. "Rome happens to love my slutty jammies, thank you very much."

"That's just because your ass hangs out of the bottom of the shorts, and that shirt is see-through." I turned back to her as I opened our door, and reached out to pinch her nipple, which was standing on end from the cold. "For example, you could currently cut glass with those puppies."

"That's exactly why I love that shirt," I heard

Roman's bass voice say—it made me jump, both because I wasn't expecting him to be there, and because he sounded, obviously, exactly like Remington. "Bring those glass cutters over here, sex-kitten."

I rolled my eyes at Roman, who was lounging on the couch, big bare feet kicked up on the arm, watching an old Oklahoma football game on our little TV. "Sex-kitten? Really?"

I was facing away from the couch as I set my purse down and slipped off my cardigan, moving gingerly; I happened to glance toward the couch just in time to see Kitty lift her shirt, flashing Roman. She shook her sizable tatas at him and then shoved her shirt back down, laughing hysterically as she realized I'd seen the whole thing.

"You weren't supposed to see that!" she said, cackling.

"No kidding," I said. "Do you need me to leave again?"

"Yep," Roman said.

"Nope," Kitty said, overlapping Roman, smacking him on the chest as she climbed onto the couch, draping herself on her side between Roman and the back of the couch. "We got out of bed ten minutes ago, you ravenous beast."

He idly twiddled her peaked nipples over the shirt. "Yep. And I was ready for more after five."

He lifted her up his body so her breasts draped against his face. "Mmmm. Kitty's titties," he said, nuzzling them. "I'm in heaven."

"Stop that, you pig!" Kitty said, shifting down his body.

"Oink, oink, sweetheart."

I faked a gag. "Okay! And on *that* note, I'm going to my room."

"If you hear loud noises from out here, just stay in there for...oh, another hour or so," Roman said.

"An hour," Kitty said, laughing. "You wish you lasted that long."

"Is that a challenge?" Roman said, his voice a feral growl.

I shivered, and my nipples ached, because that growl sounded so much like Remington's when he said things that were very similar.

"No!" Kitty said, too quickly, and far too submissively. "If you drew it out for an hour, I'd probably die."

"Of orgasms. What a way to die, huh?"

I heard her slap his hand. "Quit that! Rome... stop! Not with Juneau here."

"You know you can be quiet about it. They didn't even hear me come in last night...or you coming this morning."

I closed my door on them, muting their voices

to a dull murmur…but the sounds I heard told me I needed more than a closed door to block them out, so I turned on some Harry Connick Jr.

I barely recognized Kitty now that she was dating Roman. She was far more outgoing, far less reserved both in the way she dressed and how she behaved. The Kitty I'd known before Roman wouldn't have even held the hand of a guy she was seeing around us— but with Roman, they all but have sex in front of us, as evidenced by the current scene in the living room. I could hear Kitty laughing, and it was a… certain type of laugh. I was right here in the apartment, but she clearly just couldn't help herself.

I sank onto my bed, kicking off my wedge heels and unbuttoning my shirt, carefully shedding it. I had a full-length mirror on the outside of my closet door, and I twisted to view Ink's latest artwork—it was, unsurprisingly, incredible. You could almost reach out and pet the cub's fur, which was so detailed you could see individual strands of fur. The bears' noses looked almost wet, and he'd somehow made it look like the bears' paws were leaving footprints in my skin.

I wondered, if I were to try, if I could achieve artistic skill of that level. Certainly not without a lot of time and practice, but…I think I could. I'd done a couple of pretty elaborate pieces on Ink, and I knew part of the reason he always went shirtless was to display his tattoos…most of which were mine. He displayed them proudly which was, I guess, a testament to my skill.

I sighed, unhooking my bra and tossing it on the floor. It felt good to get that off, and I needed to get the strap away from the fresh tattoo. I hadn't been intending to put it on at all, but if I hadn't Remington would have been looking at me for far longer, and that would have been…awful.

In a lascivious sort of way.

The instant his eyes flashed on my bare chest?

My heart had slammed in my chest, and my stomach had been flipping, and I had kind of liked it.

I had to admit there was a part of me, buried way deep down, that had wanted his eyes on my bare flesh.

The look in his eyes…

…was very nearly worshipful.

Whether it was the tattoos, or the tatas, I wasn't sure.

"STOP!" I moaned to myself, scrubbing my face with both hands in frustration. "Stop thinking about him."

Focus on work. On the law.

Not on art. Not on tattoos. And not on Remington.

And then I remembered.

"He has my note," I said out loud to myself. "And you know he's going to read it."

SEVEN

Remington

I WASN'T GOING TO OPEN IT.

Nope.

Definitely not.

Snatching her little note or whatever it was and keeping it was a way of teasing her, taunting her. But actually reading it *would* be an invasion of her privacy.

It was in my wallet in my left hip pocket, and it was burning a hole in my leg. Somehow, I knew it was about me. She wouldn't be so upset about me taking it if it was just a random reminder to herself, or a grocery list, or something. No, that little square of folded yellow paper was definitely about me.

Doodling my name? Drawing cocks?

Ha, no. Not likely. Did girls draw dicks? Somehow, I didn't think so.

Was it a note to me? Something she wanted to get out of her system without actually letting me read it?

Was it dirty?

It was probably dirty. Something sexual, for sure.

"Rem?" I heard Rome's voice behind me, snapping me out of my daydream.

"Huh?" I said, spinning around in the office chair. "What?"

He was standing in the doorway to the office of Badd Kitty Saloon, a clipboard in his hands. I'm guessing this was a list of supplies we needed to order. I could see from where I was that most of the items were either circled, or crossed through. He was obviously following Bast's suggestions.

"The hell are you doing in here, Rem? Doodling?" His eyes went past me to the paper in front of me that contained a summary of our finances. Between the three of us, I was best at numbers and I was here to get a handle on where we were financially.

On the paper was a jumbled mess of figures—subtractions, additions, and tallies from where I'd started going through our expenditures and subtracting them from the total amount we'd gotten from the bank. That took up roughly the top quarter of the sheet.

Beneath that was…well, it wouldn't be fair to call it a doodle, honestly. It was more of a sketch. It was a counter with a jumble of supplies on it, and in the foreground was a tattoo chair with the outline of a body on it—front and center. The true subject of the sketch was a woman. All you could see was her naked back as she bent over the tattoo chair, the back of her head, a black braid draped over her shoulder. On her back was a rendering of nature's wonder—the salmon, the wolf tracks, the fjord…

The strong, delicate, sinuous curve of her back and the luscious round spread of her buttocks on the stool, these were all lovingly detailed in my sketch. It was, very clearly, Juneau.

And it was, in all honesty, a pretty nice sketch. There was a lot of emotion in it, and a lot of detail.

I'd started drawing her almost unconsciously.

Rome was suddenly beside me, staring down at the sketch. "The fuck, dude? *You* did this?"

I shrugged; my brothers knew I sketched as a hobby, but I was very private about it, and very defensive and possessive of my sketchbooks, so I wasn't sure either of them realized I was as talented as I was. "Yeah, I guess."

"You guess." Rome's voice was baffled. "You *guess.*"

I flipped the paper over to hide the sketch. "Yeah, I guess. What do you want?"

He reached down and snagged the paper, dancing out of reach as I swiped a punch at him. "Dude, you did this?"

"No, fucker, it drew itself. Yes, I did it. So the fuck what?"

"It's amazing, bro! She's sexy as fuck!" He squinted at it. "Wait, is that…" He glanced at me, and then at the paper again. "It is! That's Juneau!"

I snatched at the paper, but he kept it out of my reach. "Give it back, ass-licker, or I'll kick your fucking teeth in."

Rome just cackled, jogging out into the bar, shouting for Ramsey. "DUDE! RAMSEY! C'MERE!"

"Behind the bar," Ram called. "What are you two hooligans up to now?"

Rome vaulted the bar to get away from me, shoving the sketch into Ram's hands. "Look what our brother drew."

"That's Juneau." He glanced at me, frowning. "She's got tattoos? No way. She didn't seem like the type."

Knowing how defensive she'd gotten about them, I didn't want to get into that with my brothers. "It's just a stupid drawing. Give it back."

This was standard Ram and Rome strategy, and

I'd been dealing with it since I was a kid: they'd take something of mine and play keep away, and no matter how big and strong and fast I got, I could never win against the two of them. Not short of doing actual harm, at least, and they were my brothers after all.

Today, though, I wasn't playing around. I slugged Ram in the gut, snatched the paper while he was gasping, vaulted the bar and donkey kicked Rome across the room as I landed, and then stood, swiveling to flash them both the bird.

"Fuck you both. I hate it when you two fucking assholes do that."

"Dude. Unnecessary roughness," Ram gasped.

"He's touchy about Juneau," Rome said, clutching and rubbing his chest where I'd kicked him with my heavy steel-toed boots. "Probably because she won't touch him."

"Awww. Are you getting shut down?" Ram teased. "Poor Remy."

"Call me Remy again and see what happens, asshole," I snarled; I hated that nickname with a violent passion.

"He's cockblocking himself, probably," Rome added, and then wiggled his eyebrows at me. "You know, she came home last night acting awful weird."

"We're not talking about Juneau," I said, heading for the office. "I'm almost done going through our finances. Basically, if we don't open soon, we're gonna be fucked."

Rome ran his hand over his spiked hair. "Yeah, I figured that much. But Bast and I are in the final stages of negotiating this deal. That'll save our asses."

"Do we really want them all tied up in our shit, though?" Ram asked.

I shot him a look. "You really don't understand the state of our finances, then, Ram. We're down to beans and rice, basically. We blew three-quarters of our entire loan buying and renovating this place, and then we blew most of the rest on shit we don't need while not getting enough of the shit we *do* need. We *need* Bast and his brothers to bail us out."

Ram laughed sheepishly. "Wow. We really dicked this up, didn't we?"

"Yeah, we kind of did," Rome agreed, not seeming upset by it at all. "But I got Kitty out of it, so I'm cool."

"Well whoop-dee-doo for you," Ram said, dryly. "If only that meant shit in a bucket for Rem or me."

Rome lifted his eyebrows, shrugged, and headed for the storeroom. "Well, I mean…Izzy isn't so hard on the eyes. And neither is Juneau. Play your cards right, boys, and things could get pretty awesome for all of us around here."

"Not so hard on the eyes? Have you *seen* her

cleavage, or her hip-to-waist ratio?" Ram asked, incredulous. "Kim Kardashian who? Izzy's where it's at,
man."

I shook my head at my brother. "So have you
hooked up with her, then?"

He abruptly clammed up. "We need a few more
bottles of Patrón. According to Bax, the cruise ship
yuppies love their high-end tequila."

I laughed. "That's what I thought. So don't give
me shit about Juneau, and I won't give you shit about
Izzy. Capiche?"

Ram cackled and whipped a cardboard coaster
at me. "Capiche? What are you, a mafia hitman?"
He waved me away with a shooing motion. "Get out
of here. There's nothing to give me shit about, anyway. We messed around at the hospital, and that's it.
Nothing to talk about."

"Messed around? Where, in the janitor's closet?"

He turned away and adjusted the display of bottles. "Something like that. Don't worry about it. It
was a one-and-done sort of thing, and not even worth
talking about."

"If you're not willing to talk about it, it *is* something worth talking about."

He quirked an eyebrow at me. "So. Tell me how
you know Juneau has tattoos on her back."

I ground my molars together. "Point taken." I

folded the sketch and shoved it into my back pocket. "You know, if you ever want to, like, talk this shit out, let me know. Rome has his whole thing with Kitty going, and good for him, but it seems like you and me have our own weird situations."

He stared at me. "*Talk* about it? What are we, women? Go crunch some numbers, dork."

I flipped him off and returned to the office, forcing myself to focus on the tasks at hand. After the numbers were in, I wrote our remaining budget on the dry erase board and underlined it, intending to subtract each week's total expenditure—and then, when we opened, what we made each day and how it broke down. Then, I went to work organizing the office—filing receipts, setting still-to-be-paid invoices in the appropriate box, etc.

While doing all of this, I was fighting my own brain.

Fighting my all-too-vivid memory of seeing Juneau putting her shirt on in the tattoo parlor. I found my pencil moving across a blank sheet of printer paper, sketching the image in my mind. I caught her in mid-movement—one arm angled backward toward a sleeve, and the other down at her side, already in the other sleeve.

Her breasts were the focus, and I stopped every few seconds to close my eyes, recalling the memory of them. Big enough that I'd need two hands for each one—full, round, tear-drop shaped…perfect. Areolae almost as big as my palms, with thick, protruding, hard nipples. A little dark blemish on the left breast, on the inside, low down, near her sternum. In the sketch, she was twisted in the act of putting the shirt on, and I captured the way one breast hung lower than the other, swaying with her movement, the other breast lifted up and draped sideways against her chest.

Her… anatomy sketched, I closed my eyes again and called up what I'd seen of the tattoos: dots, circles, lines, triangles during the brief instant I'd been granted that glimpse at heaven. It was hard to remember the specifics I'd seen; a totem-type orca, I think, a wolf, more bands of the repeated shapes in an upside down V from under her breasts to each hip bone—or, so I guessed.

"Jesus fuck, dude!" Rome's voice from behind me, startling me so badly I jumped, and then abruptly threw my elbow back, catching him in the gut. "Ooof—dude, chill. I'm sorry. I didn't mean to snoop, man."

I flipped the paper over. "Quit sneaking up on me, Rome," I said, spinning in the chair to face him.

He rubbed his belly—he had a bottle of whiskey in his hand, and two glasses. "I was bringing us a shot to make up for teasing you. I remember how I was with Kitty, and I'm sorry." He poured a finger for each of us, and we clinked, tossed them back, and he poured more. "Honestly, the only reason we're even together is because she's patient and understands my caveman ass."

He nodded at the sketch on the desk. "You're seriously talented, Rem."

I lifted a shoulder. "It's a hobby."

He eyed the paper again. "So…is that what she really looks like?"

"For the most part…yeah."

He laughed, shaking his head. "I would not in a million years have thought she was the type to be covered in tats."

"Makes two of us," I said, chuckling. "She's weird about them, though."

"Kitty mentioned recently that she and Juneau are a lot alike in some ways—they're both more naturally reserved and conservative. Like, modest and shit." He shrugged. "So if you managed to see her like that—" he gestured at the paper—"I can see why she might be weird about it."

"It's…more than that, but I get your point." I glanced at him. "Is Kitty still that way?"

Rome shrugged as we both sipped the whiskey. "Not as much. She's loosening up. I actually kind of like that she doesn't put it all out there, though, you know? Like, that shit is *mine*." He gave a slow grin. "Gotta say though, she was never exactly shy, once things got going."

I lifted an eyebrow. "It's always the quiet ones, huh?"

He laughed, rubbing the back of his neck. "Bro, you have *no* idea. They *do* say good girls are the ones who like to get the dirtiest."

I folded the sketch in quarters, shoved it into my back pocket with the other one, and tossed back the last of my whiskey. "Come on. Let's lock up for the day. My brain is fried."

He chuckled. "Yeah, daydreaming about them big ol' titties will do that to a guy."

"Shut up. I *was* working."

"Yeah…on your hard-on."

"Rome, for the love of—" I snapped.

"Chill, chill—I'm fuckin' with you, bro." He halted, frowning at me. "Was I as testy about everything as you're being?"

"Before you figured out your shit with Kitty?" I said. "Yeah. You were."

He stopped, nodded, making a face. "Oh. Well. You'd better figure this shit out quick, then, because it's getting seriously old, bro."

We finished up a few more odds and ends, locked up, and headed for the three-bedroom apartment we rented a few blocks from the bar.

Alone in my room, I unfolded the sketches I'd done, laying them out side by side.

The one of her facing me, the look in her eyes that I'd captured—fierce, defiant, angry—was almost *too* good. Meaning, too much of a turn-on. It evoked one brief moment—less than fifteen seconds—that I'd never forget.

I lay on my bed and let my mind wander. Thinking of Juneau, of the moment that shirt moved aside to reveal those incredible breasts. You'd think I was a horny teenager, getting all hard from a few seconds' glance at a pair of tits, like I'd never seen them before.

But there was just something about *her*. Something exotic, alluring, and intoxicating.

My wallet was still in my pocket—drew it out, found the square of paper, and toyed with it, scraping with a thumbnail at the edge where she'd tucked the paper into itself. Telling myself not to open it, not to read it.

Playing games is one thing, actually opening her private shit was another.

I'm an asshole—but am I that much of a dick?

I threw the square of paper across my room with a frustrated grunt.

Now I was horny *and* irritated.

Great.

I pulled up a porn site on my phone in an attempt to distract myself and alleviate the situation, but the moment I closed my eyes and wrapped a fist around my engorged cock, all I could see was her. Those eyes, so defiant, so fierce, so conflicted. Her skin, dark and smooth and soft and so beautifully illustrated. Those breasts, pendulous and heavy, lifting and swaying with her ragged breathing...

My fist moved, gliding as I thought of her, just standing there, staring at me. In my runaway imagination, the moment lasted a lot longer. She just stood there, staring at me—letting me look at her. No shirt in her hands, just bare, confident—but slightly hesitant. Not ashamed of her nudity, but unsure of me. Maybe she'd wrap an arm under them, try to cover them—I'd stop her with a word, tell her never to cover up such beauty. Such perfection.

Fist flying faster, I wondered where else she had tattoos. If they covered her hips, her thighs. That skirt was held up by one lonely little zipper—I'd just have to give one good tug and it would float down around her feet...she'd be wearing white lacy underwear. Not a thong, nothing so daring as that. The kind of underwear that are cut high up around her hips, showing off the sexy wedge where her thighs met. She'd have tattoos on her thighs, I decided. High up. All the way around. She'd trace the bands of ink with her fingers, teasing me, drawing those thick, strong thighs apart, showing me the design as it worked its way around the tender inner part of her thigh. Maybe she'd tug aside that bit of lace covering her, and show herself to me.

Touch herself.

Those plump lips I wanted so badly to bite down on, to kiss, to lick...they'd part, and a breath would escape, and her eyes would be on me as she whimpered and writhed.

Fuck...

My cock ached, throbbed. I yanked my shirt off, tossed it aside, and gave in to the fantasy. I'd thought about her plenty since meeting her, and my imagination had run amok quite a bit in wayward moments, but I'd never done this. Never jacked it while thinking of Juneau.

Those eyes, they'd watch me so raptly, so curiously, so eagerly, if I were to do this in front of her. She'd watch my hand sliding up and down my thick, hard cock.

She'd want it. Want to help.

I'd let her.

Her hands were small, but strong looking. Soft. Warm. Her fingers would wrap around me, sliding down and gliding up, and her eyes would watch as I gasped, and her tongue would dance along her lips as she hungered for me, for my release. When I couldn't hold back anymore, she'd accept my cum in her cupped hands. Or maybe on her belly, all over those beautiful tattoos.

Or releasing across those plump, heavy, luscious breasts, swaying as she came beneath me.

I exploded, imagining Juneau underneath me, head craned backward, eyes clenched shut, breasts shaking and trembling and bouncing as she came, calling my name...

I was a mess, then—it was all over my stomach and chest. I snatched a handful of Kleenex and cleaned up, feeling relieved but still dirty, and more desperate than ever to see Juneau again.

If all I ever got of her was the one look I'd go crazy. Thanks to my rampant, dirty imagination I needed more of her. I needed to know if the reality was as incredibly sexy and fierce and shy and intoxicating as my imagination made her out to be.

I had to have Juneau Isaac.

It was no longer a mere desire.

It was need—a pure, raw, unadulterated, insatiable *need*.

EIGHT

Juneau

MOM SAT UNDER HER COLLAPSIBLE AWNING, HER wares spread out on the folding table, which was sitting on a colorful rug she'd woven herself. Her little hut was set up on the wharf near where most of the cruise ships docked, to take advantage of the streams of tourists disembarking and reboarding. She was one of a very few vendors licensed to operate on the wharf itself, mainly because she'd been doing it for so long. Her mother, my grandmother, had sold similar pieces of handmade art on these docks decades ago, and my mother had continued the tradition.

She had a small carving knife in one hand, and a tiny block of wood in the other, and she was slowly, methodically whittling away at the block, revealing, stroke by stroke, the shape of a hedgehog. I saw her plan for the little piece of art: it was small enough to sit in the palm of her hand, and she was carving the face, legs, and body out of wood. The actual spikes, however, were created out of tiny pieces of jade and lapis lazuli, which she'd already shaped for her purposes. A piece of wood she'd procured from the forest, a few dollars worth of stones, and several hours of work would probably yield her a hundred dollars, all told.

I had expected, from a young age, to carry on the tradition myself—I loved the art, the focus, the creativity. Whittling animals from wood, shaping pieces of stone, creating necklaces and earrings and bracelets and figurines. From the time I was able to walk on my own, I spent my every waking moment with Mom huddled under this awning on the wharf, playing with a carving, helping her, charming customers and passersby, running off to find a snack with the handful of dollars and change Mom would give me.

The bellowing yawp of the cruise ships as they entered the channel and came in to dock was imprinted on my very being, as was the constant chatter of voices, the laughs and the shouts and the cackling of scampering children accompanied by the worried yells of nervous parents, and the *clap-lap-chuck* of the waves against the docks and piers, and the discordant, mischievous *scree* of gulls.

As I grew up I was sent to school instead of staying home to help Mom. Grade school, middle school, high school—*see to your education, Juneau*, they would tell me. Keep the grades up. You could go to college, they told me. You could be the first in our entire family to go to college, to leave Ketchikan, to get a job. You could even go the lower 48. Become something. Forget about art, baby girl—just focus on learning. Apply to UA-Anchorage. Apply for scholarships, student loans.

They'd scrimped and saved my whole life to send me to college. Even my sisters—all older than me, the next oldest was five years my senior—had contributed from their savings to send me to Anchorage.

How could I say no? How could I tell them I didn't want a college degree, I didn't want to go to Anchorage, much less to the lower 48. I didn't want a job with the *cheechakos*. I wanted to make hedgehogs out of wood, jade, and lapis lazuli. I wanted to make necklaces from deer bone and driftwood and thread woven from hide and sinew. I wanted to work at Yup'ik Tattoo with Ink.

That was my dream, all my life.

Art—in whatever form—is all I've ever wanted.

We would talk about it, Ink and me, late at night,

making plans as we huddled side by side in the pup tent outside my parents' house, listening to Mom and Dad and my aunts and uncles and older cousins laughing around the fire.

"I hear you thinking, Juneau," Mom said, not looking up from her whittling.

"I was just thinking about how much I used to love playing here as a little girl," I said, running my fingers through the Tupperware container full of tiny pieces of jade and lapis lazuli.

"Always underfoot," Mom said, a ghost of a smile on her weathered features. "But you had a way with the tourists, you did. A little smile, a joke, a question, and somehow they'd always buy something if you were around."

"I loved it."

Mom eyed me, then. "You're thinking deeper thoughts than that—I can tell. Out with it, then." Her lips thinned, then, pressed together as she anticipated what I was going to say.

I toyed with a piece of jade. "I never wanted to be anywhere but here."

"I know, but you're too smart to waste your brains and talents sitting making trinkets for tourists." She carved at the hedgehog, a little too forcefully. "This isn't for you. It's not your future. You're meant for more."

"What if it's what I wanted, though?"

Mom's expression was hard. "Gonna waste all that money, all that time you spent at the university? Gonna waste the degree, and all that hard work interning for Daniel?" She shook her head angrily. "No. No. You're doing good for our people, Juneau. You're making a difference."

"I know, Mom, but—"

"You're spending too much time with Ink. You think making art is all there is."

"I learned it from you, Mom!"

She gestured with the carving in her hands. "This is all I know." She tapped my temple with the carving, then. "You know more. You're not gonna waste it."

This was an age-old argument between us. I don't know why I even bothered trying to change her mind.

I was tempted to show her my tattoos—the band of traditional symbols starting under my breasts and angling down to each hip, which I'd done to myself, using a mirror—it was the product of weeks' worth of work, done the old way: needle and ink.

It had hurt worse than any tattoo done using Ink's gun, but it was worth it—it was worth every minute of tear-jerking pain I'd endured, knowing I'd created something permanent and beautiful, something which honored our ancestors and our traditions.

She should understand.

But she didn't.

All she would ever accept was that I'm "meant for more." For the law degree, the job at the firm. She'd been pestering me for months to start working toward the bar exam, toward becoming an actual lawyer, not just a legal assistant. That's the dream she had for me.

No matter that the idea of studying for the bar made me nauseous, that the notion of spending the rest of my life behind a desk, or in a courtroom, or in a counsel's chambers made me want to claw my eyes out. No matter that I hated the fancy clothes and the high heels and the stuffy courtrooms and the arrogant lawyers and the belligerent defendants and the convoluted legal language and the briefs and the... everything.

I didn't want any of it.

But my entire family had sacrificed endlessly to send me to Anchorage. That degree sitting in a drawer in my office at the firm was bought and paid for by my family—weeks spent by my father in the bush, guiding elk and moose and deer and bear hunts, Mom spending eighteen hours a day under this awning making art and hawking it to tourists, my sisters scrimping and saving and stretching dollars to add their part. Even my aunts and uncles had contributed. The only one who hadn't was Ink, and that was because he'd understood how much I hadn't wanted to go, and had always believed I needed to take a stand for what I wanted for myself, regardless of the expectations on me.

But I couldn't do that.

I couldn't let them all down.

Could I?

"Are you going back to Anchorage soon, to take the bar?" Mom asked.

I sighed. "I haven't applied for the program."

"Why not?"

"Because I'm not ready to make that step. That's a big deal, Mom. It's years of work—it's not like I can just pop over to Anchorage and take a little test, you know. It's moving to Anchorage, assuming I get into the program there—and then spending years and tens of thousands of dollars on room, board, tuition, books…" I sighed, flipping my braid to the other side. "I'm not sure that's what I want to do. Not now, and maybe not ever."

"You've always wanted to be a lawyer, though." Mom glanced at me as she began creating divots in which to fix the pieces of jade and lapis lazuli.

I groaned. "No, Mom—*you* have always wanted me to be a lawyer."

Her eyes hardened. "I just want the best for you, and from you."

Rather than get dragged down into the same futile argument yet again, I leaned over, wrapped her up in a hug, and kissed her cheek. "I love you, Mom."

She nuzzled me back. "Love you too, Juneau."

"I have to go," I said, and slid out from behind the folding table, collecting my purse.

"Okay. Everyone says hi."

"Give them all my love."

She waved as I walked away from the wharf. "I will." She waited until I was almost out of earshot. "Take the bar!"

I just waved, not dignifying that with a response. Oh, just *take the bar*. Just like that, huh?

Right.

It was Sunday afternoon, and I didn't really have much to do today—I just had to get away from the endless debate over my future. Izzy was working at the shop, and Kitty was helping Roman at the new saloon, which left me alone yet again. I decided to visit Izzy at the store, knowing she'd welcome a few minutes of gossip with me.

Couture Ketchikan was one of the high-end clothing stores in the city, and Izzy was the general manager, second in command only to the owner, Angelique Leveaux, a French native who had moved to Ketchikan a decade ago.

Izzy was alone in the store, her laptop open,

keys clacking as she updated her blog. There were several racks of clothing behind the counter which she appeared to be in the process of sorting through. It looked like she was modeling them as she sorted through them, taking selfies and posting them to her social media accounts with hashtags that directed potential buyers to this store.

"Juneau! You're just in time!" Izzy said, closing her laptop. "I have several pieces I want you to try on."

I frowned at her. "I'll try them on, but you're not taking pictures."

She rolled her eyes at me. "Oh, yes I am. The last time you modeled for my Insta, I got a ton of likes, and several people actually came in to buy things."

"We'll see," I told her. "I'll try them on, but no guarantees I'll even come out to show you."

"You're worse than Kitty!" Izzy said, bubbling over with enthusiasm. "You never show any skin! You've got *curves*, girlfriend! Work 'em!"

I blinked at her. "Wow. Somebody have an extra shot of espresso this morning?"

Izzy cackled. "Yep! The barista messed up and made me a quad-shot latte instead of my usual triple, so I'm basically on speed right now. You should see how many racks I've been through already. Angelique is going to freak when she sees how much I got done today. She'll probably give me a raise just so I can afford a quad-shot latte every day!"

I frowned. "I'm not sure that's too great for your heart, Izz."

"No, probably not," she said, shrugging. "My pulse has been racing for the last hour. But if I have a heart attack and die, at least I'll die doing what I love: trying on clothes!"

I laughed. "You're ridiculous, you know that?"

"Yep. But that's why you love me. I'm basically all the comedic relief you and Kitty ever get. You're both so serious all the time." She made a pouty face and spoke in a whining, sarcastic tone. "I'm Juneau Isaac and I dress like a grandmother. I never have any fun, and I hate being sexy. Somebody give me a paper bag to put over my head."

I picked up a loose staple off the counter and tossed it at her. "Oh shut up—I'm not like that." I glared at her. "I do *not* dress like a grandmother."

She quirked an eyebrow at me, looking me up and down: I was wearing a loose-fitting floor-length black wool skirt, and a fuzzy peach cashmere sweater, with clunky black clogs on my feet.

"Okay, well it's Sunday, and it's chilly out, and wearing this sweater is like getting a hug from a cloud. I like being comfy."

"Those clothes are utterly shapeless, Juneau,"

Izzy lamented. "No one would know you even have such a banging body under there."

I rolled my eyes at her. "So what? I have to show cleavage all the time?"

Izzy pressed the sweater against my chest, flattening it against my boobs. "I'm not even talking about cleavage at this point, I'm just talking about wearing a sweater that makes it look like you even *have* boobs. You look flat as a pancake in that thing, and considering how ginormous your boobs are, that's quite a feat."

I shook my head. "I don't look flat. I'm just not showing off for anyone."

"And let's talk about that skirt," Izzy continued, as if I hadn't even spoken. "Sure, it's probably warm and comfy, but you've got zero ass in it. You may as well be wearing, like, a curtain or something, for all the shape that thing has."

"Not everyone wears miniskirts year round, Isadora," I said, deadpan. "This *is* Alaska, and it *does* stay cool pretty much *all* the time."

Isadora twirled behind the counter, showing off her midthigh-length white leather miniskirt, which she was wearing with a matching cleavage-baring white leather bustier-type thing…and not a lot else. She was, basically, all leg and boob and butt in that outfit. She could saunter down a catwalk in Paris and not be out of place. Not my thing, but she worked the look for all it was worth.

She rifled through the racks, plucking pieces and hooking the hangers on her finger—when she had a good dozen items, she sashayed from behind the counter in her four-inch stilettos, laid all the articles of clothing in my arms, and then shoved me toward the dressing room.

"I need to see at least one outfit," she said. "I picked pieces that are a little outside your comfort zone, but aren't into full slut territory."

"Good, because I highly doubt I'll ever be comfortable dressing like you."

"It's true—not everyone can pull off the high-class escort look," she said with a faux haughty sniff.

"I'm not making any promises that I'll show you anything, but I'll at least try them on."

I took the pile of garments into the nearest dressing room and went through them piece by piece as I hung them up. Mostly skirts I'd never wear because they were *way* too short or tight, and tops I'd never wear because they exposed my back and chest in such a way that you'd be able to see my tattoos. Which was a no-go, not ever. There were a few pieces I was willing to try, though—a knee-length skirt that was tighter than I usually liked, but would definitely be pretty sexy, and a top that left my arms bare but buttoned up to my neck and covered my shoulders and chest while still being cut to show off my curves. Izzy had also pulled a full-length dress that would flatter without revealing anything, and a sweater much like the one I was wearing but which would hug my curves instead of hiding them.

Just for fun, though, I decided to try on the other pieces first, the ones I'd never let anyone see me in.

First was a basic black miniskirt and a tank top blouse with a plunging neckline; I had to dance and tug and wiggle to get the skirt up over my rather generous backside, but once it was on and I'd sucked in enough to be able to button it, I had to admit I *did* look seriously hot. I almost looked like I had something like long legs—which at five-four was a tough thing to pull off. Plus, it was so tight around my ass and thighs that I could barely move, which made every movement a showcase of curvy jiggles.

Remington would die if he saw me in this.

Wait, crap! Did I really just think that?

The top was even more daring—it plunged down well below my breasts, baring most of my chest tattoo and the top of the one that started on my diaphragm. It was meant to be worn with some kind of support I clearly didn't own, because you couldn't wear a bra with it—the top was designed to show off sideboob... not just show off, but *highlight*; sideboob was the star of this piece. And even without any support—which I need like buildings need foundations—my boobs looked pretty amazing. My tattoos were on full display, especially my chest piece, which Ink had done using the stick-and-poke method. God, I loved this look. Deep down, I really wanted to dress like this.

But I didn't dare.

No one would understand.

Kitty and Izzy would be confused and angry that I'd hid my tattoos from them for so long, and Mom and Dad would hate me for the tattoos and for the showy, flashy, skin-baring outfit—not mention I'd get all sorts of male attention I'm not used to and don't know how to handle.

Just the way Remington looked at me when clothed modestly was more than I knew how to deal with.

No—nope. I couldn't dress like this.

I took a photo of myself in the outfit, and then took it off and tried on another outfit that was more my style.

No tattoos showed, no skin, but I still looked pretty, and even sexy…I just wasn't showing any skin.

Izzy's smile as I came out in the outfit was bright. "Wow! You look amazing! See, *that's* how you do a skirt and sweater, Juneau. You've got a butt and boobs in that outfit, but you're not showing anything you're uncomfortable with. See how that works?"

I rolled my eyes at her. "Yes, Izzy, I see what you mean. I *do* love this outfit."

I went back into the dressing room and put back on my own clothing, deciding to buy the skirt and top I'd shown Izzy. I left the rest of the clothes in the changing room, knowing she'd put them away later. I hesitated in the doorway, though, staring back in at the miniskirt and tank top I'd tried on.

I could buy them, just to have them. Maybe someday I'd have the courage to wear that outfit. Maybe owning it would be the first step in developing that courage. Or, maybe it'd be a waste of money to buy an outfit I knew I'd always be too chicken to wear.

Izzy saw me hesitating, and came to stand next to me, following my gaze; her eyes went to mine. "I was hoping you'd try that on."

"I did," I admitted.

"And? I bet you looked fucking killer in it!"

"Yeah, but I could never wear it."

Izzy sighed. "Why not? I don't get that about you, Juneau. You're not insecure; I know you're not. I get that you come from a much different background than Kitty or me, and that clothing like that isn't really natural for you, but...you have to get outside your comfort zone sometimes, babe. You can't dress in grandma clothes your whole life. You're beautiful, Juneau, and you have a beautiful body. You should show it off sometime."

I shook my head. "It's hard to explain."

Izzy stared at me, and then rolled her eyes in frustration. "You're impossible." She leaned in, snagged the two hangers, and walked around to the counter with them. "You're buying the outfit."

"I am not!"

Izzy stared hard at me. "Fine. *I'm* buying it, and it'll magically appear in *your* closet. I know where you live, you know."

I laughed at her. "I'm not buying the outfit and neither are you. It'll be a waste of money because I'll never wear it."

She scanned the tags, and then took the outfit I'd chosen and scanned those as well, and then punched in her manager's discount. "You're buying them. Because you never know—you may fall in love with a super hot and sexy guy who'll inspire you to find your inner sex goddess, and you'll start getting a little daring with your fashion choices."

"Find my inner sex goddess?" I echoed, laughing.

"Yep. I know you've got one in there somewhere."

"How do you know I haven't already found my inner sex goddess? Maybe I just keep that kind of thing to myself."

Izzy stared at me, and managed to make the expression drip with sarcasm. "When was the last time you fucked a guy reverse cowgirl?"

I glanced around the store in a panic. "Shush! You can't talk like that in public!"

Izzy cackled. "We're the only ones in here, Juneau!" She cupped her hands around her mouth and shouted. "Penis! Cock! Pussy!"

"Isadora! Stop!" I said, trying to clap my hand over her mouth.

She just cackled all the harder and fought my hands away. "Fuck, fuck, fuck!" She writhed in place, loudly faking orgasm sounds. "Ohhh, ohhh, ohhh! Yeah, baby, fuck me just like that! Yes! Fuck yes!"

I gave up, hanging my head in defeat and refusing to look Izzy in the eyes. "You are *so* embarrassing."

Izzy just laughed at me. "You're so easily embarrassed by the stupidest shit! There's *no one* here. The door is closed, so it's not like anyone outside could hear. And even if they did, so what? Like they'll never have heard dirty words before? Lighten up, Juneau."

"I'm leaving," I said, starting to walk away.

She grabbed my wrist and hauled me back to the counter. "No, you're not. You have to pay for the clothes, for one thing, and you never answered my question, for another."

I handed her my debit card. "I'm not answering that."

She swiped my card and handed it back. "You know you haven't found your inner sex goddess, that's why."

"I enjoy sex, Izzy. And probably more frequently than you're assuming."

"Then answer the question." Izzy handed me the signature slip and a pen. "When was the last time you fucked a guy in the reverse cowgirl position?"

I frowned at her. "Why? Is that, like, the measuring stick for whether you've found your inner sex goddess?"

"It's a pretty decent indicator, I'd say, yeah." She lifted an eyebrow. "Well? I'm waiting."

I blushed. "That's none of your business."

"Consider me a sex therapist. I'm interested in a purely professional capacity."

I shook my head. "I'm not telling you."

She stared hard at me. "Wait, wait, wait. You've never fucked in that position, have you?"

"I told you I'm not answering."

"You haven't!" She grabbed my wrists in both hands. "You *have* to try it. You have to. It's vital."

I rolled my eyes at her. "Can we talk about something else, now?"

"Yes—fellatio."

I groaned. "No! How about something *besides* sex?"

She tapped her chin, pretending to think. "Hmmmmm." She brightened. "Nope! Tell me—do you use your tongue when you go down?"

"Izzy!" I felt myself blushing. "Stop!"

"Do you? Because I'm telling you, if you don't use tongue, you're doing it wrong. They love the tongue action." She held her closed fist in front of her mouth and stuck her tongue out, rolling it in broad circles. "Like that. Dudes love that shit."

I covered my face with both hands. "You are so shameless."

"Duh, but you know that," she said, "Throw me a bone, here, Juneau. Tell me *something.*"

"Will you leave me alone about this if I do?"

"Tell me one dirty secret about you, and yes, I will agree to talk about something else."

I sighed, thinking. I leaned on the counter, lowering my voice nearly to a whisper. "The last guy I slept with, Chris—he liked to put my feet on his shoulders. I felt really awkward about it the first couple times he wanted me to do it, but it did feel really good once I got over that."

Izzy stared at me expectantly. "And?"

I shrugged. "And nothing. That's it."

"That's…that's not even that kinky of a position."

"It felt like it for me. Having my butt all up in the air? It was weird."

Izzy shook her head. "If that's your idea of a dirty little secret, then you *definitely* haven't found your inner sex goddess."

"I didn't say it was my dirty little secret."

She slapped the counter. "Well then come on! Out with it! Give me something that's a dirty little secret about you that I'd never guess."

"Why do you want to know so badly?"

"Because you're one of my two best friends and I feel like there's just a lot about you I don't know. You keep so much to yourself."

"I'm just private," I said.

Izzy drew an X over her heart. "I won't tell anyone. Not even Kitty, if you don't want me to."

"Does it have to be a secret about sex?" I asked. "Because honestly, I don't have any of those—you are right in that I'm probably not very adventurous."

"No, it can be anything. Any secret."

Could I tell her? Show her?

I sucked in a breath and held it. "Okay, I do have a secret. And you can't tell anyone—not even Kitty, because now that I'm telling you, I'll have to tell her and I want to do it in my own time."

Izzy frowned. "Wow—it must be pretty big, then."

I glanced around, and realized there was no way I could do this in the middle of the store. "Come on— let's go in the back."

She eyed me skeptically. "What could be so secret that you can't just tell me out here?"

"It's more of a *show* you than *tell* you kind of secret."

Izzy let out a breath, and then led me into the back room, where there were dozens of racks of clothes all jammed in side by side, surrounding a tiny little desk with an aging desktop computer and a pile of papers and receipts and invoices. There was barely room to stand back here, but it was private and windowless.

Izzy stood with her back to the doorway, blocking me in. "Okay. What's the big secret, Juneau?"

I hesitated—this was terrifying. "I...you might be mad that I'm just now showing you this."

"Now I'm scared," Izzy said, laughing nervously. "You're not gonna whip out a dick, are you?"

"Oh my god, no!" I closed my eyes, sucked in a deep breath, and then grasped the bottom of my sweater. "Ready?"

Izzy just blinked at me. "This is weird."

"Don't freak, okay?"

"Well, you're freaking me out right now, so no promises."

I let out another breath, and then peeled off my sweater in one quick movement. I stood in front of Izzy in just my skirt and a bra, with all my tattoos exposed…well, those from the waist up at least—I had a few more a little lower down on my hips, but I wasn't ready to strip down to underwear just yet.

Izzy's breath caught. She took a tentative step toward me, stretching out a hand as if to touch the colorful designs on my skin. "Oh…my…*god*." Her eyes met mine. "*Tattoos*?"

I turned around to show her my back, which is where Ink's masterpieces live. "This is my secret."

"Holy mother of god!" Izzy whispered. "This is…" Her fingers touched my back, making me shiver as she traced the various images. "Wow…just…*wow*."

I turned back around, biting my lip. "My cousin did most of them." I traced the bands of the traditional tattoo on my chest and belly. "I did these myself, though."

"Your cousin?"

I nodded. "His name is Ink."

She frowned in disbelief. "You have a cousin named…Ink…who's a tattoo artist?"

"Yep." I bit my lip. "And I did a bunch of tattoos on him."

Izzy shook her head as if dizzy. "Wait…*what*?"

"Surprise!" I lifted my hands in a cutesy little

gesture. "I have a bunch of tattoos!"

She traced the V running from shoulder down to cleavage and back up. "You did this yourself?"

I nodded. "Yeah."

She breathed out an amazed sigh. "That's incredible. Did it hurt?"

I barked a laugh. "Oh yeah. I used the stick-and-poke method my ancestors used, so yeah, it hurt like a bitch, to be honest."

Izzy shook her head as if to shake away the confusion. "So this is why you always change in the hot, steamy bathroom after a shower?"

I nod. "Yeah."

"And why you never wear anything that exposes your torso?"

"Yeah."

Izzy spun the office chair around and plopped down in it, putting her chin in her hand and staring up at me thoughtfully. "So…I guess my one real question is…why was it a secret? It's just tattoos. Did you think we'd judge you for them or something?"

I shook my head. "No, I just…I don't know. I'm really weird about them."

Izzy frowned, head tipped to one side. "You're gonna have to explain this one for me, honey."

I turned my sweater back inside right and shrugged into it. "Okay, so…you know that lady who sells handmade native jewelry and stuff over on the wharf?"

Izzy nodded, spinning the chair around to look for something on the desk—she whirled back around with a carving of an eagle wheeling on a wing, intricately detailed and painted, with slivers of white quartz for the feathers, and a little fish crafted from tin clutched in the talons. "I got this from her a couple years ago."

I laughed, toying with the carving. "That's my mom's." I lifted the figurine. "I actually helped her make this. I did all the painting on it."

"No way! That's your *mom*?" She took the figurine from me. "*You* painted this?"

I nodded. "Yep. Mom did the carving and inlaid the quartz, and I did the detail painting."

Izzy blew out a breath. "Okay, so you're an artist, and your mom is an artist...How does this tie into you hiding all those gorgeous tattoos?"

"Because my mom and my grandmother both have made their living as artists—and it's a subsistence living at best. My dad guides hunts and hikes in the deep bush, my sisters are all stay-at-home mothers, my brothers-in-law work in factories and fishing boats..." I sighed. "I'm the only person in my entire family—and I mean my whole lineage going back as many generations as you can count—who's ever been to college. I'm the only one to work a white-collar job. I'm the only one to leave this area for anything more than occasional trips."

Izzy just nodded. "Okay. So?"

"So…Mom, Dad, my sisters, my grandparents—everyone contributed money to send me to college in Anchorage, to get my law degree. They expect me to go back and study for the bar and become an actual lawyer."

Izzy frowned. "And? Isn't that the plan? I've heard you talking about that, as a matter of fact."

I tugged down the neck of my sweater and indicated a band of tattoo. "This is my dream. Not the law. I don't want to become a lawyer. I don't even like working in a law office. I love helping people, and I like working for Daniel, but I've always wanted to be an artist—a tattoo artist. Ink and I did our first tattoos on each when we were eleven." I tugged up the hem of my sweater and pushed down the waist of my skirt, baring my right hip bone, exposing a tiny orca in faded black ink. It's splotchy, ugly, and messy—you can barely tell what it is.

"Ink's looks about the same. We did them with pen ink and a needle. We're lucky we didn't get infections and die, quite honestly. We've talked about covering them, but we never do because it's a reminder of where we started and how far we've come." I restore my clothing. "I hide my tattoos because Mom and Dad would be super upset if they knew I have them, and if they knew Ink had done them. They'd know I don't want to do what I've been doing—that I dream of quitting and going to work for Ink."

"And? Why don't you?"

I sighed. "I can't let my family down. I can't disappoint them. They all have these huge expectations for me, and my tattoos would be...the first step in letting them all down."

"So you're ashamed of them?"

"My feelings about my tattoos are...complicated. I love them, and I'm proud of them, but I don't know how to even start the conversation about them. It was hard enough to show you—showing my parents would be...impossible."

"You know you're going to have to eventually, right?" Izzy sighed, standing up. "You're living a false life. It'll all come crashing down at some point—I know you didn't ask for my advice, but I'm gonna give it to you anyway—make the break now, in your own timing and on your own terms, rather than waiting for circumstances to decide for you."

I toyed with the end of my braid. "I'm scared that now that I've shown you, I've started something unstoppable." I laughed. "Actually, it all started with Remington showing up at the tattoo parlor Ink owns."

Izzy's eyes widened. "Wait. Remington Badd knew about your tattoos before I did?"

"By accident. I would never have shown him on purpose."

Izzy's eyes narrowed to slits. "Now, I'm mad. We're fighting."

"It was an accident! Ink had finished one of the bears on my back, and I had my shirt on backward so it could dry, and Remington came in. Ink works by appointment only, so there wasn't supposed to be any walk-ins. Much less Remington."

"We're still fighting. I'm your best friend—you should have trusted me before now." She pointed a finger at me. "You know Kitty is going to be pissed." Izzy shrugged. "Well, more hurt than pissed, but still."

"I've always been pretty conservative, but I started covering them up when I first got a tattoo, and it's been habit ever since." I met her gaze, hoping to see forgiveness there. "It wasn't about not trusting you, it was more...not knowing where to start the conversation. It became a habit to just hide them from everyone."

"I can't say I really get it, but I love you and definitely get the family expectations thing." Izzy hugged me. "But now that you're starting to come out of the tattoo closet, you can start dressing to show off that sexy ink! You can wear that outfit you bought!"

I laughed. "Yeah...no. That's as much about modesty as it is the tattoos. I've never really been into showing a lot of skin."

"I bet you look sexy as hell in it though."

I blushed, ducking my head. "I kind of do, yeah."

"Wear it for Remington, then!" Izzy said. "Show him what you look like showing off those foxy knockers of yours."

I snickered. "Foxy knockers? Really?"

"He'll spooge in his Levi's if he sees them all nakey. Guaranteed."

I bit my lower lip. "Um, well..."

Izzy's eyes widened. "What? What aren't you telling me?"

"He...he kind of already saw them," I admitted.

"Saw how much of them?"

I hesitated. "Um. All of them?"

"Like...bare?"

I nodded. "Only for a split second though. He... he sort of manipulated me into it. He snatched something I didn't want him to have, and then my bra, and told me to choose—and the only way to not play his game was to just put my shirt on. Which meant he got a quick look at my boobs, sans bra. But then he covered them with my bra anyway, which was kind of sweet, even though he created the situation in the first place."

Izzy's eyes narrowed again. "I'm not exactly following, but that's fine. The upshot of it is, he saw your tits?"

"Yeah."

"And he walked out on his own power? Without limping?"

"Why would he limp?"

"Because the hard-on he had to have been rocking must've been out of control. Makes it hard to walk, from what I understand."

"He did bolt the first chance he got."

"You're telling me you didn't look?"

I bit my lip again. "Um. I may have."

She grabbed my arms and shook them. "And?"

I rolled my eyes. "And it looked like an erection behind the zipper of his jeans." I frowned at her. "And didn't you mess around with Ramsey in the hospital or something?"

"Or something," she muttered.

"So, they're triplets. I'm guessing they're probably very similarly endowed."

"Not the point. The point is, I want details about what happened to *you*."

"I saw enough."

"Enough to know you want to jump on that monster cock and get some O's out of him?" She rocked her hips suggestively. "Yeah, baby—you know you want to."

"Izzy!" I scolded. "You are so wrong!"

"In all the right ways, Juneau." She wiggled her eyebrows at me, which was more comical than suggestive. "So? You gonna ride that D?"

I sighed. "I'm worried it'll become something I'm not ready for if I do. Either not enough, or too much, and I'm not in a place where I want either one right now."

Izzy rolled her eyes. "You're overthinking it."

I laughed. "Well, yeah. That's kind of my thing, I think."

"When are you going to see him again?"

I sighed. "Well, tonight, probably."

Izzy lifted an eyebrow. "Why do you sound both reluctant and unsure?"

I debated on how much to tell her, and decided to go for the whole truth. "Okay, so don't laugh at me *too* hard, but...you know how I take dictation for Daniel? Well, I was sort of...um...daydreaming. About Remington. And I kind of started...doodling. And ended up with a pretty...errr...graphic sketch. Of Remington...and me...in a—um—compromising position. And that sketch is what he has."

Izzy sputtered in helpless laughter, then clapped a hand over her mouth. "Holy shit. No way!"

I covered my face with both hands. "I had it

folded up and stuffed in my bra, and he found it at
the tattoo parlor. And now he has it—he kept it as,
quote, 'insurance' that he'll see me again. He said if
he doesn't see me after three days, he's going to open
it."

"Does he know what it is?"

"No, but he's got a pretty good idea it's about
him in some way because I was so crazy about him
not seeing it."

"And the three days are up…when?"

"Today. So I have to get it back from him, because
I'd die of embarrassment if he sees it."

"It's explicit, I imagine?"

I bit my lip and nodded. "Um…yeah."

"Oooh, you dirty girl."

I laughed in embarrassment. "It was an accident!
I was daydreaming and not paying attention. My pen
just sort of did its own thing and I didn't realize what
I'd done until Daniel asked me to read the dictation
back to him."

"Daniel didn't see it, did he?"

"God, no! I'd have actually had a heart attack
from sheer mortification."

"But now Remington has your dirty sex dream
drawing, and if you don't see him tonight, he'll look
at it, and know how bad you want him."

"Exactly."

She pointed at me. "You're not denying that you want him, I notice."

I covered my face with both hands, sighing dramatically, and then I shook my head. "No, between you and me—no, I'm not denying it. I want him. He's gorgeous. He's sexy. He's built like a god, and he intrigues me. He's an arrogant, manipulative jackass with a filthy mouth and filthier mind, but even that is part of what makes him attractive, I guess. It's infuriating, maddening...and sexy as hell all at the same time. Which is weird."

Izzy laughed. "Honey, welcome the world of hyperdominant alpha males. Infuriating, maddening, and fucking irresistible."

"You're an expert, I imagine?"

"I can see why you'd think so, but no. Most alpha males get sick of me being so independent and stubborn, and I refuse to play along with or do anything that reeks of submissiveness, so nothing ever works out between me and an alpha."

"Explain something for me, then."

She shrugged a shoulder. "I'll try."

"You talk about blowjobs like they're your favorite thing. Isn't a blowjob by definition submissive?"

She grinned, a feral twist of her lips. "A common misperception. A properly administered blowjob puts all the power in your hands, pun intended."

I frowned. "How so?"

"If there's a chance of getting you to put your mouth on his cock, a man will do just about anything you want. You have to be careful, though, because men have fragile egos, and if you exert that power too much, or if you don't follow through, it'll backfire."

"So, promise to blow him, and I have power over him?"

"Even tease him with it. Suggest it. Hint at it—and see what happens. But, I warn you—tease, hint, or promise too much without following through, and you lose the leverage."

"Is that why you like do it so much?"

"That's a big part of it," she said. "The other part is that I just like being able to make a big strong man go all weak in the knees, I like being able to make him gasp and whimper and shake, all just with my hands and mouth. It's not about the power or leverage, it's…" She shrugged. "It's just fun. Worth the taste and the mess, and the jaw ache, in my opinion."

"How is that different from sex?"

She waved her hands in the air. "It's totally different! Sex is mutual. For it to be good, it *has* to be mutual. You have to both get it good, or it sucks. Giving a guy a BJ? That's all about him. You're making *him* feel good. With sex, you can both do things to make the other person feel good, but a BJ? That's all you.

Just like him going down on you is all about you—all about him making *you* feel good. And that's it's own kind of very enjoyable power."

I laughed. "Oh, Izzy. You're one of a kind, you know that?"

She popped a hip and held out a hand palm up. "Well, yeah! The world couldn't handle more than one of me! The world can barely handle the one of me there is!"

I hugged her. "Okay. I'm going to go."

"Find Remington. Get your drawing back. And if he won't give it back, bribe him with a BJ."

I boggled at her. "Um, hello? Do you know me? I dated Chris for almost two weeks before I even kissed him."

She rolled her eyes. "You went on, what, four dates with him?"

"Two the first week, two the second. We kissed at the end of the fourth date, and then the next one we messed around, and then the sixth time I saw him, we slept together. And then after that, we skipped the dates and went right to sleeping together. And then, the fourth or fifth time we hooked up, he invited his friend over and tried to surprise me with a threesome. Which I believe I've mentioned."

"That's still so weird to me. That's the kind of thing you have to talk about and set ground rules for."

"I thought you said you'd never done that?"

"I haven't. But I know people who have, and everyone says you need to talk about it first and make sure everyone's on board and cool with it, and that there are ground rules. Or it has to be with random people, and not your significant other." She waved a hand. "I doubt I'll ever do that, though. I'm too ADD to be able to deal with more than one person at a time."

"You're not ADD, Isadora," I said with a sigh.

"Actually, I am. I saw a psychologist a few years ago, and he said it was likely I am—I never got diagnosed for it as a kid, but I have all the classic hallmarks—I was the bad kid, the spazz, unable to concentrate on anything for more than a few minutes. Basically, my life has always been, okay I'm gonna study for this French exam—hey look at that new top I just bought, I should try it on—wait! I have to check my email—wait! My lip gloss should be refreshed, and look, my nails are kind of chipping, so I should just repaint them…and then I never study for the French exam."

"You're not actually that all-over-the-place, Izzy."

She rolled her eyes. "Sometimes…yes, I am. When I forget to be all deep and philosophical and shit."

I whacked her on the arm. "You're not giving

yourself enough credit. There's so much more to you than clothes and makeup."

"Just like *you* have an inner sex goddess. You just have to find her, let her out, and give her the reins."

I shouldered my purse and hefted my bag of purchases. "Okay, I have to go, for real."

"I'll expect details later!"

"There won't be anything to have details about, but sure!" I called as I exited, waving at her over my shoulder.

I walked home, set the bag of new outfits on my bed, and debated on what to do next.

I was legitimately worried that if I saw Remington again, something would happen. And if anything happened, I just knew, deep down, that there'd be no going back.

He'd seen my tattoos.

And now Izzy had—and I was going to show Kitty the next time we were home alone together. And I knew it was only a matter of time before everyone else in my life found out too, and then the cat would be out of the bag, and everything would change, and I hated change.

All because Remington Badd, that stupid, too-sexy-for-his-own-good bear of a man, had seen my tattoos.

And my boobs.

Gah.

Should I take Izzy's advice?

Not about bribing him with a blowjob, of course—that would NEVER happen in a million years. But about making things happen in my time, under circumstances of my choice?

If something was going to happen, why shouldn't I make sure it was on my terms?

I laid out both of my new outfits—the one I'd normally wear, and the one that could be said to represent a potential new me.

Problem was…I wasn't sure what I wanted.

Did I *want* something to happen between Remington and me?

Did I want to risk further change to my status quo?

If I did try to make sure whatever happened was on my terms…what were my terms?

Wear the conservative Juneau outfit, and politely request he give back my drawing, and possibly agree to something I knew he'd demand? Because if I showed up to claim my sketch, there'd be some sort of demand—that was a given.

Or, go in with my new outfit, hypnotize him with my cleavage, demand he return the drawing, and go my way without agreeing to anything?

I laughed out loud. That second option sounded

nice, but it wasn't me. I wasn't like that.

But if I could show off my tattoos, why couldn't I summon a little alpha woman of my own?

Find my inner sex goddess, as Izzy put it.

Maybe I could.

And maybe I should.

NINE

Remington

My brothers and I had spent just about every waking moment over the last three days going through the list of things Sebastian wanted us to do in order to get Badd Kitty Saloon up and running. He had spent a majority of that time with us, actually, and he made it all look so easy and simple and obvious that I felt kind of stupid.

I know Rome did, too, which had us all on edge.

Plus, Bast being here meant Kitty was over at Badd's managing the place. Which meant Rome wasn't getting sex, because we'd been too busy to do anything but sleep and work—these days even eating happened on the go. And Rome without sex is a cranky little baby of a man.

I'm not sure what excuse I have, though, because no, I'm not getting sex either, but I don't have a girl-friend, and I've been focusing on other stuff since moving here. Which means I haven't had sex since leaving Oklahoma.

Okay, so there's my excuse.

Or, I'm just a cranky bastard because I hate work-ing at the bar, and I never got the tattoo I wanted be-cause of the whole scene at the parlor with Juneau.

And, to be totally honest, Juneau is part of the reason I'm cranky.

I keep having wet dreams about her, and then I wake up horny, and I look at the picture I drew of her and imagine getting my hands on those big beautiful tits of hers, and I jerk off to thoughts of her, and then I feel sleazy.

And it's a vicious cycle, which has me cranky, off-balance, and snapping at my brothers.

So, by the time Sunday evening rolled around and the list was finally done and Bast had gone home, Rome roared off in the truck to pick up Kitty for a long overdue date, and Ram hung around just long enough to get pissed at me for snapping at him about something dumb, and then took off on foot for who-knew-where, leaving me alone in the bar with nothing to do, nowhere to go, and no one to be an asshole to.

I found myself debating whether to just get hammered alone and watch porn, or admit defeat and head to my cousins' bar for company and drinks; I was leaning toward the latter simply because I knew getting hammered alone was a bad idea, and porn would only lead to pining after Juneau and those tits and those eyes and that musical, expressive voice and that long black hair and that exotic dark skin with its hypnotizing gallery of illustrations…

A quiet knock on the front door of the saloon shocked me out of my inner debate.

Who would be knocking on the door of a not-yet-open-for-business bar at six in the evening on a Sunday?

Expecting drunk tourists, I unlocked the door and yanked it open with an irritated snarl. "We're not open yet. Come back in a week or two."

"Um. Okay?" the most unexpected voice greeted me. "If that's what you want, fine by me."

I blinked, finally seeing the person who stood on the other side: Juneau Isaac. "Sorry, sorry." I stepped backward and gestured at the interior. "Come in, please."

"So you *don't* want me to come back in a week or two?" she asked, following me inside the bar.

"That, too." I closed and relocked the main entrance to the saloon, moved to lean in what I hoped was a casually cool pose against the bar. "So. What brings you here?"

She shifted uncomfortably, nervous and unsure. Now that she was inside, and I was over my surprise, I found myself openly and brazenly perusing Juneau as she stood in the middle of my bar. She was wearing a floor-length sweater buttoned up from waist to neck, which I understood, as it was pretty cold and wet today. It wasn't entirely shapeless or figure-hiding, like some of the stuff she'd worn around me, but I wouldn't call it sexy, either.

"I...you know why I'm here."

"Because you couldn't hold out against the need to finish the kiss we almost had?"

She narrowed her eyes at me, crossing her arms over the top of her chest. "No, definitely not that."

There was a glint in her eyes and a shifting of her feet and a quick glance away that told me she maybe wasn't telling the whole truth.

I kept playing dumb. "So...is it because you just can't help but to want to spend as much time as possible around me?"

She rolled her eyes. "Ummmm...no. Pretty sure it's not that."

"You wound me," I said, clutching at my heart. "For real. I might cry. I thought I had a winning personality."

"Enough messing around, Remington. Where is it?" She held out her hand. "You said I had three days—it's three days on the dot, and I want my note back."

"Just like that, huh?" I smirked, crossing my arms in a way that I knew made my biceps look good. "Just…show up and I'll give it back?"

"You said it was insurance that you'd see me again. You didn't say anything about blackmail." She gestured at herself. "Well, here I am. You see me. Now may I please have my note back?"

I shrugged and held my hands palms up. "I don't have it with me."

She huffed in frustration. "Yeah, sure. Quit stalling. You're not getting anything else out of me."

I held up my fingers in the Scout symbol. "I don't! I swear. It's at our apartment, in my room."

"Remington. Just give it to me, please."

I held both hands palms toward her. "I'm telling you the one hundred percent God's honest truth. I put it in my wallet the day I took it from you, brought it home, and took it out. Right now it's currently in my underwear drawer." I winked at her. "If I carried it around with me, I'd be too tempted to actually read it."

"What, like you haven't?"

"In the immortal words of Peter Quill: 'I may be

an asshole, but I'm not one hundred percent a dick.'" I drew an X over my heart. "I haven't looked at it, cross my heart and hope to die."

She couldn't resist a smirk. "You just quoted Starlord at me."

"I sure did."

"You really haven't opened it, and it really isn't here?"

I nodded. "Absolute truth. And, to be clear, I have been tempted to open it every single moment since I took it. It's a curse, actually. I wish I could just go over the line into being a hundred percent a dick, just so I could sate my curiosity, but I can't quite do it. I do have the tiniest bit of decency hiding somewhere inside me." I held my fingers about a quarter inch apart. "It's about this big, and it's very well hidden, but it *is* there."

She gave me a look that was equal parts droll, amused, and irritated. "You're not *that* bad, Remington."

I winked at her. "Glad you agree, babe." I jutted my chin at the door. "So. You want to pop over to my place real quick? I'll give you the note back."

She quirked an eyebrow at me. "Just like that?"

"Just like that. Just to prove I do have that sliver of decency I mentioned."

"I'm skeptical there won't be further

manipulation, but...sure." She held up a finger. "*But*—no funny business. No coercion, no seduction. You give me my note, and we go."

"We go?" I pounced on her slipup. "We go where?"

"Me. I mean...I—I go. You give me my note, and *I* go home. *Alone.*"

I stepped closer to her, giving her a smoldering grin. "I'll agree to no funny business and no coercion. I can't agree to the other one, though." I tugged on her braid, sidling closer yet; she stiffened, staring up at me with a set jaw and blazing eyes. "Being seduced is just a chance you'll have to take, Juneau."

"That sliver of decency is quickly dwindling, I see."

I stared into her eyes, meeting her bold, fiery brown gaze. "You have that effect on me."

"I turn you into a manipulative asshole?"

I snorted a laugh. "You make me a slave to my baser urges."

"Yeah...there's this thing called self-control. You may have heard of it."

"Nope. Doesn't ring a bell."

She rolled her eyes at me. "You're hysterical."

"For real. Where you're concerned, my self-control is...pretty much nil. I wish I could explain it better, but you just...you have that effect on me."

"So…I turn you into an impetuous moron?"

"I would say more of an impetuous horn-dog, but yeah. Basically."

"Wow. So flattering."

I grinned. "I mean, it should be. I've been through some of the most grueling physical training on the planet. I can cover myself in a fire shelter and stay still while a fire rages right over top of me—can, and have. I can run uphill at a sprint in full gear. Read a forest fire and anticipate where it's going to go. But resist you? Not a chance in fucking hell."

This softened her a bit—against her will, it seemed to me. "You can't resist me?" She said this with a suspicious frown.

"Nope."

"So, when I ask you to please, please, pretty please just give me my note back?" She said this with a slow blink of her beautiful brown eyes, staring up at me pleadingly.

I almost bit straight through my lip in an attempt to not groan, kiss her stupid, or rip that sweater off buttons and all—or all three.

"I'd say come with me to my apartment, and I'll give it to you."

She turned away with a blush, snickering. "That's what I'm afraid of."

I barked a laugh. "That's *not* what I meant! That

one's all on you, sweetheart. You made it dirty, not me."

She lifted her chin. "I can't deny that one." Letting out a deep breath, she smiled at me. "To your apartment then."

"Okay, let me just shut off all the lights." I hurried around shutting things down, and then led her out, relocking the door behind me. "We're about two blocks down."

"Okay."

I eyed her sideways, hoping for a glimpse of whatever she was wearing beneath the sweater. Unfortunately, I was out of luck, as the garment covered her completely—which was a good idea as a sharp wind blew, carrying with it spattering drops of rain, making her shiver into the sweater, and me wish I'd worn more than a T-shirt.

She glanced at me. "Either you're tougher than anyone has a right to be, you're used to the cold, or you're just a dumbass who didn't bring a hoodie when it's barely fifty and windy and rainy."

I laughed. "All three? I'm freezing my balls off, to be honest."

She shook her head. "It's Alaska. This is just the beginning. You're gonna want to stock up on warmer clothes." She glanced pointedly at my cut-off khaki shorts, T-shirt, and heavy workbooks.

"I was working inside all weekend, so why am I gonna dress for the weather outside?"

She tilted her head to one side. "I guess that makes sense."

I shrugged. "I can tough it out for the few minutes it takes me to go from home to the bar, or from the bar to the truck." I laughed. "If I wasn't with you, I'd be jogging about now, though. It's colder than a witch's titty out here."

She frowned at me. "Crude!"

I grinned sheepishly. "Colder than a yeti's ballsac?"

"That's even worse," she snapped, but she was laughing when she said it. "How about you just say it's very cold?"

I blew a raspberry. "Boring!"

Another cold, wet gust of wind blew, and Juneau paused, kicked off the low heels she was wearing, hooked them in her fingers, and set off in a jog. "Screw this, let's go!"

I trotted after her, and we both picked up the pace when the cold wet wind turned into a steady windblown rain. "This sucks!" I yelled, as the rain grew harder.

She glanced at me sidelong, annoyed. "You think? I'm barefoot!"

I glanced ahead to gauge our distance from the

apartment: still another half a block or so. I stopped, stood in front of her, and squatted down. "Hop on."

She blinked at me owlishly. "Um…no?"

"It'll get you inside where it's warm that much faster. We have an electric fireplace, and I have a thick fleece blanket."

She sighed. "Just don't get handsy, mister."

I smirked. "No promises. But we're not getting any drier standing out here."

With another sigh of resignation, she hiked her sweater up—I glanced back just in time to catch an expanse of bare leg, and then she hopped onto my back, clinging to my neck, her shoes banging against my chest.

I caught her easily, gave a little hop to hike her higher on my back, and then palmed a grip on her thighs.

Which were warm and smooth and bare and strong. This was a bad idea.

I set out in a jog, and then, as I became accustomed to her weight, I increased my pace—I was showing off, at this point; I was soon moving at a dead run…to show off to Juneau, yes, but also because it was really raining hard now and my teeth were starting to chatter.

We reached the building, and I jogged up the steps with her, and then squatted on the landing to set her down, and only with great reluctance did I let her warm, smooth thighs out of my hands.

For her part, Juneau was a little slow to slide off my back, and to move out of my grip.

Combine that with the hesitation around my quip about her not being able to resist kissing me, and I may just have a chance with Juneau.

Maybe.

I hauled my keys out of my pocket in a hurry, unlocked the door and ushered Juneau in ahead of me. "Second floor. There's an elevator, but I usually just take the stairs."

"Stairs are fine by me," she said, and then gestured for me to precede her up the stairs. "You first."

I laughed as I trotted up the stairs. "You want me to go first so I don't stare at your ass the whole time, or because you want to stare at mine?"

"Shut up," she muttered. "Neither. I just don't know which unit is yours."

"Sure, sure." I stopped and did a dumb pose to pop out my butt for her benefit. "You just want to look at my butt."

I glanced back at her, and sure enough, the second our eyes met, she glanced away a little too quickly.

"You're awfully full of yourself."

"You're just annoyed because you know it's true," I said, leaning against the railing and smirking down at her.

"Do you always act this way, or is just me?" she demanded, stomping up the stairs past me.

I followed her up, but sadly the sweater obscured my view of anything good.

"Stop staring at my butt," Juneau said, glaring back at me.

"Don't worry, that ridiculous sweater of yours takes care of that."

"So you admit to staring?"

"Absolutely. But currently there's nothing to see except a vague hint of motion under all that thick wool."

"Maybe that's why I wore the sweater," she said, pushing through the door and into the second-floor hallway. "To keep your eyes off me. You got more than enough of a look last time."

"See, that's where we disagree. That wasn't anywhere near enough of a look."

"Yeah, well, it's all you're gonna get, so I hope you appreciated it."

I gestured at a door on the right as she went past it. "This is me." I unlocked it and led the way in, and for once I was thankful Ram was such a neat freak, because our apartment wasn't the dirty shithole most people assumed the bachelor pad of three single men would be.

She glanced around and was clearly surprised by the fact that things were neat, tidy, vacuumed, and wiped down—thanks entirely to Ram and his OCD tendencies. "Wow. It's...cleaner than I expected it to be."

I laughed. "That's Ram. He's got issues." I gestured around. "Which works for Rome and me, cause we get a clean apartment out of it."

She stood, waiting. "So...my note?"

I sighed. "Right to business, huh?" I brushed the shoulder of her soaking wet sweater, which hung limp and clung to her body in a way I appreciated, but I knew was leaving her cold and shivering. "How about I offer you some sweatpants and a hoodie to wear while we toss your things into the dryer?"

"I'll swim in your clothes."

I lifted an eyebrow. "Hey, I'm one hundred percent in favor of you wrapping up in nothing but my fleece blanket, but I'm trying to be a gentleman here."

"The sweater is the only thing that's really all that wet," she said, her eyes flicking away from mine. "I wouldn't mind if it got dried, though."

"Give it here and I'll toss it in. The laundry room is just down the hall."

She hesitated. "Um, yeah. Okay." She slowly started unbuttoning the sweater. "Can you, um, look away?"

I snorted. "What, are you naked under it or something?"

"No, I just…" She sighed, and then set her jaw. "Fine."

She unbuttoned the sweater from the top down, held it closed, and then, with a long look into my eyes, she shrugged out of it.

HOLY. MOTHER. FUCK.

She was wearing a tight black miniskirt that only just barely covered her ass, and a tank top worn bra-less, with a plunging neckline that bared an absolutely cock-hardening amount of inner sideboob…and what with the thick straps, it also left bare an equally maddening amount of outer sideboob. Basically, the only part of her breasts that were covered was the tips.

Sort of.

Were they taped in place? If she moved wrong, a boob was sure to fly out.

Please move wrong—*please*?

And those legs? Jesus. If she stretched too far, I was certain the skirt would hike up and I'd get a glimpse at the underside of her ass, if not a hint of underwear.

And all those tattoos? Totally bared, exposed. Illuminated, you might say.

"Remington?" Her voice was low, quiet, quavery. "Say something."

"I…" My voice was hoarse. "You—you're…"

She blinked up at me, and I knew that more than tits or ass or legs, it was those eyes that would be my undoing. They were inquisitive, kind, warm, fiery, fierce, sultry…everything, all at once. "I'm what?"

She was inches away, standing in my living room with those intoxicating eyes on me, waiting for what I'd say.

"In a way it was better with the sweater on."

She frowned. "It…it was?"

"Yeah, because it was a fuck of a lot easier to keep my hands to myself when you were all covered up." I gestured at her with a sweep of my finger from head to toe and back up. "Looking all perfect and sexy like this? My self-control is a joke."

"Then give me my sweater back."

I laughed, and headed for the door. "Not a chance in fucking hell, sweetheart."

She followed me. "Remington, seriously. I just came for my note."

I paused halfway out the door. "And now you're stuck here with me for as long as it takes for this to dry—unless you want to brave the rain in just that outfit."

"You're a bastard."

"I'm drying your clothing for you, and I'm a bastard?"

"You're all but saying you plan on…on seducing me."

"Not *all but*—I *am* saying that." I turned back and sidled over to her, standing so close you couldn't have fit a piece of paper between her breasts and my chest, staring down at her. "If you're as impervious to my charms as you're making out, you're fine, right? Nothing to worry about. My attempts at seduction are doomed to fail."

"Right," she breathed.

"The only reason you'd have to be nervous about me trying to seduce you is if you *are* attracted to me—if you find me wildly irresistible despite my roguish ways."

"You've obviously read too many romance novels," she said with a snort of laughter. "Roguish ways."

"My point is, you have nothing to worry about, okay?"

She attempted a confident smile. "Right."

Impetuously, still holding her sweater in one hand, I cupped the back of her neck with my other, bent down, and kissed her.

Slowly.

Forcefully.

She stiffened at first, and then melted, and then her hand tangled into my hair and she whimpered, lifting up on her toes and pressing into the kiss, opening her mouth and offering me her tongue and taking mine.

She pressed herself against me, taking my kiss and making it something else, making it something alive and wild between us.

And when we broke apart, she was gasping for breath, and her lips were swollen, and her eyes were fixed hungrily on mine.

"Damn you, Remington," she whispered.

I just grinned at her. "Stay here," I said, and disappeared through the door, taking her sweater to the laundry room where I put it on low and warm rather than high and hot, knowing full well it would take twice as long to dry. I mean, it's wool—I'd hate to shrink it, right?

All the while, my lips tingled, and my zipper was tight, and my head spun—the girl was hungry, wild.

She kissed with a need to match the way I felt.

I had a feeling I was in trouble with this girl. A lot of trouble.

Good thing I've always been a sucker for trouble.

TEN

Juneau

OHHHHHH GOD.

Have I ever been kissed like that? Ever?

The way he cupped the back of my neck and pulled me up to meet him? Guiding, demanding, but not controlling. And his lips? Soft, yet firm; pliable, yet powerful. Damp, warm, devouring. His tongue invaded my mouth and I had no choice but respond in kind, to open my mouth for him, and taste his tongue.

My breasts flattened against him, and his heart beat hard and fast against my chest. The whole thing was completely intoxicating.

And then there was the bulging tightness of his zipper, promising something iron-hard and massive.

Lust burned through me like a wildfire.

And then, just as I was finding my equilibrium in the kiss, he broke away and that sexy, arrogant grin told me he knew damn well how the kiss had affected me.

He went off to the laundry room, and I stood in the living room of his apartment. I placed two fingers against my lips and read myself the riot act.

I was absolutely NOT going to assault him with my mouth the moment he returned. I was absolutely NOT going to let my hands get anywhere near his zipper, much less the organ behind it. I promised myself I was absolutely NOT going to let him strip me bare and have his way with me right here on the living room floor, consequences be damned.

None of that was going to happen.

We were going to remain fully clothed and conduct a civil conversation. My hands would stay on my lap, and his hands would stay on his, and when my sweater was done drying, I'd call a cab and go home. Alone.

And, once home alone, I was absolutely NOT going to use my vibrator on myself while thinking about the massive thing behind his zipper...or how thick and hard and hot it would feel in my hand as I slowly and gently stroked it.

Crap.

Crap, crap, crap.

I was daydreaming about Remington's cock. Again.

When he sauntered back into his apartment, I jumped a mile in the air, squeaking embarrassingly.

He held up his hands, moving toward me slowly, laughing. "Whoa, chill, Juneau—it's just me."

I wanted to be mad about it, but how could I? I was in his apartment of my own free will, and I knew he'd be back. "Sorry, sorry—just…"

He quirked up one eyebrow. "Thinking dirty thoughts about me?"

"No!" I protested, knowing I was giving myself away.

He grinned, a hot, knowing smirk. "I see. So… you were."

"No," I insisted. "I was just…" I sighed. "Can I have my note back now?"

He leaned in, and his lips brushed mine. "It's okay, Juneau. You can admit it." He touched his lips to the shell of my ear. "I was thinking dirty thoughts about you, too."

"You were? When?" I couldn't help but ask.

He laughed, a gruff, husky rumble. "Um…well? Just now. Last night. Three days ago. Shit—to be honest, Juneau, I'm thinking dirty thoughts about you pretty much all the time."

A heavy, pulsing, significant pause filled the air.

"Want to know what I do when I think those dirty thoughts?" he muttered in my ear, his breath hot and his voice hotter.

"No, thank you," I breathed.

"You sure?"

I nodded shakily. "Yeah. I'm sure."

His teeth sank into my earlobe, and I squeaked. "You have no interest in knowing what I do when I think dirty, filthy things about your body?"

"Nope."

He laughed, louder, and backed away. "Okay." He swaggered down the hallway, leaving me standing breathless and fighting the urge to beg him to tell me everything.

He stopped in the doorway to a bedroom on the right side of the hallway. "You coming?"

"Coming?" I jumped, blushing at the unintentional innuendo. "In—into your room you mean?" I said, my voice high and panicked.

He widened his eyes and nodded, a sarcastic expression. "Yeah...my room. Where my dresser is, which has my underwear drawer in it, which has your note in it."

"Can't you—can't you just...get it and bring it here?"

He smirked. "I mean, I *could*. But what...are you

scared of my room?"

"Nope."

"You're not scared of my room?" He leaned against the doorpost. "You're not…nervous about seeing my bed?"

"Nope."

"You're not worried because you've had wet dreams about being naked in my bed? You've never daydreamed about being bent over it?"

"No!" I snapped. "I have *not!*"

He laughed. "Yeah, okay. Whatever you say."

The sarcastic disbelief in his voice and on his face pissed me off—and loosened my tongue to an unwise degree. I stomped over to him, glaring up at him. "You want to know? Fine, I'll tell you." I stabbed a finger into his chest. "Yes, I *have* had inappropriate thoughts about you. Yes, I *am* nervous about going into your room, because I know you're trying to seduce me and yes, I *am* attracted to you, but *no*, I have no intention of letting anything happen. And you want to know why?" I stood up straight and tall, my eyes fierce on his. "Because guys like you are careless with the hearts of girls like me. You'd get what you want from me, and then it'd be over. I'm not afraid of getting hurt because I know I can survive it. The problem is, I'd have to be certain it'd be worth getting hurt over, and I'm just not sure it would be."

He winced. "Wow. Okay." He shook his head. "If that's how you really feel."

The anger and hurt on his face cut through me like a knife.

He stomped into his room, yanked open the top drawer, rummaged through it—and then stopped, abruptly spinning around to snarl at me. "No, it's fine. If you're not sure it'd be worth it, then you shouldn't be here." He went to the closet, flipped through hangers, and found a thick Patagonia fleece jacket. "Here. Take this and go. You can give it to Kitty to give back to me later. Better yet—just fuckin' keep it."

I entered his room. "Remington, wait. I didn't mean—"

His eyes blazed as he set the jacket on my shoulders. "Not worth it. What the fuck? How do you know I'd be careless? How do you know what I want?"

"It's obvious what you want!" I snapped, taking the jacket off and throwing it back at him. "You want to get me naked and fuck me. You've said almost exactly that."

"Right. I absolutely, and without a single doubt, want to get you naked and fuck you six ways to Sunday—more than I've wanted just about anything else, ever." He stood over me, staring down at me, the jacket dangling from a finger. "The question is more about what happens *after*wards, am I right?"

"Yes, that's exactly the question."

He glared down at me with hard, distant eyes. "And you're assuming I'd—what? Finish and tell you to fuck off? Get my rocks off and then never talk to you again?"

"Yeah," I murmured. "That's pretty much exactly what I'm assuming."

"And like I've said before—you're seriously underestimating me."

I hesitated. "How so?"

The distance in his eyes melted, and the hardness softened a little—heat entered his gaze. "You're assuming all I want is one time with you." He let his gaze rake over my body. "That's your big mistake. Because, Juneau, I can promise you one thing—if I were to have the *privilege* of getting my hands on you, once wouldn't be anywhere *near* enough."

I shivered at his words. "Oh."

He brushed my lower lip with his thumb. "But you're right. It probably wouldn't be worth it." He backed away, then.

Remington went to the open drawer, found my little square of folded paper, and returned to stand in front of me. Instead of placing it in my upturned palm, however, he tugged the strap of the tank top away, and placed the square against the slope of my left breast, and slid it down, down, down, until it covered my thickening, throbbing nipple. "Here. Unopened, unread. As promised."

His room wasn't large and standing here in the middle, I was within a few steps of his bed, his dresser, his closet, and the small desk shoved between the foot end of his bed and the wall. In an attempt to escape the hunger in his eyes and the effect it had on my determination to escape him unscathed, I shifted my eyes away. It wasn't safe to look at the bed, because I had, in fact, had a dream about him and his bed, to match the contents of my sketch. In the dream, I'd been on my hands and knees, and he'd been...well... rough with me in a way that I enjoyed so much in the dream that I'd woken up on the edge of orgasm and had needed only a few quick circles of my fingers to bring myself to shuddering climax. The dresser wasn't safe either, because it had his underwear in it, and if I thought about his underwear, I'd think about what was inside them.

Surely his desk was safe to look at.

Only, instead of random books or bills or a computer, what I saw on his desk was a piece of paper with a sketch on it. At first, it was just a sketch on his desk that drew my attention, because as an artist, I can spot talent, and this drawing had it in spades.

But then the subject of the sketch filtered through my shock. Remington had clearly drawn it,

as evidenced by the careless way the paper was partly covered by another paper, and the way the pencil
and a chunk of white eraser block were placed on one
corner.

It was a sketch of a woman in the act of don-
ning a button-down shirt. The woman wore a skirt,
and her breasts were bare, and he'd captured a kind
of sensual, sexual elegance in the way she was twisted to slide her arms into the sleeves. He'd captured
the sense of weight and movement in the sway of her
heavy breasts. He'd depicted her breasts with loving
attention to detail, even down to the shading of light
on them and the bumps around her wide, dark areolae, and the thick plump protrusions of her nipples.

Then other details hit my awareness, and I drifted over to the desk on autopilot, picked up the sketch,
and examined it.

It was me.

My tattoos, the bands on my chest and diaphragm were accurate, and some of the ones on my
belly and sides were, others he'd clearly guessed at or
made up. He'd even gotten the blemish on the inside
of my left breast.

I twisted to look at him. "Remington…"

He shrugged, looking away from my eyes. "It's
just a drawing."

"It's amazing. You're *really* talented."

"I had to guess at or make up some of the tattoos—I really did only see you for a split second."

The drawing told me more about how he saw me than anything he could say.

And I thought of the sketch folded into a two-inch square hidden inside my shirt, cold against my skin.

"Do you have any other drawings of me?" I asked, genuinely curious.

"Yeah, one other." He waved a hand. "It's not as good, though."

"Can I see it?"

He smirked. "Sure. If you show me what's on that piece of paper in your bra."

"I'm not wearing a bra," I blurted, and then blushed. "And that's...private. And...personal."

He indicated the sketch in my hands. "You think that's not?"

I glanced down at it. It was, very obviously, a drawing of a highly personal memory.

I couldn't show him my sketch, though. He'd... he'd know what I wanted. That I wanted him. *How* I wanted him.

But then...he clearly was able to read that in me without needing a sketch to prove it.

I sucked in a breath, held it, and met his wild blue eyes.

A crazy recklessness thrilled through me, and I knew I was about to do something really stupid.

"Fine." I clenched my jaw and breathed out slowly. "But you can't use it against me."

He grinned slowly. "No promises—you should know that about me by now." I made to reach for the note but his hand intercepted me, latching onto my wrist. "Please...allow me."

I lifted my chin, keeping my eyes on his; the hungry, amused, sarcastic smirk on his lips was maddening and irritating and sexy all at once.

He reached in behind the strap of my tank top, gathering the note in his fingers...and in the process, his hand covered my breast. It was a slow, deliberate act—designed to provoke...or request tacit permission by gauging my demurral.

My pulse slammed in my veins, and I trembled... my flesh tingled and burned where his hand touched me. The corners of the paper poked into me, and his hand cupped, squeezed, caressed, and then released.

He withdrew his hand, and I watched him lick his lips, then clench his jaw, and release a pent-up breath. The note in his hands, he held my gaze. Hesitated. And then slowly unfolded the piece of paper, placed it face down on his thigh and ran it over his leg a few times to smooth out the wrinkles. And then flipped it around to look at it.

He gazed at it for a long, long moment, and then his eyes locked on mine. "Fucking hell, Juneau. No wonder you didn't want me to see it."

"It's just a stupid doodle," I muttered.

He barked a laugh. "Just a stupid doodle?" Remington held the drawing so I could see it—him, gorgeous and in profile, his massive cock in a fist, my ass spread out as I waited on hands and knees in front of him, ready for him to take me doggy-style. "Don't bullshit me. Does this look like a stupid doodle to you?"

I closed my eyes for a second, and then met his gaze. "No."

"No, it's not." He indicated his drawing, still in my hand. "No more than that's a stupid doodle, either."

I sighed. "I wasn't aware I was even doing it," I admitted. "My boss almost saw it."

Remington laughed. "That'd have been bad."

I shook my head. "I don't even want to imagine." I indicated my sketch. "I've...I've never, *ever* drawn anything that X-rated."

Remington passed his hand through his hair. "I can't say I've never drawn a naked woman before, but...this? Of you? Definitely the most...artistic." He met my eyes. "You were obviously just using your imagination when you drew that, though."

I raised an eyebrow at him. "Oh? I didn't get the…anatomy right?"

He smirked arrogantly. "No, babe, you didn't." He tapped my depiction of his penis, which was, in my estimation, probably rather generous. "My cock is nowhere near that small."

I rolled my eyes and snorted a sarcastic laugh. "Yeah, okay. Keep telling yourself that, pal."

His eyebrow slid up. "Think I'm joking?"

My eyes, involuntarily, jumped down to his zipper—the bulge against the denim and the zipper was, errr…rather sizable. "I'll take your word for it."

"You don't want to find out for yourself?" he whispered.

I shook my head, keeping my gaze on his jaw rather than his eyes so he wouldn't see the lie. "No. I don't."

He brushed a finger across my shoulder, dancing a single fingertip along my skin; I could all but hear my flesh sizzling under his touch. "You're a shitty liar, Juneau."

"I'm not lying," I muttered.

He just laughed, shaking the drawing so the paper flapped noisily. "This says otherwise."

"It…it does?" My mind was hazy, my thoughts mixed up—he was too close, and his heat and his scent made it hard to breathe, and his finger was toying with the strap of my tank top, nudging it closer and closer to the edge of my shoulder. "What—um. What does it say, then, if you're so damned astute?"

He kept his eyes on mine as he nudged the strap until it was hanging off my shoulder by a scrap of cloth, barely clinging. "That drawing says you fantasize about me. About *us*. It says you've thought about me...about my cock. If you're drawing it like that, in that kind of detail, it says you've daydreamed about me." His voice dropped to a whisper. "It tells me you're barely resisting the urge to unzip my jeans and grab my cock. It says you want me—like this," he said, tapping the drawing.

"Not true," I murmured.

"No? You've never imagined yourself with my cock in your hand? You're not thinking about how I'd feel sliding through your fingers? You're not wondering if I'm right—if I'm even bigger than in your drawing? Or am I full of shit? You're wondering. I know you are."

I shook my head, but I couldn't make myself lie anymore—he was too good at reading my lies.

He slid the other strap to the edge of my shoulder. And now, I was a couple of flicks of his finger away from being bare for him again. My heart was slamming in my chest, and my hands were clammy and shaking, and I couldn't take my eyes off of his—and I couldn't find the drive to stop him.

"I know what you're expecting," he said.

"Oh? What's that?"

He ran a fingertip down from my nose to my chin, down my throat, over the hollow at the base of my throat, and down the center of my chest, between my all-but-bare breasts. "You're expecting me to rip your shirt off right away, aren't you?"

I shrugged, which was ill-advised, because the motion did the work for him, causing the left strap to fall off, and my breast hung free of the tank top, bare, nipple erect, swaying from the movement of my shrug. "Yeah, I guess."

"You'd be wrong."

I blinked. "I...what?"

He let his eyes hesitate on my naked breast, and then he met my eyes. "You have about ten seconds to tell me to stop. Seriously. Right now—tell me, truthfully, that you don't want me to touch you anymore, and I'll stop immediately. If you don't, you'll find out what I'm actually going to do instead of getting rid of that tank top."

I swallowed hard. "Remington..."

He smirked. "You won't say anything, though, because you like how I touch you."

"What are you going to do?" I asked, rather

than answering him.

He sidled closer, towering over me, and ran his hands down my shoulders to the small of my back. Bent over me, and I had a split second to catch my breath before his lips were on mine, and I was dizzied by the kiss, and my heart slammed and my pulse pounded and my hands shook as I caught at his shoulders and then knotted my fingers in the cotton of his T-shirt.

After a too-short, breathless moment of his lips on mine, he pulled back.

"This," he said.

And his hands slid down to spread out over my butt, cupping gently before clutching, and then kneading.

"Rem—" I managed, and then I stopped abruptly as his real intention became clear.

His fingers found the zipper of the skirt at the base of my spine. His eyes locked onto mine, watching for my reaction. My eyes widened, but my teeth seized on my lower lip and bit down, hard. Slowly, deliberately, he drew the zipper down, loosening the skirt. My nipples puckered, tightening. I caught my breath, licked my lip where my teeth had bitten. The zipper lowered, he paused, watching me, and then curled his fingers in the waistband of my underwear, preparing to tug them down.

"Wait," I murmured, and his hand stilled immediately.

I couldn't help a grin as I scratched my fingers up his back, gathering his T-shirt upward as I did so. He lifted his chin and raised his arms over his head, and I yanked his shirt off, dropping it to one side. His chest was a work of art—my drawing hadn't done it justice. He was far more heavily muscled, leaner, more de-fined. Vascular, each muscle shrink-wrapped in tanned skin. Thick slabs of pecs, flexing as he breathed, abs like blocks marching down to the waist of his jeans. He had a sleeve tattoo wrapped around his shoulder and bicep, an elegantly shaded black-and-white depic-tion of a raging forest fire, the smoke transitioning seamlessly to a murder of crows taking flight across his shoulder and over to his chest and upper.

"Your tattoo," I whispered.

He twisted and lifted his arm to look at it. "A bud-dy of mine from my unit was a tattoo artist before he got into firefighting. He got me into tattoos, and he did this one."

"He's very talented."

"Yeah, he is." He smirked. "You done?"

"Done?"

"Playing tit—" He brushed my exposed breast with a thumb, briefly but sharply pinching my nipple hard enough that I squeaked—"for tat..." he trailed off, shrugging his shoulder to mean his tattoo.

I laughed. "That was a terrible joke."

His gaze was serious. "Who's joking? Let's keep playing. Tit for tat." He brushed a fingertip over my hip. "I know you have more tattoos down here—or at least continuations of the ones here," he said, tracing an upside-down V from hip to breasts to hip, where my tattoo was.

"If we're playing that game, then I think you're already ahead," I said. "You get my skirt off, I'll be naked and you'll still have your jeans on."

"You didn't say you weren't playing, I notice." Remington's eyes raked down my body, then back up to my eyes. "Go ahead, then. I'll give you one for free."

"One what?"

He shrugged. "Whatever you want. Whatever you think will make it fair after I take your skirt and panties off."

I made a face. "Don't say 'panties,'" I said. "I hate that word."

He chuckled. "Fine. Thong, then."

I tilted my head. "How do you know I'm wearing a thong?"

He ran his hand over my ass on top of the skirt, making a rather careful examination of one cheek. "No underwear lines, and this…" He slid his fingers into the opening of the zipper, curling his fingers into the elastic of the waistband of the bright pink thong I was indeed wearing.

Instead of tugging it down, though, he reached his hand into the skirt, palming one cheek, and then the other, cupping them as if he had every right to. And I, for my part, could only gasp for breath at the brazen ownership in his touch, even as my core tightened, heated, dampened. He slid a finger along the waistband of the thong, and then under the tiny sliver of fabric right where it disappeared between the globes of my butt, drawing the panel over my core even tighter.

"See? Thong," he said, releasing me and resting his hands on my waist.

"Very observant of you."

He just shrugged. "Simple deduction, actually—a skirt that tight with no underwear lines, the only thing you could be wearing is either a thong… or nothing. And I gambled on the fact that you're not the type to wear nothing under a skirt."

"Okay, Sherlock, you win." I huffed a laugh. "I'm not even the type to wear skirts like this, usually. Or even thongs very often."

"But yet here you are, wearing the skirt, *and* a thong…for me." He grinned at me. "I must bring something out of you."

I let out a soft sigh, nodding. "Yeah, you really do."

"Sorry, not sorry," he said, and stepped back, holding out his arms wide to either side. "So. You get one for free."

He was offering himself to me. On display, for the taking. I looked him over, for once allowing my libido and impulses to rule me. Heavy chest, thick arms, broad shoulders, powerful abs; his waist was narrow, his thighs like tree trunks. It wasn't just his zipper that was bulging as he gazed at me, waiting—the entire front of his jeans were swollen, tented. He was about to burst out of the top of his jeans, I realized. Painfully erect inside his jeans.

And I was only partially undressed—tank top sagging, one breast exposed, skirt open in back and drooping.

My fingers tangled together in front of me; I was only barely restraining myself from reaching for his zipper. I hated that he could read me so easily, that he knew with unerring accuracy how badly I wanted to feel him in my hands. To see him bared for me. To know what he could make me feel. If he could set me to trembling and shaking and gasping from a mere kiss, what else could he make me feel?

God, I wanted him.

I almost didn't care what happened afterward, I

just wanted him now. I was delirious with wanting him, needing to feel his body under my hands and his mouth on my skin, and my lips on his...

Well...

Everything.

For him, I'd even consider what Izzy had talked about, earlier.

I bit my lip, my eyes on his. Did I want to give, or take? Or give in order to take more for myself?

A smile tilted my mouth, a sultry curl to my lips. If I could wear this outfit here, for him—if I could stand here, partially unclothed under his gaze—then surely I could allow my desires to take the reins, just give in for now and accept the consequences, come what may.

"What are you thinking, Juneau?" Remington murmured. "I can tell you're thinking something."

I just smiled at him. I stared at his beautiful, masculine, powerful body, and let myself want. Let myself *need*.

And then I gave in to it, completely.

Reaching down, I gathered the hem of my shirt in both hands, arms crossed in front of my belly. Pausing, my eyes on his, I telegraphed my intentions. And then I slowly peeled my tank top off, letting the shirt lift my breasts till the last possible moment, and then it was off and my breasts were bouncing free, swaying and jiggling. I heard him catch his breath as I tore the tank top over the top of my head and tossed it to the floor next to his shirt.

I felt no fear; the hunger in Remington's eyes erased any misgivings I may have had about being naked in front of him—it was obvious just from his eyes that he was only just barely restraining himself from taking me in his hands.

"Jesus—*fuck*, Juneau," Remington growled.

I held my arms at my sides and just stood there, enduring his hungry, scrutinizing stare—not enduring, soaking up. *Enjoying.* I *liked* his eyes on me. I liked the need I saw painted so indelibly in every line of his body, every twitch of his muscles, every shift of his virulently blue eyes.

"What, Remington?" I asked, even though I knew.

"You." He took a step toward me, hands reaching. "So—*fucking*—perfect."

I caught his wrists. "Ah-ah-ah. Not yet. It's still my turn."

He snarled in raw frustrated need. "I need to touch you, Juneau. I *have* to. Right the fuck now."

I ran my hands up my belly, over my tattoos, and then slowly, sensually cupped my breasts, lifted them, and then let them fall. "You want to touch these?"

"Touch 'em?" he snarled. "I'm gonna devour

them. I'd fuck 'em if you'd let me."

I felt myself blush even as my core tightened to drumhead tightness, weeping my need. "You never know what I might allow, Remington." I pushed his hands down to his sides. "I have desires of my own, though."

He shoved his hands in the back pockets of his jeans, a slow, feral, cocky grin curling his lips. "That so, darlin'?"

I laughed at the unexpected twang in his voice. "Your country boy is showing."

"Well, you know what they say—you can take the boy outta the country, but you can't take the country outta the boy." He jutted his chin at me. "And, Juneau, honey, you turn my mind into mush. I can't think about a goddamn thing except getting my hands and mouth on those perfect tits of yours."

"Just my tits?" I asked, shuffling closer to him, until inches separated us and the rigid tips of my breasts brushed his hard, muscular chest.

"Don't be stupid, babe. I plan on putting my mouth on every...single...inch of your sexy body." His eyes blazed, his abs rippled and flexed as his breathing came rapid and shallow, and his hands were knotted into fists at his sides. "You were saying you have desires of your own, though. What is it you want?"

I shrugged, and enjoyed the way the small, simple movement drew his attention. "Just…you."

He grinned. "Well, you got me, darlin'." He rolled a heavy shoulder, hands still in his back pockets. "I'm here for the taking."

I bit my lower lip, letting my eyes slip from his downward—taking in the hypermasculine musculature of his physique, his massive shoulders and thick chest and bulging arms and furrowed abs…and the sleek grooves of the V leading under the waist of his jeans. His zipper was straining to bursting, and I felt my fingers twitching, burning, aching to alleviate the pressure I could see him visibly struggling to be nonchalant about.

"See somethin' you like, Juneau?" Remington drawled, a cocky, arrogant grin heating his sexy, rugged face.

"You know I do."

"Then what's holding you back?" he asked. "I won't bite." Another grin, this one even more ravenous and primal. "Unless you want me to."

What *was* holding me back? Worry for what will happen when it's all over?

"Promise me one thing, Remington," I said, tangling my fingers together to keep them from wandering prematurely.

He frowned. "I don't like promising things, 'cause

I don't make promises I can't keep."

I sighed. "That's exactly it—please, whatever happens between us, just…please don't lead me on. Don't make promises you don't intend to honor just to get something from me. Be honest, be open, and be real. That's all I ask."

His smile was…well—honestly reassuring. "Juneau, baby—I give you my word that I will not ever lead you on, I'll never blow smoke up your ass just to get you to do something, and if things aren't working out, I'm not gonna drag it out or be a dick about it."

"Your word of honor."

He nodded. "Absolutely. My word of honor."

I let my hands follow the wandering journey of my gaze, then. Across his shoulders, down his chest, over the ridged plane of his stomach. Tracing the lines and valleys and ridges and curves of his muscles. My hands explored around the waistband of his jeans. I paused at the center, just beneath his navel. I met his gaze, and saw patience warring with need.

Lip caught in my teeth yet again, I felt an eager grin curving my lips, felt my eyes sparking and dancing as my fingers worked the button free of the loop, and then I dragged his zipper down. Immediately, his erection sprang hard against the black cotton of his underwear, pushing through the opening of his fly.

And god—the bulge was *massive.*

He was probably right about my sketch's under-estimation of his endowment.

Which made me tingle all over.

I hooked my fingers in his hip pockets and tugged down, and Remington shimmied his hips, stepping on the ends of his pant legs to jerk his legs free, toeing the jeans aside. He stood before me in just a pair of tight black briefs, the front tented with the bulging curve of his erection, which was bent almost double inside his underwear, the tip straining and nearly poking over the top of the elastic.

I reached for him again, but this time he caught my wrists. "Nope. My turn now."

Remington captured both of my wrists in his hands, pressed his body against mine, flattening my breasts against his chest, and nudged me backward a few steps, until I bumped up against his closed and locked bedroom door. And then he lifted my arms over my head, pinning my wrists against the door—my breasts were lifted, suspended, and my ragged breathing had them jiggling and swaying. I met his eyes, seeing the hunger, and felt lightning sizzling and searing through me even before he touched me.

"Keep 'em up there, Juneau," Remington growled, releasing my hands.

I layered my hands one behind the other and

rested my head against them, keeping my elbows up.

"Atta girl," he murmured, his eyes dancing and fiery with need. "Just like that. Don't move."

And then he knelt in front of me, and his palms raked down my chest, capturing my breasts in his hands, the mounded flesh spilling out of his grip, and then his fingers traced furrows down my belly and snagged into the front of my skirt, hooking around the waistband of both skirt and thong.

I had barely enough time to catch my breath before he dragged them down together in one smooth motion. Automatically, I stepped out, and he tossed the last of my clothing aside, leaving me utterly and totally naked, clad only in ink and goosebumps.

"Holy fuck," he growled. "So gorgeous."

He rocked backward, his hands on my hips, and let his eyes roam from head to toe, up and down, several times, pausing at my breasts and then my core each time.

And then, as if unable to help himself, he nuzzled his nose and lips against my left breast, tongue flicking, lips hunting. I gasped. He smirked. And then he was cupping my right breast in his big rough hand and his lips were capturing my left nipple, and I was fighting for breath, and he was trading hands for lips, cupping and kissing. Licking and nipping, kneading and flicking. Nipples, inside, underside, the entire heavy globe—Remington paid attention to every part of my breasts, both of them, until I was breathing hard and my core was soaked and if he flicked his tongue over my nipple one more damn time I was sure need would leak liquid down my thighs.

"Remington…" I breathed.

"Yeah, sweetheart?" he asked, staring up at me between my breasts, cupping them both in his hands.

"I…"

"Say it."

"I need—" I bit down on the phrase lodged just behind my teeth.

He nuzzled between my boobs again, keeping them in his hands and running his lips and nose and tongue all over them. "What do you need, Juneau? Tell me."

I felt my hips flex, rock. "More."

He just chuckled. "More, huh? What kinda more? Just…more? Or something specific?"

I glared down at him. "Don't play games with me, Remington. You know exactly what I want."

"Yes, I do." He ran his hands down the outside of my thighs, and then up the fronts, his palms flat against my hip bones, his thumbs grazing over the valleys to either side of my core.

At even the teasing promise of his touch, my hips flexed forward. "Touch me, Remington," I breathed.

"Oh, I am, babe. I'm just taking my time." He grinned up at me. "Can't rush perfection."

"Perfection, huh?" I asked, smirking down at him. "Awful confident in yourself, aren't you, Mr. Badd?"

He grazed his thumbs over the top of my pussy, down the lips, and then back up over the seam. "Absolutely." He pressed his lips against my belly, planting a line of quick kisses following the chevron of my tattoos, licking the montage of images on my stomach and hips, and then flicking his tongue in the hollows between my hips and my sex. "I am absolutely confident in the fact that you're about to have the best orgasm of your entire goddamn life, and when I'm finally done making you come, Juneau, you're gonna be desperate for more."

"I already am and you haven't done anything yet."

He just laughed. "Question for you, honey: are you a screamer?"

I shook my head, sucking in a sharp breath as he slid an index finger up and down my seam. "Not...not usually. But then, you have a way of bringing things out of me I didn't know I had, so anything's possible."

I couldn't resist the allure of his taut skin and hard muscle—my hands settled on his broad shoulders and trailed up his neck, back down, over his shoulders, caressing anywhere I could reach while his lips danced here and there—hip to thigh, then nuz-zling in between thigh and seam…everywhere except where I wanted it.

He pressed his thumbs to my nether lips, spread-ing me open. "You've had this before, haven't you? You've had this done to you, right?"

I nodded, breathless, speechless. "Y-yeah, of course. But not…" I lost my train of thought as he ran his tongue up the outside of my sex, the tip of his tongue sliding wetly along the outside of my nether lips. "Not like this…not the way you're doing it."

"Good." He grinned up at me. "Feel free to scream, sweetheart."

"I can't breathe right or I probably would," I gasped. "God—please, stop teasing me."

"Don't you know teasing's half the fun?"

"Fun for whom?" I growled.

He just laughed. "Me. And by the time I give you what you want, you'll be such a mess you'll fall apart for me so hard you won't know which way is up."

"Up?" I asked, only partially kidding. "What's that?"

He chuckled, but then his mouth was otherwise occupied, his thumbs caressing my seam, spreading me open, letting go, dragging his finger through my damp, slick, swollen lips, and then, finally, finally, he dragged his tongue along me where his thumbs had been. My knees buckled, and I had to grip his shoulders for balance.

"Oh...oh *god*." This was a whispered squeak, breathless and shrill.

His tongue drove suddenly against my clit, and my knees buckled again, and my grip on his shoulders went white-knuckled. His eyes met mine. "Hold on tight, now, Juneau."

"I am—" I started, and then he slid a long, thick middle finger inside me and curled it, and his tongue slathered against my clit, and I lost my voice and my breath all at once, and my knees gave out completely. "Remington!" I cried out.

I had to stiffen my knees and claw at his shoulders as my hips tilted, flexing spasmodically, driving my clit against his tongue, which was flicking and licking and circling maddeningly slowly. He knew I wanted it faster but was denying me. I gulped air as my lungs clenched, heat searing through me, pressure building and ballooning to crushing intensity as his thumbs pried me open and his tongue slid into my channel and lapped at my dripping sex and flicked in wicked circles around my hard, aching clitoris. My fingers clawed into his shoulders, my knees buckling in rhythm to the flicking of his devilishly unpredictable tongue. He lapped and lapped and lapped in slow time, and my hips flexed and flexed and flexed to meet him; and then he'd change his pace and his tongue would stiffen and drive in quick circles and my hips would try to keep up and as I grew more and more unable to keep up with his driving pace, I'd gasp and whimper and huff, and then, right as I was moments from falling over the edge into a molten pool of white-hot orgasm, he'd slow back down and I'd snarl and mewl like a feral kitten.

"Rem—" I gasped, unable to even articulate his full name. "P-p-please…"

I was a writhing, seething mess, my pussy drenched with my own need and his smeared saliva, my belly taut and clenching as waves of pre-orgasm intensity racked me, my hands clutching at his shoulders and his head, pawing and gripping and clawing for purchase, trying to grind him harder, closer, force him faster. I was a wanton mess of sexual need, is what I was, and Remington had me exactly where he wanted me.

I would do absolutely anything he asked of me in that moment, if only he would let me come.

"Oh—oh god—" I gasped, feeling myself hitting the edge, reaching the peak, my climax coming to a full boil inside me. "Rem—please. Please don't stop me, this time. Fuck!"

"I love it when you curse like that."

"You like making me desperate? You like making

me beg?" I wrenched my eyes open and fixed them on his—his mouth and upper lip and chin were smeared and glistening.

He grinned. "It *is* fucking hot as hell, knowing I can make you beg." He licked at me, keeping me teetering on the edge. "You're right there, aren't you?"

I nodded, gasping. "Yeah—so close."

"You'd agree to do pretty much anything I asked as long as I let you come right now, wouldn't you?"

I nodded, biting my lip. "Yes, Remington. You know I would."

He smirked, and then buried his face between my thighs and drove his tongue against my clit and devoured me, pushing me to the edge, making me gasp and whimper and writhe...

"If I make you come, as soon as you could function again, you'd drop to your knees and suck my cock, wouldn't you?"

"Is that what you want, Rem?" I snarled at him. "You want me to suck you off?"

"Maybe, maybe not. I just want to know how desperate you are." He glanced up at me. "I need you to do something for me, Juneau," Remington murmured, in between lapping at me with his fiendish tongue.

"What?" I rasped. "Tell me."

He slid two long thick fingers inside my tight,

spasming channel, curling them, dragging them out and drilling them back in, curling as they entered me. Then, he suctioned his mouth around my clit as he finished issuing his order, sucking hard on my clit and flicking his tongue against it in quick, ravaging circles.

"I need you to come for me," he murmured, and then—oh god, and then...

He didn't stop. He buried his mouth against my pussy and ate me to completion, devouring my clit, two thick fingers slicking in and out of me, driving me to the edge and past it, to the peak and over it. I screamed, a quiet breathless shriek that was all I could manage as I was racked by an orgasm so potent my knees gave out completely and even my grip on his shoulders couldn't keep me upright; Rem was there, though, holding me up, draping my thighs over his shoulders and powering upright with me sitting on his chest and shoulders, his tongue lapping at me. My spine slid up the cold wood of the door; I reached up and braced my hands against the low ceiling just over-head, shrieking and writhing as he drove his tongue against me side to side so fast and hard it shook my whole body, but maybe that was the climax shatter-ing me. Remington continued to devour me until the orgasm punched the last of my breath from my lungs and left me limp, and still his tongue circled and lapped and swiped and darted, making me curl in and clutch at his hair, knotting my fingers in the fine thick blond locks.

"Rem—Rem—god, fuck, oh god…"

"Such a dirty mouth for such a good girl," he muttered, his voice muffled against my pussy.

"I'm—I'm *still* coming."

He just laughed, walking with me across the room, carrying me easily and letting me fall backward onto his bed. I curled up in a ball, racked by waves of violent spasms. He hovered over me, grinning arrogantly down at me. "Are you done yet?"

I forced my eyes open, forced myself to uncurl and lay gazing up at him, trembling with aftershocks—I couldn't help laughing as I saw how wet and smeared his mouth was; I reached up and wiped his face clean, but then he caught at my wrists. He guided my right hand down to my sex, pressed his middle and index finger to mine and curled our joined fingers against my seam, dipping my fingers into myself, gathering my essence, and then, his eyes locked on mine, he slid my fingers into his mouth. Licked them clean.

My mouth fell open, and I groaned. My turn: I drove his same two fingers against me, and he played along, sliding and curling his thick digits inside me, then he pulled them out. His fingers were slick and sticky with my juices, and I brought them to my mouth.

I wrapped my lips around his fingers and licked between them, drawing them out. I slid my mouth down around them, bobbing on them—simulating the act of going down on him.

I tasted myself, and wished it was him.

And then, abruptly, he stood up. Backed away, an opaque expression on his face.

I frowned. "Rem? Where are you going?"

His grin was positively wicked. "Checking on your sweater."

"Screw the sweater," I said, sitting up to prop myself on my elbows. "Come here. I want you."

He shook his head slowly. He bent over and snagged his jeans, and stepped into them, his eyes on me. "Nope."

I blinked. "What? Why not?" I licked my lips, sensually, the gesture full of erotic promise. "I thought you wanted me to drop to my knees and suck your big hard cock?" God, was that *me* saying that, talking like that?

He growled, struggling to stuff his erection into his jeans. "More than you could possibly imagine."

"Then why are you stopping? Where are you going?"

He finally got himself crammed—painfully, it seemed, judging by the wincing—into his jeans, and then sauntered over to me. Bending over me, his eyes raked over my breasts and then my core, and then back to my eyes. "Because Juneau, sweetheart, when you drop to your knees and suck me off—or do anything else—I want it to be because you *want* to, not because I just gave you the best fucking orgasm of your life." He grinned at me, a cocky smirk. "And darlin'? Don't try to pretend it wasn't the best. I watched you come so hard you couldn't stand up."

I caressed his shoulder, his bicep. "I'm not pretending—it *was* the best orgasm I've ever had. I've never come that hard, ever." I ran my fingers down his side. "And I *do* want to—touch you."

He backed away. "I know you do." Bending to grab his shirt, he shrugged into it, sadly hiding all that delicious muscle. "There's another reason why I'm stopping us right here."

I frowned at him. "Do share."

He paused with his hand on the knob. "I'm proving a point."

My frown deepened. "And what point would that be?"

"That I can give without asking anything in return." His eyes devoured my body, splayed out for his gaze—my breasts hung heavy, my knees sagged apart, showing my sex, which was damp and slick, the close-trimmed patch of dark fuzz beaded with my essence and his saliva. "That I'm not just chasing you to fuck you once or twice and then ghost. I want more than that, Juneau, and this is me making sure that point is crystal fucking clear."

And then he was gone, the door closing softly behind him.

Shit.

This was not in any way, shape, or form how I saw this going.

Angry, stunned, confused, turned on, relieved, disappointed, horny as hell…I was all this and more, a tangled jumble of thorny, spiking emotions.

I dressed quickly, alternating between being horny, angry, and stunned. I shrugged into my tank top, snagged my thong and skirt…

And then made a quick decision, an impulsive decision.

I stepped into my skirt, zipped it, and then shoved my thong—which, after a sniff, I realized with some satisfaction, smelled of my ripe desire—into his underwear drawer. Before I closed the drawer, I took a moment to appreciate the sight of my dainty little thong bright pink against the dark grays, blacks, and blues of his underwear.

I closed the drawer and stepped away just as he entered with my sweater in his hand.

"There, all dry and warm." He gestured at the window. "It stopped raining for the moment, so I'll walk you home."

I stared up at him. "You don't have to prove anything, Rem."

He smiled at me. "Yeah, I do. To you *and* myself." He shrugged. "I ain't ever really been accused of being a selfless person. Gotta start somewhere, I guess, right?"

"I suppose. But I didn't come here expecting you to be selfless or chivalrous or anything."

"What did you come here expecting?" he asked, ushering me out of his room and then into the hallway outside the apartment, heading for the stairs.

I shrugged. "Honestly, I'm not sure." I blushed. "Sex, I suppose."

"Be honest—you expected me to take what I wanted—a quick, hard fuck, probably—and then for me to kick you out and never call you again."

I ducked my head and focused on trotting down the stairs next to him. "Honestly—yeah, something like that did occur to me."

We hit the sidewalk, and it was cold and damp but not raining, although the scent of petrichor in the air told me it would again, and soon.

Remington did something else totally unexpected then: he took my hand, our fingers twined together, and walked with me in companionable silence all the way back to my apartment.

When we reached the bottom step to my building, he stayed on the bottom step while I ascended to pause at the top, my key in the lock of the building door.

That's when he finally answered me. "If that's what you were expecting, Juneau, then that's why I'm doing this." He grinned at me, his signature cocky smirk. "To make sure you understand how much you've been underestimating me."

I let out a breath, yanking open the door and withdrawing my keys; I stood in the doorway, looking down at him. "Point taken, Rem."

His grin softened. "I like you calling me that." Then the cocky grin was back as he waved and turned away. "So, I'll see you soon?"

I put my fingers over my mouth, and smelled myself on my them—the scent aroused me, made me flush, and I dropped my hands and knotted them hurriedly behind my back.

"Yes, Rem," I murmured, just loud enough for him to hear me. "You will."

Then he was gone, and I watched as he disappeared down the street and out of sight.

Holy shit.

That did *not* go as expected.

ELEVEN

Remington

I SAT RECLINED IN THE BLACK LEATHER CHAIR, MY FEET propped up on the footrest. I was twisted watching Ink carefully drag the tattoo gun across the skin of the outside of my left bicep. The design was one I'd been toying with for some time, but until moving to Alaska all the pieces hadn't quite fallen into place. And now, finally, it was happening.

The tattoo Ink was doing depicted a pair of crossed fire axes with an oxygen mask and helmet in the space above the crossed ax'

heads—to the left was the outline of Oklahoma, my home state, to the right was the outline of California, where I'd lived the majority of my adult life, and beneath was the outline of Alaska, where I intended to spend the rest of my days.

Ink didn't say much while working, which suited me fine. He finished the outline and then sat back, shutting off the gun. "Break time."

I nodded, rolling my shoulder. "Sounds good." I glanced down at what he had done so far. "Dude, you are an amazing artist."

He stripped off the black rubber gloves as he headed across the parlor to the kitchen area. "Thanks." He opened a mini-fridge hidden under the counter and grabbed two bottles of local beer. "Now that I'm not in the middle of inking you, I gotta ask: what's up with you and my cousin?"

I accepted a beer from him and cracked it open. "Um…I'm not really sure, to be honest."

He was quiet for a moment. "Better be sure with that one, bro. She don't waste her time, and she don't play games." His eyes were fixed on mine, and I saw no humor or friendliness there. "And if you break her heart, I'll break your pretty face, and don't think all those abs of yours'll save your ass if I light into you."

I held up both hands. "Hey, man—I have no intention of breaking her heart, okay? I honestly don't know how things are going to play out—it's just that I'm into her. I really like her. That's all I know, okay?"

He nodded, and we finished our beers in silence,

and then he clapped his huge hands together. "Let's get back to it. Another hour or two and you're done."

It ended up being more like two and a half hours, but when he was done, it looked incredible, and I was giddy with excitement. He went through the usual aftercare spiel, wrapped it, and then stripped off his gloves, washed his hands, and went to write out the bill—which I knew would be steep, but for the quality of the art he'd put on me, I'd gladly pay it and a bit extra besides.

I was counting my cash when the bell over the door jangled; Ink and I both looked up at the same time.

Juneau stood just inside the door, eyeing me like a mouse would eye a hungry tomcat before making a break across the kitchen floor.

I laughed at her. "Don't worry, Juneau. I won't bite."

She rolled her eyes at me and huffed. "I just wasn't expecting to see you here."

It had been a little less than a week since I'd walked away from her apartment building—sporting the most painfully massive erection of my life. I still had blue balls from that whole situation, but I was confident I'd played it right.

"Avoiding me, are you?" I asked, carefully slipping my T-shirt on.

She came over and lifted the sleeve of my T-shirt and part of the dressing to examine my new tattoo with a critical eye. She glanced up at me. "This is cool." She looked at her cousin. "You did a great job, Ink."

Ink just grinned. "I always do a great job." He waved the invoice he'd finished writing out. "That's why I can charge this kinda price."

I took the invoice, glanced at it, and then clutched my heart, faking a pained gasp and staggering backward. "Good lord, that's a lot of money!" I straightened, handing him the stack of cash—which totaled the amount he'd charged me plus an extra fifty. "Kidding. Worth every penny, my friend."

Ink took the cash, counted it, and held up the stack to me in gesture. "Thanks, I appreciate it." He glanced at Juneau. "So. What brings you here, cuz?"

She lifted a shoulder. "I can't just want to come see you?"

He snorted. "It's only been a week since the last time. You never come to see me this frequently."

She sighed. "I told you I'd start coming more often, didn't I?" She was wearing a thigh-length raincoat to protect against the heavy rainfall we were getting; she unzipped it, throwing back the hood, and slipped out of it.

I did my best to stifle the growl of appreciative

arousal I felt boiling in my throat at the sight of her: she was wearing a pink skirt that hugged her ass like a glove before loosening to swirl around her ankles; her top was a gauzy, filmy white short-sleeve blouse thing with a plunging neckline that revealed her tattoos and clung to her breasts. The outfit was sexy but still classy, and the band of tattoos decorating her chest was on full display.

Ink's eyes widened. "You wore that to work?" He sounded legitimately flabbergasted.

Juneau nodded, then shrugged. "I guess I figured it was time to stop hiding so much of myself."

Ink frowned. "I've been telling you that for years, June-bug." He tucked the cash into the register and then glanced back at her. "What changed?"

Her eyes went to me, and then back to Ink. "I guess when Rem saw me, it prompted me to show my tattoos to Izzy, and then Kitty. And they both were kind of baffled as to why I'd ever hidden them in the first place."

Ink snorted. "Well, no shit. It's 2018—who hides tattoos anymore, unless your job requires it? And I know for a fact Daniel Ulujuk doesn't give a rat's ass."

He knew that because Daniel had a small tattoo on his left wrist, done by Ink.

"I just…" I shrugged. "I don't know."

Ink's eyes were fixed hard on his cousin.

"June-bug, we both know you never hid your tattoos because of work, or your friends—none of that. It's always been about your mom." He lifted an eyebrow at her. "She see 'em yet?"

Juneau shook her head, the end of her braid swaying. "No."

"She going to?"

Juneau shrugged, looking miserable. "Maybe someday?"

"Sooner than later is better." Ink waved a hand. "You know how I feel, no point getting into it again."

"I say you just show her. What do you have to lose?" I asked.

"Everything!" Juneau snapped, sinking into the chair I'd vacated. "Them! My family. Their respect, their love."

I wrinkled my brow in confusion. "Over tattoos?"

"Over what the tattoos *mean*, Remington. You wouldn't get it." She toyed with a jar of ink.

I growled. "We talked about this—you keep underestimating me."

She sighed. "Me having all these tattoos means I've never let go of art. They told me years ago to give it up—to focus on law, on my career, and then on finding a husband and having a family. Those should be my only priorities, according to my parents. My tattoos are a symbol of my rebellion against all that, even though they're not visible to anyone. I've toed the line and gone almost a hundred grand in debt chasing a degree and spending years of my life pursuing a career I never wanted."

"See, I *do* get that," I said. "You've met my brothers: Roman and Ramsey are *not* the kind of guys who appreciate art. They look at Van Gogh and see messy swirls of paint—I see a masterpiece. They have tattoos, sure, but more because they're cool to have, and serve as reminders of certain events. They don't really see them for the art—at least not the way I do. And I'm not sure they would understand me wanting to be a tattoo artist."

Juneau's eyes widened. "You want to be a tattoo artist?"

I nodded. "I have for years. It's always just been this thing I dicked around with as a hobby—I did a few on my buddy who did the piece on my shoulder, and a few for some of the other guys in the unit, but I never really considered it a viable way forward until recently." I hesitated. "I've wanted to get into tattooing for years, but I'm worried my brothers won't understand if I tell them I'm gonna quit working at the saloon—and sooner than they think—to work on my art. And maybe even have a place like this one day," I said, gesturing around. "They'd shit bricks."

Juneau made a face. "I get the impression you

three support each other no matter what."

"Yeah, of course. But that doesn't mean we always agree with or like each other's choices, though." I let out a sigh of exasperation. "See, I thought from the very start that this whole bar in Alaska thing was a bone-headed mistake, and that it was doomed to fail. I just didn't have any better ideas as to what the fuck the three of us were going to do after we quit smoke-jumping, so I went along with it."

"Yet here you are, close to opening your new bar."

I laughed. "Yeah, and truth be told, I actually hate it. And so does Ram. But we can't quit on Rome now—he needs us. Maybe when things are up and running Ram and I can start figuring what we want to do, and how to go about getting it."

Ink waved a hand. "Hey, I'm still here, you know."

Juneau glanced at him, and then dropped her eyes. "I know, sorry, Ink. I...um..."

Ink frowned, leaning back against the cash register, twirling a pen between two fingers. "Spit it out, cuz. What's on your mind?"

"I want to work here with you," she blurted, getting up from the chair. "Like, professionally."

Ink dropped the pen. "Say *what?*"

She grinned. "You heard me." Her grin faltered a little. "Quietly, on the side, to start with."

"Still scared of your mom, huh?"

She shrugged. "I'm not ready to tackle that yet. I just want to try this and see if I'm any good."

Ink bobbled his head side to side. "That's tricky, June-bug. There's requirements you gotta meet in order for me to let you do clients. I let you do tattoos on me because you're my cousin and we're doing it for fun—and because I trained you, so I know you know what you're doing. But for me to let you take on paying clients? You gotta go through an official apprenticeship program, and we gotta log the hours, and you gotta have a certified CPR and blood-borne pathogens card...there's some other shit, but that's the gist of it. I can't skirt those rules just cause you're my cuz, cuz."

She nodded. "I know. I'm not in a hurry to get licensed, I just...I want to do it."

He was quiet a long moment. "If you're sure you want to, I'll get some things together to start the application, and we'll get you in the apprenticeship program. I'll open up my hours here so you can start taking appointments." He eyed her steadily. "This is a big step, June-bug. Your mom is gonna find out, you gotta know that. Best you tell her yourself rather than her finding out from someone else that you're doing tattoos. Especially because she'll come after me, and I do *not* want to face a P-O'd Aunt Judy. Nuh-uh, cuz.

You better handle that shit so it don't blow back on me, yeah?"

She sighed. "I'll handle it."

Ink nodded. "Good." He glanced at her again. "You want a tat? Or did you just come here to tell me your news?"

She shrugged. "I came to tell you that. I've got a few ideas I'm working on for new pieces, but they still need some fine-tuning before they're ready." She paused. "Plus, the ideas I have are all for places I can't cover up, and I need time to work up the courage for that."

Ink grinned. "Well, you know I'll be ready when you are."

She walked over to him and wrapped him up in a hug, her arms barely reaching halfway around his enormous torso. She rested her head on his chest briefly. "Love you, Ink."

He kissed the top of her head. "Love you more, June-bug."

"Okay, I'm gonna go now," Juneau said.

Ink waved. "See ya. Come back in a couple days and I'll have some paperwork for you to fill out to start the official apprenticeship."

I felt my heart skip a beat as she glanced at me and then headed for the door. That glance—that look in her eyes…was it an invitation?

I jumped for the door. "Juneau—you want a ride somewhere?"

She let out a long breath, gazing at me steadily, her expression inscrutable, and then she nodded, smiling. "Yeah, sure."

Ink watched us both very carefully. "Remember what I said, bro."

I met his stare. "I got you."

"Good. Don't forget it."

I held the door for Juneau and then followed her out as she shrugged into her raincoat, tugging the hood up against the cold drizzle. I indicated my truck, which was parked across the street and down a ways, and she accompanied me over to it. I went with her to the passenger side and reached over to open the door for her; she glanced at me in surprise.

I just laughed. "What? Shocked that I can be a gentleman?"

She laughed. "Yeah, kinda."

I shrugged and nodded, still chuckling. "Ehhh… fair enough, I guess. But I can be, when I want to be."

She waited until I got in and started the engine before responding. "So it's a choice, then? When you're a rude, arrogant, selfish prick, you're just choosing to be that way?"

"Ouch," I said, clapping a hand over my heart. "Rude, arrogant, selfish prick? That stings, boo."

"Boo?" she echoed, cackling. "That's dumb, and also, I'm not your boo. Or your bae."

I shuddered. "Yuck—no way I'd ever say bae."

"Good. But boo is just as passé as bae, I think."

I pulled away from the curb and into the sparse traffic, heading back toward downtown Ketchikan. "So. Where to, June-bug?"

She glared at me. "Only one person has ever or *will* ever call me that, and hint—it's not you."

My brows rose. "Okay. Duly noted."

She huffed a laugh. "Diminutives, nicknames, and terms of endearment tend to irritate me. Ink only gets away with it because he's my cousin and we've been best friends since birth."

"Anyway—where to, babe?" I asked, grinning at her.

She rolled her eyes. "Annoying me won't win you any favors, Remington."

"I'm just messing with you."

"I know, and that's the only reason I'm still in the truck with you." She shrugged. "I don't know. I usually just go home after work, make some food, hang out with Kitty and Izzy, and then go to bed."

"Lame," I teased. "How about I take you to dinner?"

She didn't answer immediately; she just stared at me with a curious intensity, and then spoke slowly and carefully. "Take me to dinner?"

I nodded. "Yep. It's a thing people do when they like each other. We choose a restaurant, we have a nice meal together and talk, I pay...and then I take you home. At which point I either leave alone...or I don't."

She kept her expression neutral. "What if I don't like you?"

I just laughed. "You could pretend you don't, but you'd be lyin', sweetheart."

"So you're asking me out on a date?"

I nodded, acting as casual as I could, leaning my shoulder against the window, my left wrist draped over the steering wheel, fingers dangling, right hand resting on the console between us. "Yes, I am." I glanced at her. "You want me to do it more formally?"

She hid a smirk behind her hand. "Yes, Remington. I need you to formally ask me on a date."

"Fine. Juneau Isaac, would you do me the honor of going on a date with me?"

"Yes, Remington, I will, but on one condition."

I frowned. "Hmmmm. I don't like conditions, but I'll hear you out."

"You have to be on your best behavior. That means *choosing* to be a gentleman." She quirked an eyebrow at me. "Which means no crude innuendos."

"Jeez, take all the fun out it, why don't you," I

muttered out loud, then: "I accept your condition. I shall be a gentleman for the entire duration of our date, Miss Isaac."

"Very well. You may take me on a date, Mr. Badd."

We were both laughing, because the arch formality of the whole thing was just so comically stupid. "All right," I said. "Got anywhere you like best?"

She shrugged. "Not really. We can go wherever you want."

I held up a finger. "No—NO. We are *not* doing that. I got stuck in an 'I don't know, where do you want to go' time loop with a chick once, and I almost went bonkers." I laughed. "So. I'm going to name three places I know of that I like, and you can either pick one, or tell me to pick."

I named three restaurants in the area, and Juneau listened with a smirk.

"Gee," she said in a breezy, faint voice. "I don't know. I just can't decide."

I growled. "God, women are so difficult."

She burst out laughing. "I'm trolling you, Remington. A burger and a beer sounds good to me," she said, referring to the third of the places I'd named, which was actually a pretty direct competitor to both Badd's Bar and Grille, and the soon-to-be-opened Badd Kitty Saloon, but they had great burgers and a killer IPA selection, so…

We chatted about our workdays as I drove to the pub, found a parking spot nearby, and headed to the pub. We got a booth after a few minutes of waiting and, once seated, we perused the menu, decided, and set them aside. Within seconds, a waitress appeared, took our order, and sashayed off—not without a noticeable huff at the fact that I'd blatantly ignored her attempts to flirt with me.

"So," I said, when we both had our pints. "Here we are. On a date."

Juneau sighed. "You know, honestly, I kind of can't believe I'm here—that I agreed to this with you."

I frowned. "Really? Why not?"

"Because this is blurring the lines."

I nodded, taking a sip. "Ahhh, blurring the lines. A mortal sin, to be sure."

She snorted at me. "No, but I just…I *do* like you—a tiny bit, at least—but I don't have space in my life to complicate things…especially now that I'm taking steps toward tattooing."

Our food arrived, and we spent a few minutes digging in, and then, after a few bites, I washed it down with a long swig, covered a burp, and eyed her. "It doesn't have to be complicated, Juneau."

She rolled her eyes. "I'm not interested in a just-sex thing with you, Remington." she said. "I've read those books too."

"I have no idea which books you're talking about, number one, and number two, I'm not suggesting a just-sex agreement."

"Good, because that's not happening."

"Good, because I don't want that any more than you do."

She stared at me, chewing slowly. "Then…what do you want?"

I blew out a sharp breath, and then lifted a shoulder. "I honestly don't know. I just know it doesn't have to be complicated."

"It doesn't?"

I tapped the table between us. "Is this complicated? What we're doing right now?"

She shrugged, a tiny, unsure gesture. "No, I guess not."

"Was what happened the last time we were together complicated?" I asked.

She stopped chewing and carefully set down her burger, wiping her lips with a napkin. "I thought we agreed to no crude innuendos?"

"We did. That wasn't an innuendo, crude or otherwise. It's just an honest question." I let silence hang for a moment. "So? Was it complicated?"

She stared at the table, tracing lines in the sweat on her pint glass. "Yeah, actually. Kind of."

I frowned. "How do you figure that?"

"What happened—the way it happened…it's not how it usually works."

"No?"

She shook her head, and then took a sip of her beer. "No. There's usually a…a back and forth. You know…one thing leads to another." She shrugged one shoulder, not looking at me. "In that instance, the one thing led to you stopping us and taking me home. It was confusing."

"I thought you'd appreciate not being pushed into anything," I said.

She let out a breath—somewhere between a huff and a sigh. "I—I didn't feel pushed into anything. I showed up knowing something would happen. And, if I'm being honest with…well, both of us, I *wanted* something to happen."

"Wow—some honesty about what you want, finally," I said, finishing my burger and wiping my lips and fingers with a wad of paper napkins.

"Hey, don't be a dick," she snapped.

I reared back in the booth. "Whoa, okay. I wasn't—it's just the honest truth, Juneau. You haven't been exactly truthful or forthcoming about how you feel about me, and whatever the hell this thing we're doing is."

"Because I'm conflicted about how I feel."

"Clearly. And my decision to stop things last time was, at least in part, a way of…slowing things down for you, I guess. Giving you something to process in a…bite-sized chunk, you might say."

She eyed me warily. "Make any jokes, Remington, and I swear I'll smack you."

I lifted both hands in surrender, laughing. "Never even crossed my mind."

She sipped her beer, toying with her braid with her other hand. "So stopping things and making me leave wasn't you playing mind games with me?"

I lifted an eyebrow. "What kind of mind game would it be?"

She shrugged. "I don't know. Teasing me. Making me…" She dropped her voice to a whisper. "Making me want…certain things…even more, because we got so close and then stopped."

I groaned, rubbing my face with both hands. "I promised no crude innuendos, but I didn't expect it to be this hard." I cackled abruptly. "And no, that wasn't one either."

She covered her mouth, coughing through clamped lips as she tried not to spit out her mouthful of beer. After she'd swallowed, she glared at me. "Except you made it one by saying it wasn't." She wiped at her mouth and then her fingers. "So. Was it a mind game?"

I eyed her. "I don't know—depends on if it's working or not."

Juneau huffed an annoyed laugh. "Wouldn't you like to know."

I leaned forward, the humor gone from my face. "Yes, Juneau, I'd very much like to know."

She knotted her fingers together on the table, her eyes dropping from mine to my lips, and then away. "A little. Maybe." As if realizing that her knotted, fretting fingers were giving away her nerves, she flattened her hands on the table to stop them from fidgeting.

"A little, huh?" I traced a fingertip from her thumbnail to the web of her hand, and then down and back up each finger in turn. "So you're just think-ing *a little bit* about…what you want. And how you didn't get it." I grinned at her, keeping my voice near-ly inaudible. "Thinking…*long*…and *hard*?

She frowned at me. "Hey, you agreed to no crude innuendos."

I shrugged. "Sorry, I must have forgotten."

"You're a shitty liar, Remington."

"What happened to calling me Rem?" I asked.

She just blinked at me. "That's awfully familiar."

I smirked at her. "I can still taste you, Juneau. That seems awfully *familiar* to me."

I was beginning to be able to tell when she was blushing, not from the tinge of her skin, but by her body language—she shifted uncomfortably, ducked her head, avoided my gaze.

"Rem—don't, please," she whispered.

"Don't what, Juneau?"

"Embarrass me."

"How am I embarrassing you?" I asked.

"Talking about…that."

I leaned even closer, trailing a fingertip over the back of her hand. "Talking about what? How I can still smell you on my fingers, and taste you on my lips? How I can still hear the way you moaned as you came all over my mouth?" My whisper was so low I could barely hear myself in the din of the crowded pub. "How I can still feel you writhing against me? How I can still feel you tightening around my fingers and squirting around my tongue?"

"Stop!" she hissed. "And I did *not*…squirt."

I laughed. "No, but I could make you." I eyed her. "Have you ever come so hard you squirted, Juneau?"

She shook her head. "No. There's nothing special about it, though—it's just pee, I think."

"I've heard varying reports about that, actually," I said. "And by all accounts, it's wicked intense."

She narrowed her eyes at me. "And you can just make that happen, huh?"

I sensed a trap in her words. "I told you I was gonna give you the most intense orgasm of your life, and I delivered, didn't I?"

Juneau toyed with her braid and looked away. "You're pretty cocky, you know that, Rem?"

I noticed she was using the short, familiar version of my name—I didn't call attention to it, though.

"It's not arrogant if I'm just stating a fact. I know myself and my abilities, and I'm confident in them, yes." I let a wicked grin curl my lips. "But yeah, Juneau—I am pretty...*cocky*."

She bit her lip, and then huffed in irritation. "I knew you couldn't keep your promise to be a gentleman."

"What can I say? You bring things out of me, too."

"Not yet I haven't, but I'd like to." She said this, and then abruptly clapped her hand over her mouth. "I can't believe I just said that."

I laughed loudly, unable to help myself. "Ho-ly shit—good one, Juneau!"

"If you make fun of me for that, I'm leaving."

I leaned close again. "I'd never make fun of you, babe." I shifted on the bench. "To be honest, it turned me on more than it should've."

"It was a stupid joke, and a crude one at that."

I slid one finger between two of hers, tracing between the knuckles and then over the back of her hand, and then up her forearm. "True, but it's hot.

And in my book, at least, there's absolutely nothing wrong with a little sexual banter between two people who have seen each other naked."

"Only one of us has seen the other naked," she pointed out.

I grinned, her tilted lips and hooded eyes more of a heated, explicit innuendo than anything I could say. "We could leave right now and rectify that, if you want."

She bit her lip. "We could."

I wanted to exult in victory and excitement, but I'd worked hard to remain nonchalant. "Sounds like there's a *but* in there somewhere."

"But Izzy and Kitty are probably both home. And I'm assuming your brothers are too."

"Do you have a door that closes?"

She frowned. "Yeah, but—"

"Then we can figure it out. You'll just have to be quiet."

"*I* will have to?" she said. "If we're still playing tit for tat, then it's *my* turn. Which means *you* will have to be quiet."

"You put your hands on me, I can't make any promises I'll be able to keep mine to myself," I said. "And if I get my hands on you again, what happened the last time we were alone together will seem like high tea with the goddamned queen compared to what I'll do to you."

"You can't talk to me like that, Rem," she whispered, her voice hoarse and raspy.

"No? Why not?" I leaned closer yet, so I was a few inches from her face, our eyes locked. "Does it make you uncomfortable?"

She nodded.

"Does it make you want…certain things? Does it make you squirm?" I was barely even whispering now, so she had to lean close enough that my lips were touching the shell of her ear. "Does it make that sweet, tight, hot little pussy of yours all wet?"

"Rem…" She was breathing hard, her chest heaving, which was…distracting.

"Yeah, babe?"

She bit her lip, glancing down for a moment, and then her eyes met mine. Her fingers were knotted together again, twisting and fidgeting. "Get the check."

I grinned, unable to restrain my eagerness. "Good idea."

I got the check, tossed enough cash to cover the bill and a fairly generous tip, and then we headed out for my truck. Once again, I helped her in; this time, though, I planted a foot on the rusted metal step, leaned in, grabbed the buckle, and slid it across her body to buckle her in.

"I could have done that myself," she muttered, as

I adjusted the strap to sit nice and flush between her boobs. "You're not subtle, you know."

I laughed as I hopped down and circled around to climb in behind the wheel. "It's more fun to do it for you," I said. "And I wasn't trying to be subtle. Not really in my repertoire, as you may have noticed."

"Yeah, I noticed," she said, her voice dry.

I pulled away from the curb and then stopped, idling partway out into the road. "My place or yours?"

"Mine," she whispered. "If someone is going to know what we're doing, I'd rather it be Kitty and Izzy than your brothers."

I chuckled. "Yeah, probably smart. They'd be all over that shit like white on rice, and then neither of us would hear the end of it."

We drove in silence toward her apartment, both of our hands resting on the console between us. Her eyes locked on mine, I tangled our fingers together, palm to palm, fingers threaded. Intimate, more than just familiar. Juneau's eyes widened, and her fingers tightened, squeezing hard as if to alleviate her nerves.

"You never cease to surprise me, Remington," she murmured.

I grinned, a cocky smirk. "Sweetheart, I have so many more surprises in store for you...you don't even know."

"What kind of surprises?" she asked, her voice

suggestive and her eyes sultry.

"You'll see," was all I could manage, sounding raspy and guttural.

Juneau's laugh was amused and knowing—she'd seen exactly how affected I was. "Having problems, Rem?"

I growled, not liking the way the tables were suddenly flipped. "Nope."

She let go of my hand, only to wrap her thumb and index finger around my middle finger, sliding her hand up and down in a blatantly suggestive movement. "No? No...issues...you may need help with?"

I shifted, trying to alleviate the aching pressure of my cock, which was folded painfully into my jeans. "Nope. No issues."

"Now who's lying, Rem?" she whispered. Her lips brushed my ear, her whisper tickling. "You're so hard it hurts, doesn't it?"

"Quit that, goddammit."

She huffed a laugh. "Why? Does it *bother* you?"

The only way to reclaim the advantage was to play her game, but better. So, I met her eyes. "Yeah, sweetheart, I'm so hard right now it fucking hurts like a bitch. I'm so hard I could come just from the way you look at me. So anytime you want to reach down there and help me out, feel free."

She gnawed on her lip, her gaze going from my

eyes to my zipper—almost as if she was contemplating taking me up on my word.

I gave her a look of warning. "Don't start something you won't finish, Juneau."

She only narrowed her eyes at me. "And you say *I* underestimate *you*."

I lifted an eyebrow. "You want me to believe you'd help me with my little…issue…right here, right now, in the truck?" I indicated the road ahead. "Especially when we're less than five minutes from your place?"

"You don't think I would, if I really wanted to?" she said, challenging me.

"No, not really."

She lifted her chin and her eyes blazed. "Both hands on the wheel, eyes on the road."

"Juneau—" I started, but the look in her eyes stopped me, and I just smirked as I grabbed the steering wheel in both hands, doing my best to look cockily skeptical. "You know what? I'm all yours, darlin'."

She reached across the console, and the way she gnawed on her lower lip gave her away—she was nervous. I wasn't sure what she thought she had to prove, but the way her anger provoked her was hot as fuck.

Pulling up to a stoplight, I said, "You know, Juneau, you don't have to prove anything to me."

Which only served to feed her ire. "I'm not trying to."

I glanced pointedly at her hand, which was resting on my thigh, exploring the muscle there. "No?"

"If I'm proving anything, it's that you really don't know me, or what I'm capable of, or what I will or won't do—if I *want* to."

I gripped the wheel hard, twisting the leather. "In that case, carry on."

She rolled her eyes at me. "I'm glad I have your permission, *sir*," she murmured, tracing the outline of my erection against the folds in my jeans.

I eyed her, resisting the urge to flex into her touch—which would have been a blatant plea for her to touch me more, and I was determined to stay cool no matter what.

"Everything okay down there?" Juneau asked, knowing full well I was beginning to have trouble keeping my cool.

"What, that li'l ol' thing?" I drawled, nodding to the front of my jeans.

Juneau's teeth sank into her lower lip, a habit I found unbearably sexy. "Not so little anymore, Rem."

I huffed a laugh. "Matter of opinion I suppose."

She frowned at me in confusion. "Aren't you the one who told me my sketch hadn't done your godlike endowment proper justice?"

"Don't you think my cock is godlike?"

"Well...I don't know yet. I haven't been properly

introduced to it."

I lifted an eyebrow at her. "I thought that you could make the necessary introductions right here, right now."

"What would you think if I did?" she asked, her eyes seizing on mine. "About me?"

I just stared at her. "What would I think about you?" I laughed. "What a bizarre question."

"No, it's not," she argued.

"Yeah, it is." The turn that would take us to her apartment was coming up, but I passed it by, and she didn't seem to notice. "What do you expect me to say? Like, what, I'd call you a dirty slut or something?"

She shrugged. "I mean...kind of, I guess?"

I cackled. "Juneau, babe. For one, do I *really* seem like that kind of a guy?" I glanced down at her hand, which was now resting on my thigh, covering my erection. "If you were to...uhhh...explore...a little bit, I'd be too busy enjoying it to think about what it said about your character. And considering I've already eaten you out, I'm not really in any kind of place to be judging you for getting a little handsy."

She ducked her head. "Yeah, I guess that's true." She looked around us, then. "Hey—you missed the turn."

I grinned. "I guess I did. I'll swing around the block."

She eyed me suspiciously. "You missed it on purpose."

I rolled a shoulder. "Maybe, maybe not."

"Don't you want to get somewhere more private where I'm likely to be less inhibited?" she asked.

"Yeah. But I'm also just curious whether or not you're all talk right now."

She stared steadily at me, her expression hardening into resolve. "I'm not all talk."

I just held a steady grin. "Okay. I believe you."

Her gaze turned fierce. "No, you don't."

"Fuck, man—I can't win! I admit I'm curious as to what you'll do, but if you're gonna turn it into something weird, then forget it. I'm not a manipulator, Juneau." I held her gaze. "If I was going to try to get you to put your hand in my pants, I'd be upfront about it."

"Yeah?" She made it sound like a dare.

"Yeah, actually." I grabbed her hand, placing her palm over my erection. "I'd be very, *very* clear about what I wanted." I thrust suggestively into her hand. "There would be absolutely *zero* doubt."

Juneau let out a tight breath. "Oh," she breathed.

"Yeah, oh."

We were making a turn that would lead us down the last couple miles back to where her building was. I put both hands back on the steering wheel, pretending to not care at all about the outcome of this odd little exchange.

I watched Juneau, though.

She was chewing on her lower lip so hard I was worried she'd hurt herself, and she was breathing hard—which was distracting, to say the least, what with the way her breasts lifted and fell, swelling against the confines of her shirt.

She noticed my gaze, and her grin turned amused and seductive at once. "See something you like, Remington?"

I growled. "Fuck yes, I do."

She glanced around quickly, seeing that we were alone on the road for the moment and then, unexpectedly, she twisted to face me, hooked her fingers into her top, and tugged it down to flash her breasts at me. "What, these li'l ol' things?"

The sight of her bared for me sent all the blood in my body flooding south, and I went fully rigid, swelling in my jeans so hard a groan of pain escaped me. "Shit, Juneau. You don't play fair."

She laughed, and I realized I'd played right into her trap. Not that I wanted to fight this at all, but still. The point remained, I had played right into her hands.

Acting with abrupt confidence, she reached across the console with both hands and unfastened the fly of my jeans, and then tugged down the zipper.

Immediately, my erection sprang into the opening, swelling hard against the confines of my underwear, curling awkwardly down and away from my body in a painful, unnatural angle. Hesitating only a split second, Juneau glanced at me, at my groin—and then she delved her hand under the elastic of my underwear and palmed my cock.

I nearly drove off the road.

"Ohhh...*shit*," Juneau whispered. "You're *huge*."

TWELVE

Juneau

HOLY MOTHER OF ALL COCKS—YOU HEAR ABOUT OR read about guys being "hung like horses" or whatever, but feeling the reality in your hand? A whole different ball game.

I slid my hand under the elastic of his underwear and cupped my hand over his cock—and the words that came out of my mouth emerged unbidden. "Ohhh...*shit*. You're *huge*."

His grin was lazy, arrogant, and simmering with lust. "Told ya."

"Guys who brag about the size of their dick are almost always lying out of insecurity," I said.

He shifted, flexing his hips as if trying to alleviate

discomfort. He was stuck, I realized—his cock trapped down against his thigh inside his jeans. "Yeah, well, I wasn't bragging when I said that, just…informing you that your drawing wasn't accurate."

His cock was so warm, so velvety smooth, and I just wanted to get it out in the open, bare, and look at it, caress it, stroke it, discover it, explore it. I wrapped my hand around him, and my shock over the sheer size of him only magnified—he was so *thick*, my hand could barely make it all the way around, my thumb and forefinger only just meeting.

"Seems like you're trapped in here," I said, sliding my fingers from the base toward the tip, following his thigh.

"Yeah," he growled.

"Is it uncomfortable?" I asked, lifting my eyes to his.

He narrowed his eyes, and all but snarled at me. "Fucking hurts like a bitch."

"So…you need some help."

"Now who's playing games, Juneau?" he rumbled. "Yes, I need some help."

I lifted the waistband of his underwear away from his belly and guided his erection to slide upward into place against his body, the fat, gleaming, bulbous head bobbing near his navel; a droplet of precum beaded on the tip.

He sighed in relief. "Thank fuck."

I had him in my fist, the elastic waistband pinning my hand inside his underwear. "Looks like you're… leaking a bit." I grinned at him, licking my lips at the beautiful sight of the upper couple of inches poking out over the top of his black underwear.

"Yeah, well, I'm hard as a fucking rock and you've got your hand on me. I'm about to do a fuck of a lot more than just leak a little bit, babe."

I bit my lip at the thought of him exploding, right here, right now. "That'd be messy," I said. "You should wait until we're somewhere more private for that."

He just smirked. "Then you better get your hot little hand off my cock and put away those tits." He indicated ahead of us with a jut of his chin. "We're here."

We were pulling up to my building, I realized. I hurriedly released him, tucked him back into his underwear, and zipped him up—but I wasn't certain the fly would button closed again, not with the gargantuan presence of his cock in the way.

"Leave it," he muttered.

I tucked myself back into my shirt as he pulled up to the curb outside my building and into a parking spot. "You're going to go in there with your fly open?"

He shrugged. "My shirt'll cover it, I hope." He quirked an eyebrow at me. "That thing ain't going back in all the way, Juneau. Not after the attention you paid it. He's sitting up begging for more."

I huffed a laugh. "Well, let's hope your shirt covers it, then."

He shut off the engine and we both got out; I rounded the hood to the sidewalk and found Remington standing facing his truck, tugging the front of his T-shirt down in a comically vain effort to cover the obvious erection. No way were his jeans buttoning again, and no way was his tight, fitted black T-shirt hiding anything.

I bit my lip in an attempt not to laugh. "Might have to wait until it subsides before we go in," I said.

"Fuck that," he growled. "That'll take way too long. I keep thinking about getting you alone and naked and I get hard all over again."

"Stop thinking about it, then?" I giggled again as he winced, trying to get his jeans to button. "That's not working, Rem. It won't fit." I could tell my laughing wasn't helping his current attitude any, which was irritated and aroused and impatient. "What do you do when you're trying to…errr…hold back or whatever? Do you, like, think about nuns or something?"

He grumbled wordlessly for a moment. "Nah, that shit doesn't work. Just makes me lose it completely. Only way to hold back is to use the muscle to hold it, and even that only works for so long." He stared at me, his gaze white-hot with lust and need and promise. "I don't hold back. I just make sure my partner gets hers before I get mine."

"Oh," I said. "I see."

"Like I said earlier—once I get my hands on you, Juneau…you have *no* idea how hard or how many times I'm gonna make you come."

"With the way you made me feel last time, I'm starting to believe you."

He sucked in his belly and tried yet again to button his jeans, to no avail. "This conversation is *not* helping my situation."

I glanced into his truck. "Do you have a hoodie or something? You could tie it around your waist and pretend you got hot and took it off?"

He nodded. "Hmmm. That may work. I do have an old hoodie in here." Rem jerked open the back passenger seat, leaned in and snagged a faded, well-worn gray hoodie off the floor and then closed the door again, wrapping the sweatshirt low around his waist and tying the sleeves in a knot directly over his erection. "Well…it sort of works."

I covered my mouth with a hand, stifling a laugh. "I mean, sort of." I took his hand and led him to the door of my building. "Enough to get us inside."

"Maybe we'll get lucky and your roommates won't be there," Remington said, following me up the stairs to our unit.

We approached my door, and I heard voices—Izzy and Kitty bickering about something. I laughed again. "No such luck, it seems. You should just stand behind me as much as possible, I guess. Izzy will take one look at you and know what's up, and then she'll make all sorts of filthy jokes and it'll be awkward."

"Sounds like Ram," Remington muttered.

I opened the door and led the way in. Izzy and Kitty were on the couch, watching Netflix and arguing about which of their favorite characters was better. Remington stayed behind me as we moved into the living room, and as we paused to talk to Kitty and Izzy, he sidled up behind me, pressing against me and rested his hands with possessive, familiar intimacy on my hips. I stifled the urge to toss his hands off me—and the equally powerful urge to push back into him, to writhe against the thick ridge of his erection I could feel nudging against my buttocks.

Izzy and Kitty went silent, and Izzy lifted the remote and paused their show.

"Well. Um..." Kitty blinked at us, a puzzled frown on her face. "Hi?"

"Ladies." Remington waved a hand, immediately replacing it on my hip, smoothing his palm down to my thigh and back up, even circling back to caress the outside of my right ass cheek. "How's it going? Nice to see you both again, Kitty, Izzy."

Izzy just stared. "Remington. Fancy seeing you here…" She eyed the way he was posed behind me, her eyes going to his hands, which were brazenly roaming my hips. "With Juneau."

There was a slight emphasis on the word "with", making it a question, to me, of how *with* we were.

There would be no way of hiding what we came here to do, I realized. So I may as well just own up to it, bold and open—for once in my life.

Kitty glanced at my outfit—the skirt, the blouse showing off my tattoos. "Juneau, you look…amazing." She eyed Remington behind me, his hands, the way we were standing together. "I have to admit I'm a little…surprised."

"At what?" I asked.

Kitty shrugged, gesturing at me. "Everything. Showing off your tattoos, and now this thing with Remington…it's just a different side of you, I guess."

"I've been hiding parts of myself for too long," I said. "Maybe I'm just getting tired of it."

She held up both hands palms out. "Hey, look— I'm all for it. God knows I've changed a good bit myself lately." She smiled. "I like this new you."

Izzy seemed less certain. "Is the new you about to tell Kitty and me that you and Remington are going into your bedroom?"

Remington went still behind me, his hands tightening on my hips. It was a subtle thing, but I felt it. He was very interested in how I would play this, I realized.

I bit my lip, brows furrowing, a grin curling my lips, and then I nodded. "Yeah. That's exactly where we are going."

Remington chuckled quietly behind me. "Atta girl. Own it."

I twisted to frown up at him. "Hush, you. This is girl talk."

He rumbled another laugh. "Yes ma'am."

Izzy's eyebrow curled up. "Do we need to, like, give you two privacy? Or just turn up the volume?"

I shrugged. "You don't have to leave if you don't want to. I just don't want to make this weird between the three of us."

Kitty laughed. "Too late, babe. But then, I've brought Roman over and made it very clear we were just here to have sex. And god knows Izzy has brought over *plenty* of boy-toys, and not been in the least tactful about it."

"Tact is for people who give a shit," Izzy said, her voice arch and haughty. "And I give zero shits."

"The point *is*," Kitty said, rolling her eyes at Izzy, "neither of us have any cause to be making it weird for them."

"You know what'll make it weird?" Remington said. "Continuing to talk about it." He tangled his fingers into mine, the backs of my hands nestled against his palms, and rested his chin on my head; it was an oddly and almost uncomfortably intimate pose. It made my heart thump in a strange way. "So let's just wrap it up by saying Juneau and I are going to go into her room and hang out now, and let's all just be adults about this."

"Something'll be hanging out, all right," Izzy said, cackling to herself.

"IZZY!" Kitty snapped. "Inappropriate!"

Remington laughed, though. "Woman, you are so right." His chest vibrated with another laugh. "You and Ramsey would like each other, I think."

Izzy's expression went opaque and unreadable. "We've...met."

Remington laughed. "And I think I'll leave that one well enough alone." He patted my hips with both hands. "So. Which room is yours, Juneau?"

I stepped away from him, pulling him by the hand into the short hallway and toward my room. All three of us kept our doors closed pretty much all the time, mainly since none of us were the neatest people in the world and it was easier to close the door on our messy rooms than to pick them up.

I opened my door, let Remington go in before

me, and then closed the door behind me, twisting the lock and then pressing my back to the door. Remington was standing just inside, taking in my room—there was a laundry basket with dirty laundry spilling out of it, a chair in one corner with my clean clothes piled on it, my dresser opposite the foot of my queen-size bed, a few drawers cracked open. My closet was open as well, dresses, skirts, sweaters, and blouses stuffed into it to overflowing so the bifold doors wouldn't close. There were at least four bras hanging by their straps from the knobs of each bifold door, and my shoe collection spilled out of the bottom of the closet—snow boots, mukluks, dress boots, flats, slides, sandals, heels, wedges, clogs, knee-high boots…my shoe collection was even more extensive than my clothing.

"I wasn't expecting to bring you here," I said by way apology for the mess. "I would have cleaned up if I had."

Remington just waved a hand dismissively. "Nah—I like it like this. I like seeing how you are when you're not expecting company. It's the real you." He crossed the room to the dresser and examined my other collection—figurines I'd made over the years while sitting under the folding awning with my mother. "What are all these?" he asked, picking up a little carving of a hare sitting up on its hind legs, head turned to the side, ears tall—a little pink stone made the nose, bright chunks of turquoise for the eyes, polished ovals of agate inset in the ears.

"That's what my mother does for a living—she makes and sells stuff like that. Not just animal carvings, though, but necklaces and other kinds of jewelry, ornamental knives and letter openers, door stops and paperweights, all sorts of stuff, all handmade."

He set the hare down and picked up a little fox—carved from deep red Spanish Cedar, with turquoise for the eyes, its jaws open and real pieces of fox teeth sanded down to size and inset. "So your mom made all these?"

I fidgeted with the collection—a hundred or so little animals, most small enough to sit in my palm. "Actually, all these ones I made. I grew up helping her make and sell her art. She's a better woodcarver than I am, but I've always had a better knack for polishing and setting the stones and painting them."

He shot a surprised glance at me. "You made these?"

I nodded, smiling shyly. "Yeah."

He put his back to the dresser, staring down at me. "You're a wicked talented artist, as in sketching and tattooing, *and* you do this?" He frowned down at me. "And you're playing the legal game?" Remington shook his head. "That's a goddamn crime."

"What do you mean?"

He threw up a hand. "Art is meant to be shared with the world, Juneau. If you have talent as an artist, I've always felt you have almost an obligation to share it with the world—there's so much ugliness and violence out there, if you can do something to make it more beautiful, you should."

I stared up at him. "I suppose at this point I shouldn't be surprised to hear a sentiment like that coming from you, but I am." I rested a hand on his chest. "More of me underestimating you, huh?"

"I grew up around a lot of that ugliness, Juneau. My dad was a drunk, and we lived in a shithole. We were surrounded by violent, drunk, drug-addicted fuckheads. I didn't go to college, and I barely graduated high school. We only avoided becoming the kind of people we grew up with by leaving as soon as we could and never going back." He shrugged nonchalantly, but I could tell this was a deep, difficult subject for him. "As a kid, I always wanted to spend more time in the library. I wanted to look at art books. It was the only time I ever felt...at peace, looking at those photographs of famous paintings from around the world. But my brothers were always more interested in getting into trouble, as you can imagine, and I always got dragged into shit with 'em." He laughed ruefully. "Honestly, I was always willingly in the thick of things. But I did find art peaceful. I would sketch just to get my mind off of our shitty, leaky trailer, and Dad being passed out on the floor. Art was my escape. So yeah, I can see how you'd be surprised to hear a roughneck kinda guy like me talking about the obligation to share art, and making the world a better place, but there it is."

I ran my hands over his shoulders, down his arms, slipping my fingers under the tight sleeves to trace around his tricep. "You really are a man of endless surprises, Rem."

"It's just because I'm so damn good-looking," he said, dryly. "People look at me and just see another big, pretty piece of man meat and assume there's no brains or depth in here." He tapped his temple.

"I admit I'm guilty of making that assumption," I said, and untied the sweatshirt so I could dip my hands under his T-shirt and slide my palms over his ridged, rock-hard abs. "But there are brains and depth in there. And a surprisingly sensitive heart in here," I added, palming his chest over his heart.

His skin was warm under my hands, and smooth; his muscles bulged, and as I ran my hands over his pecs and up over his shoulders—pushing up his shirt, but being careful to avoid his new tattoo—he tensed his muscles, involuntarily. Abandoning pretense, I shoved his shirt up and off, baring that magnificently sculpted body of his. I couldn't help but let my hands play over his torso, exploring the curves and lines of muscle, flicking my thumbs over his flat nipples, carving my fingers through the valleys of his abs, traipsing down his wedge waist to the denim loose around his hips, his jeans zipped but not buttoned. He was still hard—not all the way, the intervening conversation having allowed it lessen a bit, but as I let my hands wander closer, I watched him thicken and lengthen inside the constraint of the tight, stretchy black underwear.

"It'll be kinda hard to get those jeans off if you're still wearing boots, you know." I let my eyes and the curve of my lips fill in the rest for him.

He put a hand on the dresser to steady himself, lifting his foot to untie the boot, loosen the laces, and then tug it off, tossing it aside, and then repeating it on the other foot. He toed off his socks, and then he was, deliciously, clad in nothing but a pair of blue jeans. His abs rippled with each breath, a vein in his throat pulsing, his jaw flexing and releasing as he stared down at me, waiting.

Now that I'd gotten to feel him, to wrap my hand around him, I was eager for more—I wanted to see him, totally bare. I wanted to get both hands around him. I wanted to make him groan.

I wanted to see if I could bring this mighty man to his knees with just my touch.

"See something you like, Juneau?" he murmured, grinning.

I smiled back, mischievous and eager and full of lust. "Not yet, I don't." I rubbed a hand over his hard stomach. "I mean, this is pretty nice, don't get me wrong, but there's something else I want to see a little more of."

"Just a little more?"

I shrugged. "Yeah, just a little."

He stepped on the cuff of his jeans and yanked his leg free, and then kicked them off, standing now in just a pair of skin-tight black boxer briefs that left very little to the imagination. His erection was a thick bulge behind the black fabric, straining against it; he pinched the material over his cock between thumb and forefinger and tugged it down...just enough that the broad round head popped out to peek over the gray elastic of the waistband.

"How's that?" he teased, that maddeningly arrogant—and maddeningly sexy—smirk tilting his lips. "That enough?"

I slipped my hands over his shoulders, palmed his shoulder blades, resisting the urge to just rip the stupid underwear off—I wanted to play this game with him; I was enjoying the push-and-pull, the tease, the game, the waiting despite wanting.

I pretended to be unaffected, although I couldn't

take my eyes off what I wanted to have all to myself. "Pretty nice," I said, running a fingertip down the center of his chest to his navel, stopping there. "I wouldn't mind just a *tiny* bit more, though."

He rumbled, a huffing laugh. "Cool as a cucumber, aren't you?"

I knew my tendency to chew on my lip gave me away, so I fought the urge to do so. Instead, I attempted to satisfy my lust for Remington by wrapping both hands around his enormous bicep, and then the other, and then scraping my palms down his abs yet again—those arms and those abs were worthy of a magazine, of a feature film, of his own woman-oriented pornography channel, if such a thing were to exist. Maybe it did—I wouldn't know because I wasn't really into porn, but seeing Rem like this made me think maybe I should start.

He laughed, probably because he saw through me. He hooked his thumbs into the elastic on either side of his cock and slowly, sensually pushed downward, gradually exposing a couple more inches. I couldn't help the slight intake of breath as the true scope of him was revealed. Feeling it in my hand was one thing—*seeing* it was another.

His underwear was around his butt, now, and if I had to guess, I'd say he was roughly halfway bared. And that half was already more than I'd ever experienced.

Ohhhh god. Oh god. I *wanted* him.

My lip stung, aching where my teeth had involuntarily sunk in and bit down hard.

The rough pad of Remington's thumb gently tugged my lip free of my teeth. "Quit that—you'll hurt yourself."

"It's an unconscious habit."

He ran his thumb over my lip, and I slid my tongue against the salty flesh. "I could kiss it all better."

"I wouldn't mind that," I said, breathless.

He leaned in, closed both lips over mine where I'd bitten myself, and I felt the soft wet touch of his tongue and then his lips were covering mine and I was dizzy and throbbing everywhere. His kiss was a wilding onslaught against my senses and my restraint. He kissed me as if it were the last time, or the first time. He kissed me as if trying to fuck me through the kiss—with such hungry abandon I whimpered and clutched at his sides with clawed fingers and tangled my tongue with his.

He pulled away, grinning wickedly. "There. All better."

I curled my fingers into the elastic of his underwear, but instead of pulling them off just yet, I grinned back at him…and bit my lip, hard, intentionally.

He laughed and frowned, shaking his head. "Why'd you do that?"

I shrugged, a cute, demure little roll of the shoulder. "So you'd kiss it all better again."

He laughed, his hands curling around my back and teasing the space between blouse and skirt. "You know, you could just ask me to kiss you."

"Sure. But this is more fun." I bit my lip again. "Plus, I have a feeling it makes you a little crazy when I bite my lip."

"Drives me fucking wild," he growled.

"How wild?" I breathed.

He pressed up against me, trapping my hands between us, sliding his hands up my back under my blouse, his lips slashing across mine, demanding a fiery kiss, slanting and touching, pulling away, teasing, licking my lip where I'd bitten it, then delving in for a kiss that scorched away my breath. He broke away, tugging my blouse up—I cooperated, slithering my arms out and letting him tug it off and toss it aside, leaving me in bra and skirt and heels.

"That wild enough for you?" he murmured, tugging down the zipper of my skirt.

I wiggled my hips side to side, letting the skirt droop, sag, and then fall free to billow around my ankles. "It's a start," I said.

He stepped backward, openly admiring me. I was clad in just the lingerie I'd chosen for the day—and it was, truly, a lingerie set. I'd dressed for myself today, wearing a comfy but sexy skirt and pairing it with a top that showed off my tattoos and made me feel sexy. And, underneath…royal blue lace, comfortable but not entirely practical, a demi-cup push-up bra that my breasts didn't need but which I knew made me look even more stacked than I already was, and a thong with a wide band and low waist.

He shook his head as if in disbelief, passing the back of his wrist over his lips. "Damn, Juneau."

I popped a hip. "See something you like, Remington?"

He growled. "You know I do." He reached for me, grabbing me by the ass with a rough handful of flesh and tugging me toward him. "Gimme."

I laughed, dancing backward. "Ah-ah-ah." I pushed his wrists down. "My turn, remember?"

"Fuck—I didn't think you were serious." He tested my grip, my resistance. "Mine. I need to touch you. I need my mouth on that tasty fuckin' skin of yours. I need to bury my face between those gorgeous tits of yours." He fought my grip, and I fought back, knowing he could overpower me if he really wanted to, but I was determined to show him I was strong—and serious. "I need you naked. I need you under me."

"Yes, Remington, I was serious when I said it was my turn." I pushed his hands down and then held up a forefinger in warning. "Stay."

He laughed, an impatient, amused, feral sound. "You have a few seconds—*very* few. So make 'em count, babe."

I gazed up at him, hooking my fingers in his underwear on either side of his erection. "You want me naked and underneath you?"

He nodded. "*Need* is the more accurate word here, sweetheart."

"Then you'll give me all the time I want."

"What are you going to do?" he asked, eyes narrowing suspiciously.

"Whatever I want." I tugged downward. "I'm guessing you'll probably enjoy it, though, so it's in your interests to just play nice and cooperate."

"Neither of those things are really in my skill set."

"Time to learn, then."

I had his underwear past his hips, past that taut, hard bubble of his ass, and he bent, shoving them down and stepping out of them, and I finally, finally got to see all of him, totally bare, and all for me.

And oh...my...*god*—he was glorious.

That V-cut was like an arrow from God to the promised land, pointing directly to the giant, veined, straining colossus that was his cock. I couldn't even begin to guess at measurements, and comparisons were futile. As big as a...? What? What in my life could compare to that beautiful organ? Nothing. Absolutely nothing.

I groaned, my lip between my teeth. "God, you're beautiful, Rem," I whispered.

He didn't laugh, gave me no arrogant smirk. Just gazed levelly at me. "I'm glad you think so," was all he said, in a quiet murmur.

I wanted to grab it and do all sorts of wicked things to him, but instead I took my time exploring the rest of his body. I arced my hands over his narrow hips, scratching my fingernails up over his hard round ass, then palmed the globes and caressed them, then up his back and over his shoulders. I nuzzled against his chest, caressing his arms and his sides, and his hips again, and my lips danced across his sternum. He sucked in a breath, a long, slow, deep inhalation, which he held; his hands went to my butt, caressing and cupping as I had his.

I pushed his hands away. "Ah-ah. My turn, remember? I told you to stay."

He snarled. "Can't help it." He clutched my ass, squeezing in gesture. "Got this beautiful thing out in the open, and I gotta get acquainted with it."

"Fine. But that's it."

He laughed, a quiet huff. "Yes ma'am." He continued his explorations of my backside and hips, toying with the strap of the thong. "You know, I never thought it'd be my thing, but I kinda like the bossy version of you. In this context, at least."

"I'm glad you like it," I said, echoing what he'd said when I got my first glance at the glory of a naked Remington Badd. "Because I'm not sure I can help it. I'm not usually like this, but as we've established, you just bring something out of me."

"You can make demands of me any time, sweetheart," he murmured. "I can't promise I'll always hop to obey you, 'cause taking orders ain't my style, but I'll do my best…just to make you happy."

I just laughed, a sniff and a huff of amusement at the idea of a man like Remington taking orders, using words like "obey." He was dominant, all alpha, but he could also be sweet and thoughtful…when he wanted to be.

"You can take off my bra if you want," I said to him.

He bared his teeth at me—less of a grin and more of a feral, animal gesture, a primal display of virile sexuality. He made quick work of my bra, unhooking it and stripping it off me before I knew what happened, and then, before he could do anything else, I pushed his hands down to his sides and touched my lips to his chest.

"Need," he muttered, the word more of a growl than speech.

I cupped my breasts, rubbing the hardened tips against his chest. "These?"

"Fuck…" he breathed. "You're really fucking with my self-control here, babe."

I was at the end of my own self-control, truth be told. I pushed up against him, pressing my breasts against his chest—I felt his erection as a hard hot ridge between us, and I was afire with need—it was all I could think of, all I could comprehend, the only thought or emotion within me was need.

My fingers curled around him, seizing the thick shaft. I pulled away a few inches, watching as my fist slid down and the fat tip popped out of my fist and his shaft sprouted upward through my hand. I wrapped both hands around him, caressing his full length with slow strokes, exploring him.

Not to harp on size, but he was so damned massive it made my head spin and my pussy ache just thinking about it. Each stroke of my hands around him took an eternity, traveling from root to tip and back, and each time, he hissed, his abs tensed, flexing.

"I've been hard for fucking *hours*, Juneau," he growled. "You keep that up and this'll be over before it starts."

"We have time," I said. "Unless you're in a hurry?"

He groaned as I continued to caress his cock with both hands, without rhythm, just petting him, thumbing the precum-smeared tip, just playing with him, learning the feel of him in my hands. "Yeah, I'm in a hurry. I need to feel you. I need to watch you come apart under me."

"What if I want to watch *you* come first?" I asked, meeting his gaze. "What if I want to just touch and you feel you…" I hesitated "…And taste you? What if I want to come apart on top of you instead of under you?"

He closed his eyes, abs flexed, hips subtly flexing forward as I let my caressing strokes find a rhythm. "Fuck, fuck, fuck." His eyes flicked open. "I want to let you do what you want, Juneau, but I'm not sure I'll be able to stop myself."

"Stop yourself from what?" I asked. "Coming?"

He laughed. "No, that's a goddamn certainty at this point—especially the way you're touching me right now. You're about to have a fucking mess on your hands, and I mean that literally." He swallowed hard, breathing deeply as I pumped his length with both hands. "No, what I mean is I'm not sure I'll be able to stop myself from bending you over this bed and fucking you."

"Oh," I breathed, my lungs seizing as images of him doing just that bashed through my lust-hazed mind. "That would be…yeah. Wow."

"I've never needed anything in my life the way

I need to fuck you, Juneau." He pressed against me, grinding. "And I don't mean just *fuck*—I mean…" He struggled for words. "I mean…everything. God, I don't know what I mean."

I wasn't ready for him to come, yet. I wanted more time with him. I wanted…just more. More touching…I wanted to taste him.

I clutched him in one hand and walked backward toward my bed, pulling him after me, using his cock like a handle. He grinned, half laughing and half groaning as I twisted, pushing him gently toward the bed. He sat down on the edge, reaching for me, reading what he thought was my intention to climb astride him.

I pushed his hands away, giggling breathily as I nudged at him, meaning for him to scoot further up the bed.

"Juneau, I—" he started, scooting up so his head was on the pile of pillows.

I touched his lips, pushing his hands up over his head. "You had your turn. This is my turn."

"Juneau—"

I bent over him, the erect tips of my breasts draping against him, palmed the rough stubble of his cheek, and then kissed him. My kiss wasn't the scorching, wild thing his was—my kiss was slow, delicate, soft, probing.

I kept my palm on his cheek, feeling it move under my hand as our tongues danced, and I let my other delve between us to grasp at his erection. As we kissed, as my lips searched his with soft, damp eagerness, I felt him throb harder in my fingers, I felt him burgeon, grow harder yet, larger yet. He was slightly thicker in the middle than at the head or base.

His hand descended, resting on my spine, and then carving down to curl possessively over my ass, and then his touch continued, delving under to find my damp seam, pressing his fingers against my clit. I gasped into the kiss at his touch, my caress of his cock halting as I shuddered under his touch. I nearly lost myself in it, then, wildness lacing into the kiss, hunger setting me afire as his fingers pressed and circled, touching just gently enough, fiddling and tweaking my aching clit. I groaned, my hips jutting, pushing, finding the rhythm as he touched me, our kiss synching to it, tongue probing and withdrawing to the rhythm of his touch, of my fist pulsing and sliding around him.

"No…" I whispered, breaking away. I laughed as I pulled back. "Bad boy. You almost had me, there."

"Couldn't help it."

I sidled downward, kissing his chest, his diaphragm, his side…I ran my tongue down one groove of his V-cut and then the other. I ached, throbbed—he'd gotten me moments from the edge before I'd remembered myself.

I glanced up at him as I tossed my braid aside and lay my cheek on his belly. "I told you—*my* turn."

His eyes blazed. "Juneau—"

I let a sultry grin curve my lips. "My…turn."

"Fuck." He let his head sink back down to the pillows, but then immediately curled upward in a crunch, neck craned, to watch, one hand hooked behind his head. "Juneau, you do that—"

I stroked him slowly, one-handed, feeling the veins and ripples of his flesh stutter in my palm. "I know exactly what will happen, Remington." I smirked. "Maybe that's what I want."

He closed his eyes briefly, and then opened them again, watching as I kissed his belly, and then his hip bone, and then, slowly, I opened my mouth, extended my tongue, and licked the plump head of his cock—tasting his flesh, his essence. "Ohhhh fuck, Juneau."

"Fuck…what?" I murmured. "Fuck…me?"

"Uh-huh," he grunted, struggling to formulate words as he watched me tease him, tonguing his shaft, kissing the side of it. "Fuck your mouth. Fuck your tits. Fuck that sweet tight pussy…"

Apparently he'd found his words.

"In that order?" I said, laughing as he just grunted at my suggestion.

"I won't last that long," he muttered.

"Doesn't have to happen all at once you know," I said, in between flicking my tongue against the thick, heavy shaft. "You could take your time. Let me fuck you with my mouth, let me fuck you with my tits…and then let you fuck me until I scream."

He flexed his hips, seeking my mouth. "Holy shit, Juneau. You know what it does to me when you talk like that?"

I ran my tongue over the tip, tasting his musk. "Yeah, I can taste what it does to you."

"Such a dirty girl. I had no idea."

I kissed the very tip, and then kissed it again, letting my lips split over him a tiny bit, swirling my tongue against his tangy, salty, leaking head. "I didn't either."

"I bring it out of you. I turn you into a dirty girl."

"Something about you just…makes me crazy." I shrugged. "I don't know what it is, or how to describe it, I just know I can't fight it."

His eyes flicked open and he watched, unblinking, as I continued to kiss his hot, throbbing cock, slowly, gradually taking more and more of him in my mouth with each wet kiss. I clutched him in both hands, holding him away, bringing him to my mouth, stretching him away.

I let my hands move, then, needing to feel him throb in my hands, feel him pulse and shift and thrust. Faster, then, letting my lips reach further and further down his enormous, straining cock. He was huffing between clenched teeth, eyes narrowed to slits, watching, his abs flexing. He let out a grunt, and his hips pulsed, pushing him into my mouth—he groaned and forced his butt back down to the bed, forcing himself to stillness.

I cupped one hand around his tight, heavy sac, gently caressing them, stroking them with my thumb, massaging and rolling them in my hand, using my other to continue stroking his length just under my chin, keeping my mouth locked around him, swirling and flicking my tongue against him as he filled my mouth and then receded.

"Ohhh god—" Jis voice was a rough rasp. "Fuck...ohhh *fuck*, June—Juneau. God, June." I didn't correct his use of the shortened version of my name, something I allowed very few people to do. But from his lips, like that, it was beautiful. It was delicate, a whimper of my name—excuse the pun, but it was an involuntary ejaculation, an affectionate form of my name torn from him.

I felt him throbbing in my hand, his balls tensing, his cock pulsing against my lips.

Soon.

He growled, a purely animal sound, and with a wrenching heave, he tore himself away from me. Leaped with primal agility, to stand beside the bed, sweat beading on his skin, every muscle tensed and standing out hard, his cock bobbing against his belly, gleaming wetly.

"Rem, I—"

He yanked open my bedside table drawer, correctly guessing where I would keep things. He found a strip of condoms, ripped one free from the strip and tore it open with his teeth, sliding the ring free and rolling it onto himself in two smooth strokes; he pawed through the drawer, found my vibrator.

"Remington, what are you—"

He knelt on the bed, and his rough, powerful hand gripped my hip and flipped me to my back. "Had your turn, sweetheart."

"I wanted to—"

"First time you make me come, June, it won't be in your mouth." He levered over me, turning on the vibrator to its highest setting. "First time you make me come, you're gonna be screaming my name. You wanna make me come in your mouth, babe, you'll have plenty of opportunity. I'll let you and ask for more. But this first time?" He touched the humming tip of the vibrator to my clit, and I jumped, shrieked, clapping a hand over my mouth.

"It's for *us*. It ain't for you or for me—it's for us, sweetheart."

"For…for us?" I reached for him, curling my fingers around his latex-sheathed cock, guiding him to me.

He nudged my opening, and I let my thighs fall apart wider. "For us."

My eyes slid closed as I felt him press against my tight slit. "God, Rem. Please."

He circled the tip of the vibrator against my clit, setting my hips into motion, flexing, thrusting, questing for him as the maddening intensity of the humming, buzzing device against my sensitive clit sent me to the edge. "Come for me, June."

I shrieked breathlessly through clenched teeth, writhing against the vibrator, feeling his cock sliding against me. Control or leverage or power was out the window—it didn't matter, and never did, I realized. This was beyond that.

For us? What did that mean?

I couldn't fathom it, had no space to ponder it as I exploded, coming after mere seconds of the vibrating touch. I cried out, not caring who may hear, needing only to feel him, to have more of him.

"Rem—*please*," I said, not caring how desperate I sounded—because I *was* desperate.

He pressed himself to me—I gripped him in one

hand, taking the vibrator from him with the other, changing the angle of it and adjusting the pressure of it.

"Juneau…" he growled. "I fucking need you."

I writhed, thrusting, whimpering. "Take me, Rem. Please, *please* take me. I'm yours—right now, I'm yours." I couldn't begin to fathom why those words came out of my mouth.

I am no one's but my own—ever.

Yet, in that moment, it was utterly true: right then, I was his.

He sank slowly into me, inch by inch, carefully. Watching. He sank into me as I came, and I felt myself pulsing around him as he slid into me, gradually filling me. Each inch split me wider and wider; each inch made me ache, made the stretching ring of my pussy burn with the strain of accepting his unbelievable size. I whimpered, moaned…I cared not what noises I made or how loud they were—all I could do was manipulate the vibrator to bring me further pleasure, to make me come again, or keep coming, I wasn't sure which. All I knew was Rem, his huge hard body above me, all around me, the wedge of his waist pressing between my thighs, his shredded abs tensed and flexing as he pushed into me slowly, slowly…*so* slowly. His shoulders were mountains, his chest a cliff, his arms thick and rippling as his hands began to roam my body, caressing the tender silk of my inner thighs, palming my trembling breasts, tracing the splayed flower of my pussy.

I kept the vibrator against myself, playing with the setting, pulling it back in intensity so I could focus on him, on the delicious ache of him inside me, on the fullness of him. With my other hand, I touched him. Delighted in the bulge of his biceps and the flat slab of his pecs, tracing the ripples of his stomach and cupping the tensed hardness of his ass.

It felt like a thousand delirious years as he pushed into me, until finally he was fully impaled in me, his hips against mine. Once there, he sank forward, a groan slipping from him. "Fuck, June—*so* goddamn tight."

"Don't—don't stop."

He rumbled a hoarse laugh. "Haven't even started yet, sweetheart." He caressed my breast, and then my cheek. "Eyes open, babe. Watch us."

I realized my eyes were closed only then, and I opened them. Watched as he withdrew as slowly as he'd thrust in. The vibrator hummed, buzzed, pushing me closer and closer to another orgasm. I cried out—or just flat out cried, perhaps—as the edge washed over me. As the climax hit, I turned the vibrator up all the way, and then I was coming again, and I knew I was screaming but there was a hot rushing roar in my ears and a blasting inferno inside me, a tangling tornado of heat and pressure. I felt myself clenching in waves around him, squeezing his cock so hard he grunted—and then he began to move.

He had no choice. I watched him succumb, watched him lose himself in me as much as I was already lost in him. I writhed through the climax, and he met me there, pushing into me, gripping my hips in both hands and pulling me toward him.

I screamed again, this time gritting my teeth and screaming through clenched jaws as the climax ripped me to pieces, his thrusting cock hitting every nerve ending I had and setting them on fire, the thick shaft splitting me open and searing against a place inside me that turned the orgasm into something else, into something more than just mere release—a clenching of body and soul and heart and mind, my clit blasted with searing spasms like bolts of lightning and my channel racked and detonated. I tossed the vibrator aside, no longer needing it, needing only my fingers and his cock—and then I needed nothing but him, one climax tumbling and twisting and shearing into a second and third…or just one, long, undulating orgasm.

He was moving, then, thrusting, driving.

I felt him nearing his own edge, knew it in the way his rhythm stuttered.

Instead of driving through it, he growled in his

chest and yanked out of me abruptly. "Not ready for it to be over, yet," he snarled.

"Me—me neither," I gasped. "I want more."

His grin was hot and ravenous. "More? You've come half a dozen times already, you greedy girl."

"I want more." I reached for him, clutching at his swaying cock, the latex dripping with my need. "I want everything you can give me. I want *you* to come."

He grabbed me by the hips and flipped me, physically tossing me onto my belly; he yanked my hips upward, grabbing the vibrator and sinking to his belly behind me. He slid the vibrator into me and his tongue flicked against me, and I flinched, whimpering as I was launched into immediate bliss. I couldn't help but grind against him, feeling the vibrator slide in and out of me—it was a pale and sorry imitation of the real thing, nowhere near as large as Rem, and I needed him, not this, but I was lost in the rush of it.

Dirty girl, he'd said.

God, he had no idea how dirty and sinful he made me want to be.

I've never known need like this, never known the rush of lust to be so all-powerful, so deliciously potent. I wanted anything and everything with this man, and I knew he could make everything perfect, make me come a million different ways.

Yet, in that moment, all I wanted was to feel him lose control. To feel him go weak. To bring him to that, to be the one that could weaken him and make him go limp and to cradle him against me in his most vulnerable moment.

Instead, I knelt on the bed, ass in the air, and felt him lashing my clit with his tongue, fucking the vibrator in and out of me, sending me surging to the edge.

"Rem—" I breathed, and then lost the ability to speak as ecstasy lanced through me.

And yet again, at the moment I reached the very peak of my climax, I felt him lift up, felt the vibrator slide out of me, leaving me clenching around nothing, writhing against nothing, crying out as he touched the humming device to my clit. I wanted to tell him I didn't want to come any more, that all I wanted was to feel him explode inside me, but I couldn't—I didn't want it to stop. I wanted to come and come and come forever, as long as he would keep touching me and kissing me and licking me and fingering me and—

Oh god—

And thrusting deep inside me as I came, pushing all the way in with one smooth, fast movement. My low, guttural moan ripped apart abruptly, shifting into a hoarse cry of surprised ecstasy as he filled me, stretched me…

And began fucking.

Oh, such bliss—such glory—such wild, wicked, sinful perfection. I felt him withdraw, slide in. Shift his position, shuffling his knees closer so his quads brushed flush against the backs of my thighs and his hips pressed into my ass cheeks. His hands carved over my ass, and then spread me apart as he drove in...

Once. Hard.

His hips slapped loudly against my ass, and I cried out, a shrill, breathless cry.

Again. Once...hard. A quick, rough thrust, followed by his hands caressing my ass ever so gently, lovingly, tenderly, possessively—and then he gripped my ass cheeks in a rough squeeze and slammed into me, his grunt laced over my whimper.

"Yes..." I breathed, as he repeated this. "Rem—yes. *Yes*."

"You like this?" he murmured, caressing, petting, and then thrusting. Fucking.

"God...*yes*," I rasped. "So much. Don't stop."

He kneaded my buttocks, petted them, caressed them in slow circles, patted them. Then, without warning, he smacked my ass. Not hard, just a playful little whack. "How about that?" he asked, spanking me again, a little harder. "You like that?"

"I—I don't know," I admitted, truthfully. "Keep doing it and I'll let...ohhh god, *oh* god—I'll let you know."

He laughed, thrusting slowly. "You'll let me know."

I tried to come up with another witty piece of snark in reply, but he fucked it out of me, slamming his cock into me and slapping my ass cheek in unison, my genius reply turned into a breathless whimper.

Again, a slow wet glide as he pulled out, his hand smoothing and caressing, and then a hard thrust and a smack.

And each time, he smacked a little harder, left side, right side, alternating. My ass burned at first, but then as his thrusts grew faster, closer together and his smacks grew harder, the burning pushed through me, searing into my core and turning to heat, turning to need, turning to an orgasm barreling through me like a hurricane. I felt it hit and couldn't stop it, could only bury my face in the mattress and let myself scream.

"Rem…" I murmured. "What are you doing to me?"

"Everything."

His hands palmed my ass, no longer spanking, just holding me as he thrust, pulling me backward into him.

Harder, then. Faster. More, and more. Moving, thrusting, pulling me backward by the hips, our bodies slapping together. I could feel his heavy balls tapping against me as he moved, and even that, for some reason, was unbearably erotic. The grunt of his exertion was erotic. The way he gripped my hips and then palmed my butt as if he couldn't decide which he wanted more was erotic.

"Rem…" I breathed his name again. "Come for me, Rem."

He grunted. "Soon, baby. I'm close."

I felt him nearing the edge, and I knew something was missing.

I couldn't think straight to figure out what. I just knew I needed something, something from him, something more to make this every dream and fantasy I've ever had come true.

Right as I felt him shuddering and stuttering to the edge, he stopped.

Pulled out.

"Rem!" I cried, aching for him, needing his completion. He was rough, demanding, and ungentle as he flipped me back over, abruptly enough and roughly enough that I gasped in shock. "What are you—"

Then, gentling, he took me by the hand and pulled me upright as he lay down on his back. Instinctively, without thought, I knew what he wanted, and it was exactly what I needed—what I hadn't known I needed.

I climbed astride him, knelt above him, fondling his massive, gleaming erection, stroking him as I guided him to me. I pressed him to my seam, split myself open with his cock, and sank down onto him. No hesitation, no drawing it out—I slipped him against my opening and impaled myself on him hard and fast, crying out.

"I need to see you when I come," he growled. "You're gonna make me come, and I'm gonna look you in the eyes while you do it."

"How do you know?" I breathed, whimpering. "How do you always know what I need?"

"Because it's what I need, and for some fuckin' reason, we seem to be built to need the same things." His eyes were locked on mine as I rose up, hesitated a brief instant, and then slammed down to sink him into me again. "We're just…"

He couldn't quite say it.

I could. "Made for each other."

"Yeah," he groaned, his hands on my hips again, thumbs pinioning against the hollow where hip meets thigh, letting me decide the rhythm, the speed, the force. "That scare you at all, June?"

I shook my head. "N-no."

"Take your hair out of the braid," he ordered.

I balanced myself on him, still rising and falling slowly, rhythmically. Snapped the tie off the end of my braid, worked my fingers through the woven strands to free my hair from the braid, and then shook it out.

Loose like this, my hair draped around my shoulders and obscured my breasts. He brushed it back, fingering through it.

"Fucking gorgeous," he muttered. "You are so goddamn perfect, June."

I rode him, then. With wild fury and primal abandon, I rode him. Braced my hands on his chest and slapped my ass down against his hips, spearing his cock into myself, screaming breathlessly with each thrust.

"Oh fuck, June," he breathed, and I felt him drawing close again—I knew, now, without a doubt what he felt like as he reached the edge.

There would be no stopping it, this time.

"Come, Rem," I gasped. "Come for me. Give it to me."

He strained up into me, face twisted in the agony of ecstasy. His fingers gripped my hips with bruising strength. He fucked wildly. Madly. Furiously. Driving up into me—and all I could do was take it, ride through it. This was all him now—all control was his.

I was his. He took me, made me his own.

If I was orgasming, it was a climax of the heart, a release of the soul—I felt it in my pussy, felt it searing through me like a physical orgasm, but it was detonating in my very being. It was brought on by him—by his power, his utter male beauty, his driving, primal, possessive strength, his raw need. I shook, trembled—my breasts jounced painfully as he fucked me, and I gloried in that ache, seeing how it maddened him all the more. I clutched my breasts, pinched my nipples, and let them bounce, thrusting down against him with absolute abandon to make them bounce all the more just for his benefit.

"June!" he whispered my name as he came.

"Rem…yes!" I cried out, uncaring how loud I knew I was. "Rem…god—Rem. Come for me, right now. *Come!*"

"Fuck, oh fuck, oh fuck, *June*—I'm coming!" This was a tense roar, not loud but searing in intensity. "Look at me! Look into my eyes."

"Say my name while you come, Remy."

He palmed my breasts for a handhold and I clutched at his hips, and then I sank forward onto him, smashing my breasts against him and snaking my arms around him. His hands sank into my ass and lifted me, slammed me down onto him.

"Juneau—" His voice was hoarse, now.

"June…" Stripped of power, dominating in its vulnerability.

"Oh god, June. *Juneau…*" Exquisitely surrendered.

I felt him, all of him. Felt his cock spasm as he emptied himself inside me, thrusting madly through it—he clung to me, hands clawed into my ass cheeks, guiding my movements, his face buried in my throat. I felt each juddering slap of my buttocks onto his thighs, felt each spearing thrust of his cock into my spasming channel, felt his voice shudder as he lost the ability to speak, and could only grunt helplessly. I felt him throb, felt the warmth inside me as he came and came and came.

He wasn't grunting, I realized—he was saying my name. Groaning it.

June—June—June. Juneau—Juneau...

Again and again as he ravaged into me, our bodies writhing together, my own unexpected final climax coming on the heels of his, brought on by him, by his, by this, by everything.

My arms were wrapped around his neck, my face in his chest. His hands roamed my body, caressing me everywhere as he stilled, finally, panting breathlessly.

How long did we cling together, like that? Just breathing together, gasping. Bodies joined, sweat-slick and trembling.

I lifted up, eventually, and his eyes met mine.

Something moved between us—an awareness, a knowledge that what just happened wasn't at all normal.

"June..." He sat up, keeping me on his lap, and I wrapped my legs around him, sitting on him, facing him, my arms on his shoulders, one hand brushing affectionately through his thick blond hair. "That was…"

"Everything," I finished.

He released a pent-up breath, running his hand compulsively over my breasts, as if making the most of the opportunity to just touch them. "Yeah. It was everything."

"More than everything."

He looked…shaken. "Juneau, we…" He shook his head, hunting for words. "What did we just do?"

I felt as shaken as he was, but I was less surprised by it. This was why I'd resisted him for so long, why I'd tried to keep this from happening.

"What we just did is what happens when things go way, *way* beyond merely fucking."

He exhaled sharply. "Yeah, that was a *lot* more than just fucking."

"A lot more." I toyed with his hair. "You look scared."

He laughed. "Yeah, I am."

"Why? Of what?"

"Because I'll never want anything else but that." He clamped his jaw shut, flexing it, and then spoke as if the words were being torn from him. "And I'm not sure I know how to do that."

I laughed, falling against him, burying my face in the side of his neck, my words muffled against his salty skin. "Why do you think I tried so hard not to like you?"

"Because you saw this coming?"

"Hell yeah, I did."

He frowned. "And you assumed if it did—*when* it did—it'd only end up with me leaving you hurt."

I nodded, not even pretending otherwise. "Yes, exactly."

He cupped my cheek in his big, rough hand. "You're always underestimating me, Juneau."

"Even in that?"

"Especially in that."

I felt a pang in my heart. "Rem, I..." I breathed slowly through my nose. "Remember what you promised—no promises you can't keep, and no bullshit."

He cupped the back of my head, stared into my eyes for a long moment, and then...

He kissed me.

And this one eclipsed all the others—it was manic, furious, fraught with intensity, wild with desperation, tender and rough, aching with surrender, needy and confident...all of this at once.

"Look into my eyes, June." I did, and he spoke with a rough growl. "Now tell me you think I'm bullshitting you. Tell me you think I'm making a promise I won't keep."

I couldn't.

Tears burned my eyes, because I honestly wanted to tell him he was full of shit. I wanted to tell him I knew he was just saying whatever he could to get me to sleep with him once more. I could have saved him the effort—I'd fuck this man as many times as I could, and he didn't need to blow smoke up my ass about some emotional connection.

None of that applied.

The connection was real, and undeniable.

He didn't have to say a damn thing, because I *knew*.

And so did he.

We both knew, and it scared the shit out of both of us.

THIRTEEN

Remington

IT WAS FOUR IN THE MORNING. NEITHER OF US WAS asleep, though we had both been drowsing in almost-sleep for hours. I'd like to say I lost count of the number of times Juneau and I had fucked, but that'd be a lie—I never started counting.

Fucked.

That's the wrong word.

Truthfully, I knew what it was—I knew the most accurate phrase for what Juneau and I had shared at least half a dozen times in as many different positions, always fraught with manic intensity and a wild passion that shook me to my core.

I just couldn't get the phrase to go through

my brain.

"Rem?" Juneau's voice was quiet in the word-thick silence.

"Hmmm?" I rolled over and stared at her; Juneau's brown eyes glittered in the darkness, searching me.

"What happens next?"

I chewed on the inside of my cheek. "I…I don't know," I admitted.

"Neither of us is denying that this thing is…" she trailed off, at a loss for the right word.

"Something?" I suggested.

I saw the slight curve of her lips in the darkness. "Yeah," she said. "It's something."

"But then, I knew it'd be something the moment you ran into me and I caught you," I said. "I stared down into those gorgeous brown eyes and I knew…" Now it was my turn to trail off.

"Knew what?" Juneau pressed.

I rolled a shoulder. "Just that it'd be…*something*."

"Is it as hard for you to sleep as it is me?" she asked.

I huffed a laugh. "I'm fucking exhausted, but yeah, I can't sleep."

"Having someone in my bed when I'm trying to sleep is…weird."

"Same." She hesitated, but I could tell she had

something to say. I brushed a long tendril of black hair away from her face. "Whatever it is, just say it."

She bit her lip, and I only just barely resisted the urge to smooth it away with kisses—we were, even in this state of exhaustion and satiation, powder kegs of sexual tension, and if I kissed her now, the conversation would be over. So, instead, I brushed my thumb along her lower lip, tugging it free of her teeth—it backfired, because she closed her teeth over my thumb, capturing it, and then wrapped her lips around my thumb in an erotic suggestion.

I felt a growl rumble in my chest. "June—quit playing with fire."

She sidled closer to me. "You started it."

I tugged the white flat sheet up higher, covering her so I wouldn't be tempted by her flesh—I knew in my gut that whatever she was hesitating to say was important; if there was ever a time for me exercise self-control and restraint, it was now.

"I can see you mulling something, Juneau. What is it?"

She sighed. "I just...I don't want to presume anything..."

"But?"

"But right now, we're acting like two people sharing a bed. We're in this bed together behaving like two people used to sharing a fun time or two that's never going to go anywhere."

My gut flipped. "Because that's what we are—two people used to sharing a fun time or two that's never going to go anywhere."

"But if this is something—no boxes, no labels, just...*something*, right?" she prompted; I just nodded, and she continued. "Then maybe we could...act more like we're two people exploring the boundaries of our something."

I chuckled. "The S word."

She frowned, an adorable wrinkling of the bridge of her nose that had some odd part of my chest feeling all...melty. "The S word? Which word is that?"

I slipped an arm under her neck and rolled to my back, bringing her with me—like two pieces of a puzzle fitting together, she sank with instinctual, natural perfection into the crook of my arm, resting her cheek on my chest, a hand on my stomach. "Snuggle. The S word."

She giggled, a sound I felt in my heart and my cock at the same time. "Oh." She slapped my stomach playfully. "You say S word like it's some dirty secret, or a swear word."

"For a lifelong, avowed bachelor, there are three dirty, forbidden words: the S word, the C word, and... the L word." I lapsed into silence, letting her try to figure out what they were.

"Hmmm. The S word is, according to you, snuggling. Which means the C word is probably... cuddling?"

"Ding-ding-ding."

"The L word?" I could tell by the tightness and hesitation in her voice that she knew the answer already. "Love."

"Yeah," I muttered. "Got 'em in one."

"There's another C word, you know." She twisted her head to look up at me.

"Oh?"

She grinned. "Commitment."

I faked a disgusted, frightened shudder. "Ugghhh! Quiet, woman—you'll scare me away."

She didn't laugh, though I'd meant it as a joke. "Rem...I wasn't suggesting anything."

"I was joking, June. You're not gonna scare me away."

"Oh."

"I'm not that fragile, babe. The thought of what this could be...yeah, if I think too far ahead, I get a little dizzy." I tightened my hold on her. "But this, right here? This is all I need. The rest we can figure out as we go."

She nuzzled closer. "I like that answer." Her voice was drowsy. "I think I could fall asleep, now."

"Me too."

And so…we did. And I'd never slept better in my life.

We were awoken by the muffled sound of a ringing cell phone. Juneau shot up, dislodging the sheet.

"Shit!" She dove off the bed, rummaging under the pile of clothing for her purse. She found it, dug her phone out, glanced at it, and promptly freaked out.

"SHIT!" She put the phone face down on her thigh, sucking in a deep breath, holding it, and letting it out. And then, remarkably calm, she answered. "Daniel, hi. Um…I'm so sorry. I've overslept. I know you have court this morning. I'm sorry, and I'll be there in a few minutes. Twenty or so? Thanks, Daniel. See you soon, bye."

She tossed the phone onto the bed and stood up, naked and beautiful. "I was supposed to be at work thirty minutes ago!"

She quickly got dressed, finding a pair of bright, flower-patterned underwear in her dresser, and a bra hanging off the doorknob. It looked practical, functional, meant for support and comfort rather than the male gaze…not that it stopped me from gazing with great interest and attraction as she hooked the eyelets together in front of her, then spun it around, shrugged into the straps, and then tucked her boobs into the cups.

Her eyes went to mine, a grin on her lips. "What? You're staring at me."

I just grinned back. "I don't know—it's weirdly hot watching you get dressed. Don't get me wrong, I'd rather you either stay naked, or strip you all over again, but I like watching you get dressed."

She shook her head. "Weirdo."

I shrugged, not minding the term in the slightest. "This tiger's stripes ain't changin', sweetheart."

Her smile was tender as she grabbed a brush from inside her purse and dragged it through her long, raven-black hair. "Good. I like your stripes just the way they are."

After a few dozen strokes of the brush, she braided her hair with swift, practiced ease, and then went to her closet and chose an ankle-length dress with long sleeves, a high neckline, and a sweater to go over it.

Then her eyes went to me, to my tattoos, and she put the dress back, and the sweater. Instead she chose a black ankle-length skirt, and a green top that was opaque over her torso, gauzily transparent from the cleavage up—baring her tattoos.

I grinned at her. "That's my girl."

She rolled her eyes. "Don't be patronizing."

"I'm not!" I said. "I mean it. I'm genuinely proud of you for choosing to wear your ink openly. I know it's not an easy thing for you to do."

She put on the sweater while sliding her feet into a pair of black ballet slipper-type shoes. "I'm only putting on the sweater because it's chilly in the office."

I smirked. "You know, you owe me zero explanations."

Another eye roll. "Oh, shut up." She snagged her purse off the floor, shoved her brush and cell phone into it. "I have to go. Daniel's probably going to fire me when I get there anyway, though. He's pretty cool most of the time but he's got zero patience for tardiness."

I tried to bite down on the comment lodged behind my teeth, but Juneau saw, and sighed.

"What, Rem?"

"Maybe instead of him firing you, you should put in your notice."

"And do what?" she asked; I just lifted an eyebrow, and she sank down onto the bed, perching on the edge. "No. I can't. I can't!"

"Why not?"

She exhaled sharply. "I can't have this conversation with you right now, Rem. I have to go."

"I didn't mean to upset you."

She shook her head as she stood up. "You and Ink—you both act like I can just defy the expectations of my entire family, like it's as easy as just...doing what I want, regardless of my duty to my family."

I waited until she was halfway out the bedroom door. "Hey, June?"

She stopped, glancing back at me. "What?"

"Lunch. Twelve-thirty. I'll pick you up at your office."

She just stared at me for a long moment. "Make it one. And it'll have to a be a short one to make up for being late."

I pointed a finger at her and clicked my tongue. "You got it, sexy."

She laughed, rolling her eyes at me. "Are you gonna hang around naked in my bed until then?"

I slid out of the bed, sidling naked over her to her—watching the way her eyes roamed. "Nope." I yanked her up against me, palmed her cheek, and kissed her hard.

She pushed me backward. "Not fair."

I just laughed. "I never claimed to play fair." I kissed her again, a quick, soft peck. "Can I make one small suggestion before you go?"

She eyed me. "What?"

"Put on some deodorant and perfume or something, because you smell like sex."

She paled. "I was in such a rush to get dressed I forgot."

"That's why I'm reminding you."

She dropped her purse on the floor, shrugged back out of her sweater—which she shoved into my hands—and then vanished into the bathroom, closing the door. I heard water running, and some rustling, and then she came out of the bathroom a minute later, zipping her skirt back up and righting her shirt.

"Ho bath, but better than nothing," she said. "Now how do I smell?"

I sniffed at her, grinning. "Fresh as a daisy."

She took her sweater from me and put it on, and then hustled for the door. "Use my shower if you want," she said as she breezed out. "You smell like sex, too."

I took her up on her offer, and discovered that using a shower in an apartment lived in by women was a little tricky—there were roughly fifty different bottles cluttering the four corners of the tub and lining the high, frosted-glass windowsill, each one with a fancy name. In the end, I used one that had the word "shampoo" on it, although it smelled like somebody had put a bunch of lavender on top of a cupcake. There was no regular soap either, just shit like "exfoliating sugar scrub" and "invigorating citrus body wash." There was also no washcloth, just a bunch of different colorful poofy things. I ended up using the invigorating citrus body wash, glopping a bunch into my palm and doing my best to scrub it into the important places.

At least I was clean.

I dressed, and then, on a whim, made Juneau's bed. I paused in the kitchen, which was...not clean.

I hissed through my teeth. "Damn you, Ramsey," I muttered.

He had this thing about cleaning—he claimed even if he did nothing else that day, making his bed and cleaning the apartment gave him at least some small sense of accomplishment. And I'd found myself agreeing with him, lately, which was a new twist for me.

And now, standing in the kitchen of my girlfriend's apartment—wait. What? Girlfriend?

I rubbed my face with both hands. I'd just thought that, for real.

Own it, buster. It's real. It's good. Getting spooked is for pussies, and I'm no pussy.

I grinned to myself, and set about cleaning their kitchen. Dishes got rinsed off and put in the dishwasher, counters got sprayed and wiped down, the floor got swept, and when I was done, I did indeed feel a sense of accomplishment.

I also knew when Juneau realized I'd done it,

she'd probably be pretty…grateful. Which wasn't why I'd done it, but was certainly nothing to sneeze at.

I headed over to the saloon, then, whistling to myself.

Ram and Rome were sitting side by side at the bar, plates of breakfast food piled in front of them. Sebastian and our youngest—and weirdest—cousin, Xavier, were standing behind the bar. Despite the drastic difference in size, build, and age, the two were standing in the exact same pose: leaning back against the counter opposite the bar, ankles crossed, arms folded over chests.

They all heard me come in, and all eyes went to me.

"The fuck you been, dude?" Rome demanded, around a mouthful of food.

"Out," I growled. "What's going on in here?"

"Out," Rome mimicked in a sarcastic whine. "What are you, fourteen?"

"Shut the fuck up, you ugly goddamn gorilla." I took a seat next to Ram. "There any more of that?"

Xavier blinked at me owlishly. "As a matter of fact, there is. In the kitchen."

I blinked back. "Well…can I have some?" I stared at him, wondering if I was missing something in this exchange. "Please?"

Xavier scratched at his forearm, which was wrapped in a full sleeve of geometric designs, rune-shapes, and math symbols. "Yes, you may."

He pushed away from the counter and went into the kitchen, returning a moment later with a plate piled high with scrambled eggs, toast, bacon, sausage patties, and black beans mixed with sour cream and salsa—which was weird paired with eggs, but good.

"Dude, this is amazing," I said. "Who made this?"

Xavier raised his hand. "I did."

"You got culinary skills, son."

Xavier's expression didn't change, but there was a hardness in his voice. "I am not your son."

I glanced at Bast with a lifted eyebrow. "Just an expression."

"Slang is often wasted on me," Xavier said. "I tend to be rather literal about most things."

"Gotcha." I lifted a forkful of eggs. "Well, cousin, this shit is delicious. And by shit, I mean the food, not literal shit."

He sighed, a sound of long-suffering patience. "I did gather that much."

I laughed. "Well, you *said* you were literal." I glanced at him, and then at Bast. "So, what brings you guys here, and why the delicious but unexpected breakfast?"

Bast answered. "Testing an idea."

I finished the plate with a sigh of contentment. "Thanks, Xavier, that was awesome." I eyed Bast. "What idea?"

"There is a rather decided dearth of breakfast choices in Ketchikan," Xavier answered. "We thought to fill that void."

"Dearth?" I questioned. "Sorry, but I barely graduated high school, so you'll have to dumb down the vocabulary for me."

"Lack of," Xavier answered.

I glanced around at our saloon, which we'd designed and renovated intending it to be primarily a night-time-focused drinks establishment. Then it morphed into a fine-dining establishment, and now a breakfast spot, as well. Fine, but just not what we'd first intended.

"I see," I said. "And whose idea was this?"

Rome got up, vanished into the kitchen, and came out with a pot of coffee and five white ceramic mugs; he poured us coffee, set the pot on the bar, and sat back down. "It was my idea," he said.

I glanced at him in surprise, leaning forward to look at him past Ram, who was still shoveling food into his mouth. "Yours? I thought you wanted to run a bar, not a restaurant."

He shrugged. "I tried to take Kitty out for breakfast yesterday morning, and everywhere was packed to overflowing. A couple places had a wait list...for *breakfast*. I may not be the savviest businessman in the world, but to me that says opportunity. And if we're going to focus on food as much as drinks, we may as well at least think about trying to hit all the marks where we can make money."

"It's not a bad idea," Bast said.

"So we're going to be open from, like, seven in the morning to bar close? Who the fuck is going to work those hours?" I asked.

Ram finished his meal. "The idea is, we'd be open for breakfast and lunch, then close from like two to five for cleaning and restock, and then open again for dinner." He indicated Bast and Xavier. "And they'd hire people. No one is suggesting the three of us work the entire stretch."

I ran my hand through my hair. "Hmmm. This was never my shindig, so if you think it'll work, fine by me." I glanced at Xavier. "And what, you'd cook?"

He shrugged. "To start, yes. I enjoy cooking breakfast. I'd hire and train people to take over." He paused. "I would rather work early in the morning, because I do my best thinking late at night, and I am currently working on a new AI system."

I blinked. "A what?"

"Artificial Intelligence. An operating system for robots. I design and build robots."

My eyes widened. "You do?"

He nodded. "I've sold designs to automakers, tool and die companies, toy manufacturers, and such. What I'm working on now is a design for a commission by a private company specializing in space exploration and satellites." He said this with no hint of pride.

"Damn, dude. So you're like, literally, a rocket scientist?"

Xavier snorted. "More robotics and AI scientist, but I take your meaning."

I frowned. "And how old are you?"

"I turn twenty-two soon. Why?"

I laughed self-consciously. "It's just impressive." He was scratching his forearm again, drawing my eyes to his tattoos. "I like your ink, dude. Who did it?"

Xavier stared at his forearm for a moment, as if it took a moment to transition from what I'd said to whatever was going on in his head. "Oh. Thank you. An artist in Los Angeles. I admit I chose the parlor and artist somewhat at random." He tugged up his sleeve, indicating the blank space above his elbow. "I have had a thought of adding to it, but I do not know where I would go, or what I would have done."

I grinned at him. "You're in luck, dude. I know the best tattoo artist in the area."

"You do?" he asked.

I nodded. "My…um—Juneau's cousin is a tattoo artist." I tapped my chin. "Actually, Juneau is too, come to think of it." I let out a deep breath, and went for it. "And so am I."

My brothers both swiveled their heads to stare at me.

"Say *what*?" Rome asked. His eyes went to the tattoo peeking out from under my sleeve. "I know you and Mike used to fuck around with his machine, but calling yourself a tattoo artist seems like a bit of a stretch, bro."

"The half sleeve on his left arm?" I paused for effect. "I did the whole thing."

Rome frowned. "The black and white thing? All the dragons and pinup girls and shit?"

I nodded. "Grayscale, not black and white, but yes, I did that entire piece."

Ram eyed me. "When the fuck did you two have time for that? That shit takes hours of work."

I laughed. "You know all those times you and Rome went out barhopping for easy ass and I decided to hang back?" I rolled up my sleeve. "He was doing this, and I was doing his."

Ram pulled a face, nodding. "Huh. I guess that makes sense." He sniffed the air, frowned at me, and then leaned closer to me, sniffing my hair. "Dude. Why do you smell like…" He sniffed again. "You smell like a fucking girl."

I growled. "Don't fuckin' worry about it."

He sniffed me again. "It's not just your hair, dude." He eyed me. "Rem—why the hell do you smell like a chick?"

I didn't want to answer questions—not yet. "Shut the fuck up and don't worry about it."

Rome cackled, leaning back in the stool. "Oh shit! It happened!"

Ram eyed our brother. "What happened?"

Rome smirked at me. "You used the lavender cupcake shit, didn't you?"

I shot him an evil glare. "Fuck off."

He came around and sniffed my head. "You did. You used their lavender cupcake shampoo." He sniffed the back of my neck. "And that exfoliating sugar shit."

"Would you quit sniffing me?" I snarled, taking a swipe at him.

Rome slugged me in the shoulder. "Oh quit being such a defensive bitch." He bent his head toward me. "Sniff."

I whacked him. "I'm not fucking sniffing you! What the fuck is wrong with you?"

"Just take a whiff."

I groaned, but I sniffed—and sure as shit, he smelled like lavender cupcakes. "So we both smell like chicks. Awesome."

"Hey, man," Rome said, laughing. "My hair is soft as a baby duck and it was a lot easier to get it to look right this morning. Plus, I showered there yesterday and my hair *still* smells good."

Bast was trying gamely to suppress his laughter. "You three are fucking strange, you know that?"

Rome grabbed my shoulder and shook it. "Hey, Rem, answer me one thing." His eyes met mine, and I knew he was serious now.

I tried to pull away. "Fuck off, Rome."

"No, for real." He searched me, and I knew my brother saw what I was being so prickish about. "You connected, didn't you."

"Shut up," I grumbled.

Ram was watching us, perplexed. "The hell are you two sissy-ass dweebs crying about?"

Rome just grinned. "Our brother has fallen in love."

I gave him a glare—the kind that would have put him six feet under, if looks could kill. "Rome, last warning. Shut...the *fuck*...up."

He held up both hands. "All right, all right, but only because I remember feeling that same way."

Ram was still lost. "What way?"

Rome patted him on top of the head, viciously patronizing. "You'll understand when you're older, baby brother." That was a joke between the three of us, because Ramsey was the youngest of us by several minutes.

"I'll kick your ass, Rome, and don't think I won't." Ram shot him two middle fingers. "You know I can, and you know I will."

Truth be told, in a one-on-one fight, Ramsey probably could take either one of us, because he'd spent his off time—when he wasn't hiking or hunting—in a martial arts studio learning Muay Thai from a scary old Thai man.

Rome just pretended to shiver. "Ooh, I'm so scared." He glanced at me, then. "You were there all night, weren't you? That's why Kitty ended up crawling into my bed at one o'clock this morning—you and Juneau were keeping everyone up."

Ram was suddenly very interested in the grain of the bar, and I suspected there was something he wasn't saying, but I figured if I didn't want to talk about my thing yet, then I couldn't very well push him about his.

I did wonder if it had something to do with the odd way Izzy had said she and Ram had "met."

Rome shot me a look, glancing pointedly at Ram—asking the question silently—and was about to say something else when Bast slapped the top of the bar. "Are we done discussing your love lives?" he grumbled. "You're acting like you've just discovered fire, and you're trying to keep the secret to yourselves."

Rome just laughed. "Actually, it does kind of feel that way, at first."

Bast made a face and nodded. "You're not wrong." He tapped the plate in front of Ram. "So. Are we in agreement about breakfast hours for Badd Kitty Saloon?"

"Fine by me," I said. "But don't count on me being around much to help."

Rome eyed me. "No? Got something better to do, huh?"

I sat back and crossed my arms. "Yeah, actually."

Rome snorted. "Juneau doesn't count."

I glared at him. "Don't be a dick." I hesitated. "I plan on doing tattoos full-time."

"What, like your own tattoo parlor?" Ram asked, skeptically.

I shrugged. "Maybe someday. I'll probably work for Ink for a while first, though."

"Ink?" Rome asked.

"Juneau's cousin, the tattoo artist. He owns Yup'ik Tattoo just outside town." Rome was quiet, and I sighed. "Rome, look—you know I was never super thrilled with the idea of operating a bar."

"Yeah, I know. I just...I had this vision of the three of us running this place together. I thought it'd be kinda fun." He shrugged.

Ram snorted. "Dude, Rome. You *know* Rem and I hate bars. I only go when I want to pick up some fun for the night. If I really want to drink, you know I'd much rather be in front of a campfire with a bottle than in a booth in some loud bar overpaying for watery bullshit."

Rome blew out a frustrated breath. "No, I get it. I do."

I clapped him on the back. "Bro, we're not going anywhere. I'm not, like, leaving. I'll be around, and I'll pop by and take a shift pouring beer now and then. But this is your thing, not mine." I gestured at Bast and Xavier. "And look at it this way—in dragging us up here, we discovered family we didn't know we had, and they *are* into running bars. Not sure you can get much better than that."

"Plus, you managed to hook up with Kitty, and for some strange fuckin' reason, she seems to actually like your dumb caveman ass," Ram said.

Rome nodded and shrugged. "I still need help getting things running, though, so you two can't quit yet."

Bast gestured at the kitchen. "I've got a company coming by this week to get started installing the new kitchen, which means it's gonna be all hands on deck ripping shit out, because the more we do for free, the less we pay them to do, which means more money for renovations and overhead."

I rolled my shoulders. "Ripping shit out I can do."

So I found myself shoulder to shoulder with my brothers and cousins, tearing apart the dirty, dated, nasty industrial kitchen—pulling out the fryers and grill, rolling away the old refrigerators—which were older than any of us—demolishing counters, disassembling storage racks, and even scraping away the warped, filthy linoleum. At some point, word got out that a demo job was afoot, and we found ourselves crowded with help, Baxter, Brock, and Zane all showing up to help knock shit down and tear shit out. Thus, the job was on pace to get done in a quarter of the time it'd have taken ordinarily.

I was sweaty, dirty, and tired when I happened to glance at my phone: 12:30.

"Shit!" I peeled off my shirt. "I have to go!"

Rome, already shirtless, paused with an armload of ripped out flooring. "Go where?"

"I told Juneau I'd take her out for lunch. I have something thing planned."

Rome just grinned. "Fine, fine. Ditch us for your girlfriend."

I rolled my eyes at him. "Oh, like you haven't done the same thing pretty much every day since you met Kitty."

He shrugged. "Yeah, well, once a girl gets her

hooks in you…"

"You turn into a pussy with no friends and no life?" Ram snarked.

Rome and I just exchanged amused glances. "I'd watch it, bub," Rome said. "You're next and you know it."

"The fuck I am." He pounded his chest with a fist. "Lone wolf for life right here, boys."

I just cackled. "Izzy!" I said, pretending to cough the name into my fist.

Ram straightened slowly and turned to face me, taking on the body language of a predator about to pounce. "You wanna say that again?"

I waved my hand in front of my face—there actually was a fair amount of dust in the air, and my fake cough turned into a real one. "Say what again? I was coughing."

"'Say what again!'" Rome said, quoting one our favorite movies—*Pulp Fiction.*

I laughed again, still coughing through the demolition dust. "Lone wolf for life," I repeated, cackling. "What a dork."

Ram just shot me the bird again and went back to scraping dirty white subway tiles off the walls with a crowbar. "Fuck you. You two assholes can fall in love all you want. It's not happening to me."

Bast just laughed in mockery, joined by the rest

of the cousins.

Bax had a shovel and a bucket, and was scooping up the tiles Ram had scraped free; he paused to lean on the end of his shovel, wiping at his face. "Dude, fatal mistake. The harder you fight it, the harder you fall."

"True that!" Zane said.

Brock paused in the act of piling the uprights from an old storage rack. "He's right, you know. Confucius say, the only pussy is he who rejects love from beautiful woman."

Ram frowned. "Confucius didn't say that, you tool."

Brock just laughed. "No, but it's still true."

"And anyway, I'm not rejecting anything. There's nothing to reject." Ram turned away, and went back to scraping at the tiles. "It was just fun, one time, and that's it. I don't even *like* her"

"Ah-*ha*!" I shouted. "There *is* something with you and Izzy."

He didn't look at me. "I thought you had to go."

I glanced at my phone again. "Fuck—yeah, I do." I waved. "Got to go. Thanks for the help, guys. See you around."

I made it back to our nearby apartment in record time, rinsed my face and scrubbed my pits, put on deodorant, changed into clean underwear, jeans, and a fitted polo, and then hauled ass to pick Juneau up from her office at one—making one quick stop on the way.

I had a plan, and I wasn't sure if she'd appreciate it right away, but it seemed like the right thing to do. I just hoped she'd end up seeing it that way.

FOURTEEN

Juneau

HE PICKED ME UP PRECISELY AT ONE, AND HIS HAIR WAS still damp, droplets of water beading in his stubble, and he was wearing a clean, fitted blue polo shirt instead of his usual T-shirt. He'd even put on different boots, newer ones with clean, polished black leather and crimson laces. The effect was to make him even sexier than normal, which meant my libido—in overdrive from all the sex we'd had last night and this morning—revved up to an almost unbearable degree.

As soon as I slid into his truck, he leaned across and kissed me, and just like that, it was a conflagration, a moan escaping my throat as his tongue found mine and my hand tangled in his damp hair.

I pushed him away abruptly. "Stop, stop, stop." I let out a slow, calming breath. "You keep kissing me like that and something inappropriate is going to happen in this truck."

He grinned at me, and then turned to look around. "There a private parking lot around here somewhere?"

I rolled my eyes. "No, and we're not spending my lunch hour having sex, Rem. I never had breakfast and I'm hungry."

He sighed, pretending to be saddened—or... mostly pretending. "Fine, fine. I guess I'll feed you."

"I need to restore my energy," I said, smirking at him. "Someone kept me up most of the night."

He just grinned even wider as he pulled away from my office building. He drove us toward the docks, parking at the marina.

I eyed him. "Where are we going?"

He hopped out of the truck, retrieved something from the bed, and opened my door. "You'll see."

I frowned at him. "You're being mysterious."

He just winked at me. "Yeah, well, I'm a mysterious kinda guy."

I laughed. "Right. Subtle and mysterious. That's you."

He hefted the seafoam-green Yeti cooler on a shoulder. "Picnic at the dock," he said. "It turned out to be a nice day, and I thought you'd appreciate some time outside."

I followed him as he wove his way unerringly in the one direction I didn't want to go—a certain section of the marina I was all too familiar with. "Rem... where are we going?"

He didn't answer right away, just braced the cooler on his shoulder with one arm and held my hand with the other. "You trust me, Juneau?" He paused, his eyes fixed on mine.

I met his stare, frowning. "That feels like a trap, considering where we are." A few feet away, my mother sat under her awning, polishing a piece of turquoise, watching us. I glanced back at Remington. "Why are we here, Rem?"

He shrugged his shoulder, indicating the cooler. "Picnic with your mother."

"I know what you're trying to get me to do."

"Yeah—have a nice friendly picnic lunch, in which you introduce your new boyfriend to your mother." He gazed at me innocently, but I could tell that a certain phrase in that sentence had taken some balls for him to say so casually.

"My new boyfriend." I squeezed his hand. "Is that what this is?"

He smiled. "It's as good a thing to call it as any." He lifted an eyebrow. "Unless you don't want to be my girlfriend."

I pretended to think. "Hmmmm. I don't know…" I leaned against him, laughing. "Yes, you big dork. I want to be your girlfriend."

"Even if I've tricked you into introducing me to your mother?"

"A dirty trick, to be sure." I sighed. "Why, Rem?"

"Because you'll never talk to her on your own. I figured you could use me to break the ice a little." He eyed me sideways. "Tell her about the tattoo you're going to do on me."

I lifted an eyebrow. "The what?"

He tapped his hip pocket. "I have a design, and I want you to do it." He grinned. "Plus, I also kind of told my brothers I plan on working with Ink. You know…an apprenticeship."

She blinked. "You…did?" She eyed me. "Did you talk to Ink about this?"

He just grinned a cocky grin. "Nah, not yet. But he'll be down—he likes me."

I just laughed. "So sure of yourself." I pulled him into motion, deciding I had to just bite the bullet. "What if he can only take one apprentice at a time?"

He smiled slowly. "Well…you're his cousin. I think there's probably some kind of preferential treatment for family."

"I'd hope so," I said. We were reaching my

mother's booth, then, and I spoke to him quickly, in low tones. "Let me do this my way, okay?"

He just laughed. "We're just here to have lunch with Mama Isaac. Anything else you want to do while we're here is all you, sweetheart."

I glared at him. "You are *so* manipulative."

"I prefer the term *subtle*."

I laughed. "Yeah, subtle as a sledgehammer."

Mom continued to polish the turquoise as we approached, but she did allow me a long, openly curious look. "Juneau—hi, honey."

I let go of Rem's hand and circled behind the table to hug her. "Hi, Mama."

She eyed Remington. "Who's this?"

I let out a sharp breath, steadying myself. "This is Remington." I swallowed hard. "He's my boyfriend."

Mom blinked at me in blank surprise. "Really." She frowned. "I never heard anything about him until now."

I just shrugged with a small smile. "It's...new."

Remington reached out to shake my mother's hand. "Hi, Mrs. Isaac. I'm Remington Badd." He wrapped an arm around my shoulders. "You raised a hell of a woman, ma'am."

Mom's eyebrows shot up. "I'm glad you think so." Her eyes went to the tattoo on his arm, which the short, tight sleeves of his polo left mostly exposed.

I had my sweater on, buttoned up against the cool breeze on the marina. It was actually fairly warm, now, though, and I was genuinely getting a little hot.

So…

I unbuttoned the sweater, letting it hang open. Letting my tattoos show.

Mom's eyes fixed on them, and her expression darkened. "Juneau Isaac. What are those?"

I slipped the sweater off entirely. "Tattoos."

She lifted an eyebrow. "I know that." She glared at me. "You know what I'm asking." Her eyes went to Remington. "He do those?"

I smirked. "No. We've only known each other a short time. I've had these for years, actually." I lifted the hem of my shirt to show her the ones on my diaphragm and belly. "As are these." I turned, and Rem helped me lift the shirt in back. "And these."

Mom was having trouble formulating words. "Who…who did them?"

I lifted my chin; I traced the band running from shoulder to breasts to shoulder, and then the matching one inverted on my belly and hips. "I did these myself. The rest…Ink did."

She sighed. "I knew it would have something to do with that boy." She shook her head. "Can't even see his skin for all the tattoos making him look like… like some illustrated man."

"Have you ever read that book by Ray Bradbury?" I asked. "It's amazing."

Mom rolled her eyes. "Got no time for that nonsense." She sighed again. "Why are you showing me this now?"

"Because...because most of those tattoos illustrating Ink's skin were done by me, Mom."

This caused her to put down the turquoise she was furiously polishing. "Nuh-uh. No." She fixed me with a hard look. "We talked about that years ago. You were giving that up."

I sighed. "Mom, I can't just—just give it up. It's part of me. I could never give it up. I never have." I teared up. "Mom, you're an artist. You don't do this just to pay the bills—you *love* creating this stuff." I lifted a carving of a horse which she was in the process of finishing, putting in stones for eyes and tiny strands of real horse hair for the mane. "You've done this your whole life. Could you just give it up?"

Mom took the carving from me and examined it critically. "It's all I've ever known. I wanted more for you. We all—"

"I know, I know," I interrupted. "That's why I've done this in secret for so long. Everyone sacrificed so much to send me to college, and I'm grateful. But..." I tapped my chest piece. "This is what I want."

She gazed sideways at Rem, who was watching

the conversation with open interest, sitting on the cooler. "You have anything to do with this?"

He shrugged. "Not directly."

I frowned at him. "Yes, directly."

"How do you figure?" he asked.

"You saw me doing a tattoo on Ink, and you saw my tattoos. That was the start of things coming out into the open."

"So you blame me?" he asked, his eyes cautious.

"Blame...and credit," I said, smiling at him. "Both are equally true."

Mom glared hard at Rem. "How much of her *tattoos* have you seen?"

Rem shifted, unsure how to answer.

I was more certain. "Mom!" I snapped. "I'm an adult. That's none of your business."

Rem met Mom's eyes steadily. "One thing I'm sure of, ma'am—Juneau is incredibly talented. And she's unhappy in her job at the law firm. She does it to make you happy and proud of her. But it's taking a toll on her, and I, selfishly, just want her to be happy, and not just doing something out of a sense of familial obligation."

Mom was quiet a moment. "Familial obligation."

"I don't *hate* it," I said, "I just...it's not what I want."

"What do you want, then?" Mom snapped,

gesturing at the awning. "This? Sitting on a dock selling trinkets to tourists?"

"Yes!" I cried. "It's what I grew up doing. I have a whole collection of little figurines like this I've made with you over the years, and I treasure each of them." I tapped my tattoo again. "And I want to do tattoos. I want to do art—whatever it looks like, whether it makes me a lot of money or not."

"It's never been about money, Juneau," Mom said. "It's about—"

"A lot of things," I cut in. "None of which matter in the long run. I went to school and got the law degree, and I've been working with Daniel long enough to know without a doubt that I have no interest in being a lawyer. Ever."

Mom nodded, staring at the table. "You been putting off going back for the bar so long I was starting to wonder."

"I don't want to let you down, or have you or anyone else think I'm not grateful for the opportunity to go college." I grabbed her hand. "I just...I want something else. I've wanted this since I was eleven years old."

"Eleven?" Mom asked.

I laughed and showed her the tattoo Ink had done on me with a pen and heated needle. "Ink did this one, and I did one on him when were eleven."

Mom snorted. "Lucky you didn't go septic and die, doing that crap."

I nodded. "I know. We did get sick, actually."

Mom laughed. "I thought that flu was awful sudden." She shook her head. "Ink getting sick at the same time was also kinda coincidental."

"We were lucky it wasn't worse," I said. "But we'd been drawing on each other with Sharpies and pens for years, and we wanted something permanent. We were just a pair of dumb kids with dreams bigger than our sense."

"You were always covered in scribbles, and so was he. We always knew he'd end up doing what he does. I just thought you could do something more than..." She shrugged, gesturing at the table. "This."

I shook my head, sighing. "Mom, I'm *proud* of this. You are an *artist*. I've seen photos on Facebook of people around the world proudly displaying *your* art on their desks and mantels. I'm proud to be part of something that goes back beyond you and Grandma. It's more than that." I tapped my tattoo. "This is part of that. I want to be part of this—bringing our heritage back."

Mom knew what I was referring to, and I didn't have to say anything else—her grandmother, whom I'd known as a young girl, had the ritual tattoos on her face and hands, and the tattoos on my chest were, in part, a dedication to her, modeled after what I remember seeing on her skin, and thinking were so beautiful.

After a while, Mom glanced at Rem and the cooler. "You got any food in that thing, or you just bring it to sit on?"

He laughed. "I have food. I just didn't want to interrupt." He got off the cooler and opened it, pulling out a spread of food—a cold rotisserie chicken, cheese, pickles, olives, nuts, and crackers.

We ate, and Rem charmed my mother into telling as many embarrassing stories about me as possible. Unsurprisingly, Mom ended up being as easily won by his gorgeous grin and beautiful eyes and easy good humor as I had been. Which meant he learned a good many of the most embarrassing things that have ever happened to me. Knowing Rem, he'd get Ink to tell him the rest.

After a while, I glanced at him. "Hey, Rem..."

He just grinned, standing up. "I saw a public bathroom somewhere around here—I'll be back in a minute." He winked at me, somehow knowing I wanted a few minutes alone with Mom.

She watched him go, as I did. When he was gone, she glanced at me. "Well, Juneau, you know how to pick 'em." She smirked. "You've never brought a guy around me before, so he must be pretty special."

I shrugged. "Like I said, it's…new."

Mom snorted. "He's good for you, girl. Keep him around. I like him."

I laughed. "Okay, if you insist." I sobered, looking at her inquisitively. "This wasn't quite how I saw myself revealing all this to you, you know."

Mom grinned. "Bringing a good-lookin' fella to break the news for you was pretty smart. I couldn't yell at you with him around."

I sighed. "I've struggled with this for so long, Mom."

She leaned into me, wrapping an arm around me. "Juneau, if it's what you want—if you're passionate about it? I want you happy. I just didn't want you getting stuck in it because it's all you know, just because it's some family tradition. I wanted you to have options. I'm proud of you for what you've accomplished—you're the first person in our entire family to ever go to college, and I'm proud of that." She traced my tattoo. "This is really beautiful. Makes me think of my grandmother."

"It's part of why I did it—for her. Because of her. I remember sitting in her lap as a little girl, tracing the pretty marks on her leathery skin, wishing I could have them too."

"You gonna do some on your face, too?" she asked.

I shrugged. "I don't know. Maybe." I laughed. "Not right away. I'd have to work up to that. Get some on my hands first, or my forearms."

She traced lines on her fingers, between the first and second knuckles. "Right here. Like Grandma."

A hopeful grin blossomed on my face. "I could do them for you, like Great-Grandma's. Ink has the supplies so I could do them with, like, FDA-approved tattoo ink."

Mom eyed me, touching my knuckles. "Get 'em to match?"

I clutched at her hand. "Mom—don't play with me. Really?"

"Slow day today. I could close the booth early." She smiled at me. "Think Ink will mind us dropping by?"

I couldn't help a shriek of excitement. "MOM!"

She just smiled at me, taking my hands in hers and pressing kisses to my knuckles. "I can't believe you kept this from me for so long, Juneau."

"I was afraid you'd…" I shrugged, blinking back tears.

Mom frowned. "Afraid I'd what? You're my daughter, my baby girl." She shook her head at me. "Yes, I'll admit I'm a little disappointed that I'll never get to say my daughter is a lawyer, but if that's not what you want, if you're not really passionate about it and you're just doing it because you feel obligated to me and everyone else…?" Mom sighed. "Then it's not right for you."

I hugged her. "You don't even know how relieved I am."

Mom whacked me on the shoulder. "I'm honestly a little pissed off that you'd keep secrets like having tattoos and not wanting to be a lawyer just because you were afraid I wouldn't understand." She shook her head again. "I thought you knew me better than that."

I toyed with my braid as Mom began packing up. "I do, but sometimes you build up these fears in your head, you know? Like, part of you knows it's irrational, but you've been weighed down by it for so long that it's nearly impossible to convince yourself otherwise, because you have this imaginary worst-case scenario all built up in your head."

Mom nodded. "Oh, I know. I know that feeling all too well."

I helped Mom finish packing up, and then Rem showed up and helped us carry Mom's stuff to her truck—a pickup older than me, falling apart with rust. I had as many memories of sitting in this truck with Mom as I did of sitting under that folding awning.

Remington, having tied Mom's gear down in the

bed of her truck, slapped the side of it. "So, where to, ladies?"

I glanced at Mom. "Are you serious about this?"

Mom's grin was infectiously happy. "It's something I've thought about since I was a little girl. I just…I'd never do it alone."

Rem's eyes widened. "What are we talking about, here?"

I jumped up and down excitedly. "Mom and I are getting matching hand tattoos."

He staggered backward. "You…*what*?" He straightened with a grin. "So all that secrecy and hiding was all for nothing?"

"Shut up," I muttered. "What the hell do you know?"

He raised his hands. "Absolutely nothing. I'm just happy for you." He indicated his truck, parked a block or so away. "We can all pile into my truck." He frowned at me. "Although, if this is a special mother-and-daughter thing, you guys should go together and we can catch up later."

Mom patted him on the cheek. "You're sweet, Remington." She headed toward his truck. "You're coming. I'll need something pretty to look at while my daughter is stabbing me with a needle."

He rubbed the back of his head, chuckling. "Well, that I can do."

Mom eyed him. "You could take your shirt off?" She glanced at me. "I'm assuming the rest of him is as pretty as his face."

"Mom!" I shouted. "What's gotten into you?"

She just cackled. "You're not the only one who's been holding things back, girlie."

"Well you being a freak about my boyfriend— who's only officially been my boyfriend for, like, half an hour…that part you could keep to yourself."

Mom just laughed at me. "So when you said it was new, you really weren't kidding."

"We're still figuring it out, to be honest."

We got in the truck, Mom choosing the back seat before I could say otherwise, and Rem headed toward Ink's parlor.

"What's to figure out?" Mom asked. She whacked Rem on the shoulder. "You love her or not?"

Remington shifted uncomfortably.

"MOM!" I said, panicking. "*Seriously?*"

She just sighed. "It's not that hard, you know." She leaned forward between the seat, elbows on the console. "Remington. Do you want my daughter to be happy, even if you had to sacrifice something of yourself to make it happen?"

Remington's reply was immediate. "Yes."

"If you thought it would be what my daughter needed to be happy, would you walk away?"

"As an absolutely last resort? Yeah, I would."

"Is there anyone who could compete with her for your attention and affection?"

"Not a fuckin' chance."

She patted him on the shoulder. "You love her."

"I suppose so." He grinned at me. "Subtle as a sledgehammer, your mom."

I just huffed. "You're impossible. You both are." I rested my hand on his. "You don't have to say it, Rem. We're not there yet."

He shrugged. "I ain't afraid of it." He laughed. "Well, okay...I am, a little. It's a lot really fast."

Mom snorted. "Kids these days. Knowing you love someone isn't the scary part. When you have kids together and realize you're bound to each other for life no matter what else happens? *That's* scary."

"*Mom*," I hissed. "Stop."

"What?" she asked, cackling again. "I'm just tellin' the truth."

Rem patted my hand. "Relax, June-bug. I don't scare that easy."

I narrowed my eyes at him. "I told you—Ink is the only one who can call me that. We are *not* there yet."

He frowned. "But I called you June last night and you were fine with it."

I blushed, looking out the window to cover it.

"Yeah, well…that was different."

He caught on, and just grinned. "Oh. Got it."

Mom covered a laugh with a fake cough, pretending to be absorbed in something in her lap.

"Oh, stop, Mom." I sighed. "Like I said earlier—I'm an adult and it's none of your business."

She just shook her head. "I didn't say anything."

I rolled my eyes. "Doesn't mean I didn't hear it." I glanced at my phone, and swore. "Shit! I have to call Daniel!"

That was a tough conversation—a much-needed one, but difficult. I'd started dressing to show off my tattoos, and he hadn't said anything, but I'd felt his speculative gaze and had seen the questions in his eyes. So, when I called to say I had to take the afternoon off, he surprised me.

"You're quitting, aren't you?" he asked, cutting off my explanation.

I sighed. "Yes. Not right away—I'll give you proper notice, but I just—"

His voice was soft and understanding. "You are a wonderful person, Juneau, and I've loved having you work for me, but it has been obvious from the start that your heart is not in the law." He spoke over my protestations. "I'll consider this your notice. You just let me know when your last day is. Whatever you end up doing, Juneau, I truly do wish you the best of luck."

I sniffed. "Thanks, Daniel."

We reached the parlor, then, and I said my good-bye to Daniel; Rem hopped out of the truck, opened the door for me and then my mom, helping her down with those perfect manners he could apparently turn on and off at will. I led the way into the shop, Rem behind me and Mom behind him—Mom was small enough that she was mostly hidden behind Remington.

Ink was tattooing a large, bald, muscular man with tattoos all over his bare upper body. "Be with you in a minute," Ink said without looking up. "I don't do walk-ins, so if you want a tattoo, leave your email on the pad of paper by the register and I'll get back to you."

"Just us, Ink," I said.

He looked up then, briefly. "Hey there, June-Bug. Rem—how are you, buddy?" Ink went back to the tattoo then, not seeing Mom, who was still obscured by Remington's bulk.

Mom slid out from behind him and stood next to me with her arms crossed. "No walk-ins, huh? Not even for your Aunt Judy?"

Ink jerked the gun away from his client, eyes widening. "Aunt Judy." He blinked in shock. "I…what?"

The client frowned up at Ink. "Yo, Ink. I got a

meeting to get to. Can we finish the session?"

Ink shot him an irritated glance. "Yeah, yeah. You're gonna have to give me a second—my aunt's never been in here before, so this is a big deal for me."

The client rolled his eyes. "That meeting is to secure a half-million-dollar contract—*that's* a big deal. I'm paying you here, bud."

Ink lifted an eyebrow. "I'll cut your bill in half if you shut the fuck up and let me say hello to my auntie without your bitch-ass griping. How's that sound?" He indicated the tattoo he was working on. "Good luck getting anyone else to match my style, so don't piss me off."

The client harrumphed. "You're lucky you're the best tattoo artist I know, or I'd tell you to fuck off."

Ink slugged him on the shoulder, and I realized the two were friends, and this was part of their banter—a guy thing, I supposed. "I'll get you done in a minute, Bry. No worries."

The client stood up and stretched. "I need a smoke break anyway." He exited out the back door, tugging a flattened pack of cigarettes from his hip pocket, flicking a lighter as he toed a brick in the doorway to keep it from closing and locking.

Ink set the gun on the tray and stripped off his gloves, standing up to tower over Mom. "Auntie Judy. You are, no lie, the absolute last person I expected to see today." He glanced at my exposed tattoos, and then back at Mom, and his eyes widened to saucers. "No shit! You guys talked?"

I shrugged. "You may or may not have been right when you said you thought she would be more understanding than I was giving her credit for."

"Well no shit, cuz. Don't you know by now I'm almost never wrong?" He wrapped Mom in a giant bear hug. "I been telling her for years to just get it all out there with you."

Mom patted Ink on the shoulder. "I know. You're a good boy, Ink."

He growled in irritation. "Make me sound a like a dog, Auntie."

She just laughed, and then glanced at me. "You want to tell him, or should I?"

Ink frowned. "Tell me what?"

I grinned, only barely holding in my excitement. "Mom and I are getting matching tattoos."

Ink was stunned silent for a long moment. "Nuh-uh. Say that shit again."

Mom snorted. "You kids and your cursing." She smiled at Ink. "You remember your great-grandma Irene?"

Ink nodded, his eyes still wide. "She made the best cookies."

"You remember her hand tattoos?"

Ink stared up at the ceiling, thinking. "Yeah." He shuffled over to the counter,

rummaged around for a scrap of paper and a pencil, and then hunched over it, sketching. His huge round shoulders shifted as he drew, the tattoos on his bare torso seeming to move on their own. After a few minutes, he came back over, showing us his drawing. It was of a pair of hands, a quick but accurate sketch, incredibly detailed considering how fast he'd done it. The hands were old, wrinkled, small and delicate but strong: Grandma's hands, Mom's hands, my hands. The drawing depicted lines and angles and shapes across the fingers between the first and second knuckles, with similar lines banded around the wrists.

"There it is, best I can remember."

Mom traced the lines on the fingers in the sketch. "That's it—that's exactly how those tattoos looked." She looked at me. "Just like that?"

Ink nodded. "I'll get the supplies. You want it old school, or with the gun?"

"I don't care," Mom said, smiling at me. "I just want you to do it."

Ink's eyes couldn't go any wider, but somehow they did. "You guys really *talked*."

I nodded, smiling—I couldn't remember having ever been happier than I was in that moment. "Yeah, we did."

"So…I've got a new apprentice, then?"

My grin widened. "Yeah. You do. I still have to tell Daniel when my last day will be…but yeah, I can't wait to start."

Rem cleared his throat. "Actually, I was wondering if I could log in some hours too?"

Ink chuckled. "Going from a one-man show to three of us, huh?" He shot Rem a sly smirk and reached under the counter, pulling out a thick packet of paperwork. "Good thing I saw this coming, yeah?" He pulled out another stack, and handed it to me. "For you, cuz."

Remington took the stack and thumbed through it, then sat back and eyed Ink. "I had another thought."

Ink twirled the pencil in his fingers. "What's that?"

"There's a retail space for rent downtown, just down the street from Badd Kitty. It's a prime location, right near the heaviest tourist traffic. It's more than I can swing by myself, but if there were three of us…" He shrugged, shuffling the stack of papers to align the corners. "Could be fun…and profitable."

Ink sat down in his own tattoo chair, fiddling with the jar of ink. "Downtown, huh?"

Rem nodded. "It'd need some renovation, but my brothers and my cousins and I are good at that shit, and it'd give June and I time to finish our

apprenticeships. Then we could open for business together, as three artists sharing a studio." He gestured
at Ink. "You're a hell of a selling point, though, so I
was thinking we'd just call it...Ink."

My cousin laughed. "You've got this all figured
out, huh?"

Rem laughed. "I guess I do."

Ink narrowed his eyes but I could tell, knowing
him as well as I did, that he was just playing with
Rem—he'd decided already. "How do you know I
want to leave here? What if I like just being my own
boss?"

Rem waved a hand dismissively. "Nahhh...you're
bored and you know it." He grinned. "Plus, you'd
spend time around my cousins, and I think you'd
like them. There's something about them. Beautiful
women just seem to fall from the sky when they're
around and, if you're lucky, you could catch one of
your own."

Ink snorted a laugh. "You're crazy. Ain't no pretty lady want to mess with all this." He gestured at
himself.

Rem shrugged a shoulder. "You never know,
man. Women are funny that way. They'll surprise
you." He grinned at me as he said this.

Ink's client came back in just then, trailing smoke
from his nostrils. "All right. You ready, Ink?"

Ink slapped the arms of his chair as he stood up, moving to his rolling stool. "Sure thing, Bryan. Siddown, and we'll finish this fucker."

Mom whacked him as he shoved his hands into gloves. "You watch your language, young man."

Ink ducked his head, shying away. "Yes, Auntie. Sorry."

Bryan, the client, just laughed; I knew he was laughing at the idea that Ink wasn't big enough or bad enough to ignore his aunt Judy.

We all sat around watching Ink work, chatting amiably. It took Ink another forty-five minutes to finish Bryan's piece—a wolf howling at a full moon, all done in grayscale on the back of Bryan's left shoulder. He examined it after Ink announced it was done, and nodded, pleased.

"Good shit, Ink, as always."

Ink just nodded, taping the wrap over the fresh tattoo. "My pleasure." He patted the other shoulder. "You got any more work you're gonna want done?"

Bryan laughed. "You know it. I got an idea I'm working on. I'll be back in a few months."

Ink grinned. "In a few months, I may be at a brand new place downtown."

"No shit? That'd be a hell of a lot more convenient. You being way the hell out here is annoying. Your work is worth it, but I know a lot of people who'd love it if you were more centrally located."

Rem pointed at Ink. "See? It's a great idea."

Ink wrote up Bryan's bill, settled it, and by then Mom was already sitting in the chair. Ink laughed. "I gotta clean up first, Auntie. Sanitization procedures and sh—and stuff."

"Fine, fine." She smiled at me as she vacated the chair so Ink could clean it. "I can be your first real customer."

I laughed. "I'm not licensed yet, for one, and for another you'd have to pay me to be a customer and I'd never accept your money."

Ink went through the sterilization process, and then I used a marker to copy Ink's sketch of our grandmother's tattoos onto Mom's hand. Then, with a long look at Mom, I put on gloves, picked up the gun, and started work.

Three hours later, Mom and I had matching tattoos across our hands, the traditional design ringing our fingers and wrapping around our wrists.

Mom admired hers, laughing. "Your father is going to go apoplectic."

I paled. "He's going to kill me!"

She just laughed all the harder. "Nonsense. His grandmother had them too. He'll be fine, once he gets over his shock."

I hugged her. "You really have no idea what this

means to me, Mom."

She tapped my nose with a finger. "Baby, I love you. I want you to be happy." She flashed her hand at me. "If *this* makes you happy, then do it. I only ever wanted you to have the options I didn't, honey. That's all."

I fought the tears, but lost. "I'm grateful, Mom. I always have been. But this is who I am."

Mom sighed, wiping at my face. "It always has been, sweetheart. You never had to hide it, you silly girl."

Well…I won't. Not anymore.

FIFTEEN

Remington

6 months later

"**A**RE YOU SURE, JUNE?" I ASKED, FOR THE FIFTH TIME. She sighed. "Yes, Rem. I'm sure. You've already done this on my forearms—*both* of them." She smiled at me. "I trust you."

I let out a breath, and then dipped the specialized needle into the ink jar. "Okay, here we go."

Juneau was naked, lying on her back on her bed—a new flat sheet was spread across it to catch any potential ink spills. She had her thighs splayed open, which was...distracting, to say the least. I had her leg across my lap, her silk-soft skin under my hands. I'd already outlined the design with a marker—a band circling each thigh just a few inches down from her core. The design was a traditional one, meant to mark fertility and to welcome a child into the world with something beautiful—not that she was pregnant, mind you, but it was a traditional placement for a woman's tattoo and she'd been wanting me to do it on her for months, now—ever since we'd been officially licensed, in fact. I'd wanted more time to practice before I tried working somewhere so delicate and intimate. *Especially* on my girlfriend. I'd practiced professionally, and on Ink, and on my brothers, and my cousins—and they'd all let me practice using the stick-and-poke method Ink and Juneau had taught me, and now, finally, six months after being licensed as a tattoo artist, I felt confident enough in my ability to give Juneau the tattoo she wanted, where she wanted it, using the traditional method, without fucking it up.

It was a hell of a rush, to be honest—having all this beautiful, perfect skin as a blank canvas.

I focused on the design I'd marked out, putting the rest of my thoughts out of my head, centering on the art, on the process. Dip the needle in the ink, poke, just to the right depth, just hard enough. Dot by dot, patiently.

I lost myself in it, absorbed in the process of turning the design into beautiful reality. Through it all, Juneau was still, quiet, and thoughtful. Just watching, occasionally wincing, but never making a sound. When I finally had to take a break to shake out my cramping hand, she ran her fingers through my hair.

"You're pretty amazing, you know that?" she said, her voice quiet and tender.

I grinned. "Yeah, I know."

She huffed, rolling her eyes, but had to work to suppress her grin. "And so humble and modest."

I brushed imaginary lint off my shoulder. "Yeah, well, it's hard to be modest when you're me." She tried to lean forward to look at her tattoo, but I pressed a hand against her stomach to keep her down. "Ah-ah-ah. Not yet. I'm almost done."

"I wanna see," she muttered.

"You will." I grinned. "When I'm done."

"Does it look good?" she asked, her voice anxious.

I snorted. "No, it's all smudged and looks like shit." I laughed at her. "Yes, babe, it looks amazing— if I do say so myself."

"Don't make fun of me."

"I'm not, I'm just teasing." I leaned in and kissed her thigh, the one I wasn't working on.

I watched her eyes flare with lust. "Don't start something you can't finish, Remy."

I chuckled—mostly because she'd taken to calling me Remy just because she knew how much it annoyed me. "Who says I can't finish it?"

"The tattoo you're working on, that will be super tender...it's right by my hoo-ha."

I quirked an eyebrow. "I could use my mouth... and be really gentle."

She closed her eyes and flopped her head back against the bed. "Just finish the tat, Rem. You're next, you know."

I worked for another thirty minutes or so, and then had her flip to her belly so I could bring it around the back of her thigh, where it sat just beneath her buttock. Which was another temptation, because all I wanted to do was sink my teeth into all that juicy flesh, and run my hands over it. Or slide my cock between them...

I groaned, shifting, pausing in the tattooing to gather myself.

Juneau just laughed without even looking at me. "Having trouble, are you, babe?"

"You know how hard it is to keep my hands and mouth to myself when I've got you naked in bed and all spread out for me like this?" I laughed and groaned again, clutching her backside with my free hand. "It's fuckin' torture, babe."

She glanced at me over her shoulder. "Finish that tattoo and I might take pity on you."

"By jabbing a needle into my thigh?" I joked.

She wiggled her eyebrows at me—which was comical rather than arousing. "That too."

"Don't tease me, woman."

She laughed. "Have I ever teased you and not made good on it?"

I went back to work on her thigh. "No, you haven't."

"Okay, then. Finish the tattoo. Don't rush, and make it right. If I like it enough, you may receive payment...of a kind."

I kept working. "I know what you're getting at, June, but I hope you understand just getting to do this on you is its own reward. That you trust me this much? It's...everything."

She waited until I paused and then she turned to look at me. "I know, baby." I sensed something in her silence and looked into her eyes. "And that's why I love you, Remington Badd."

She said it.

I felt my chest tighten until I felt like it might crack open from the pressure inside. "June..."

She shook her head. "I just wanted to say it because it's true, for me. You say it if and when you're ready." Then she got comfortable again and didn't say another word.

Another forty-some minutes, and I was done.

I sat back, admiring my work. "There. Finished."

Juneau's eyes met mine as she propped up on her elbow and twisted to look at me over her shoulder. "Can I look now?"

I grinned. "I mean, I could wrap it and you could wait to look at it?"

She kicked at my shoulder with her foot. "Move so I can roll over, you big dork."

I patted her ass, and then slid backward so she could roll to her back and sit up. She drew her knee up and stared at my handiwork for a long time, gently tracing some of the lines.

"It's beautiful, Remington." She blinked hard. "Thank you."

I laughed softly. "So emotional, silly girl." I smiled. "You're welcome. Thank you for trusting me." I traced a portion of the lines. "There'll be another session or two to fill in and shade."

"I can't wait," she murmured. And then she sat up, slid off the bed, and stood in front of her full-length mirror, twisting so she could see the back. "I think before you do the shading, I'll have you do one to match on my other leg, and *then* you can do the shading."

I rubbed my hands together. "Oh goody! That means more time with you naked on my lap, unable to touch you." I laughed sarcastically. "My favorite!"

She rolled her eyes at me. "It won't kill you to

want me and not have me right away. You're just getting too used to me giving it to you whenever you want."

I quirked an eyebrow. "I'm pretty sure you instigate it as much as I do, babe. If not more."

She turned back to face me, a sultry grin on her face. "Yeah, well, I can't be held responsible for what I do when you look the way you do." She swayed toward me. "I've never had any self-control where you're concerned."

I set the needle and jar of ink aside as she closed in. "Same, babe."

She sank to her knees on the floor in front of me. "Question for you, Mr. Hunk: how am I supposed to tattoo your thigh when you're still wearing pants?"

I grinned. "That's a good point."

She unzipped and unbuttoned my jeans, and then tugged them off.

"You know, the tattoo will just be a couple inches above the knee, hon—do you need to take off my underwear too?" I said this with a grin, knowing exactly what she had in mind.

Juneau just smiled then grabbed the waistband of my underwear and tugged them off, then turning her attention to my cock, which was now as hard as a rock.

"Ooops," she murmured, caressing the length of

my cock. "I must have slipped."

I laughed. "Slipped, huh?"

She fondled me, her eyes on mine as she caressed my length. "Yeah, you know me. Always slipping."

"Such a clumsy girl."

She bent forward and took me in her mouth, slurping noisily over the head, and then backing away, grinning. "Oops. I slipped again. Clumsy me." She cupped my balls in one hand and stroked me with the other. "But…while I'm here, I may as well say thank you for the tattoo."

I laughed, preparing a witty reply, but then she had me in her mouth again and I could only gasp, and then groan, and then bury my fingers in her long loose hair and let myself thrust into her mouth.

She moaned as I came, and when I was finished, she backed away, tossing her hair aside with a shake of her head, dragging her wrist across her lips.

"Wow," she muttered. "Someone was all pent-up."

"Yeah, well, I was staring at your sexy naked ass for two hours unable to touch it, so I admit to being a little pent-up." I moved to sit up, intending to toss her on the bed and do my best to be gentle around her new ink.

She knocked my hands aside and pushed me backward onto the bed. "Nope, not yet, big boy. I'm inking you first." She smirked. "And *then* I'll let you have your wicked way with me."

I groaned. "I'll be all pent-up again by then. Especially if you don't put on some damn clothes."

She just giggled. "It's almost as if I planned it like this."

"Such a dirty girl," I murmured as she settled on the bed and brought my leg to rest on hers.

"I didn't use to be like this," she said, consulting the sketch she'd done that would soon grace the front of my thigh: an outline of Alaska, with a big bright star where the city of Juneau is located. "I met this guy, and I guess his filthy mind and dirty ways infected me." She smirked at me.

It was a small, simple design, and it only took her a few minutes to trace it onto my leg, and then she began the process of making it permanent, using the same stick-and-poke method I'd used for hers.

Which required her to be in close proximity to me the entire time.

Which led me to thinking about what she'd just done.

And how good it had felt.

And what I wanted to do in return, and how she'd sound—plus the fact that she was naked, those big beautiful breasts draped against my other leg…

She huffed a laugh as someone decided to wake

up and stand at attention. She batted at it playfully. "Down boy! Didn't I just take care of that?"

I laughed. "Like you're gonna *take care* of it once and I'm not gonna need you even more? I didn't get to taste you even once while I was doing yours."

"You could've, you know."

I frowned. "I wanted to stay focused. I was worried about messing up." I reached out and touched her shoulder. "I couldn't bear it if I messed up this beautiful skin of yours."

"It's okay. I like letting you stew in your desire for me a little bit," she said, smirking at me wickedly. "Makes you that much crazier when you finally do get me."

"You like it crazy, huh?"

She paused, her eyes serious. "I love every single crazy thing about you, Remington."

I swallowed hard. "That's good, because you're stuck with me." I cursed mentally, knowing I'd wimped out.

She went back to poking. "The tattoo makes it permanent, huh?"

I waited until she was dipping instead of poking, so she didn't accidentally poke too deep. "No, me being head over heels in love with you makes it permanent."

She accepted this with a warm, tender, loving

smile, one that made my heart melt and my cock hard. "Good answer."

I grinned. "I'm full of good answers and good ideas. It's because I'm so smart."

She rolled her eyes at me. "But yet such a dork."

Later, after she'd finished, she set the needle and ink aside, leaving my leg resting on hers. Watching me, waiting.

She knew I was about to pounce, and she was ready for it in every sense of the word.

But what she wasn't ready for was me, looking directly into her eyes, telling her that I loved her with all my heart.

What made it perfect was the way she whispered back to me, "I love you," in my ear, words I never thought I'd ever hear a woman say to me.

But I wasn't ready for the way the tears clouded in my eyes, or the way she sobbed as I said it again, "I love you."

THE END

EPILOGUE

———— ⚜ ————

Izzy

RAMSEY BADD AND I HAVE BEEN SUCCESSFULLY AVOIDING each other for months, now. Almost a year, in fact, come to think of it.

And it hasn't been easy, considering both of my roommates are seriously involved with his brothers.

One or all of the three triplets were constantly swinging by our apartment to pick us up or hang out for one reason or another. Between the Badd cousins, their wives, fiancés, and girlfriends, and Remington and Roman and Kitty and Juneau there is always something happening. They're all one big happy family.

Even though everyone was so busy running the

most successful bars in town—Badd's Bar and Grill and Badd Kitty Saloon—there were always regular family get-togethers.

Badd Kitty Saloon was almost at its first year anniversary, and it was already a booming, madhouse success. The new tattoo parlor, INK, had been opened for a few months. Sometimes there was a family tattoo party at INK, because they were all addicted to the stick-and-poke tattoos that Ink, Rem, and Juneau were becoming famous for; they even had clients who would fly into Ketchikan just to get inked by them.

It was a fun time, because I always got included, and it made me feel great to be surrounded by such awesome people.

It was tricky, though, because it meant I had to see Ramsey quite often.

In fact, I saw him ALL. THE. TIME.

And it was tricky.

Because we had…history. Sort of.

And that history began that day in the Seattle hospital a year ago. I'd gone down there only intending to support Kitty and her new boyfriend in a difficult situation, and to have a little fun—meet some hot guys, and, honestly, just do something different for the weekend.

It wasn't supposed to be anything else.

We got to the hospital, had a visit and then

Juneau and Rem had gone to get coffee. Kitty had said she and Rome needed a few minutes together with Roman's dad who was in the hospital due to a vehicle accident.

No problem, I thought.

I left the hospital room, intending to look around Seattle and catch up with Kitty and Juneau later.

As I was heading toward the elevators I sensed I had a tail...one of Roman's brothers, Ramsey, was following me. They were triplets and, like his brothers, he was tall, blond-haired, blue-eyed, massively muscled, and intensely gorgeous. His shaggy hair and thick beard immediately got my imagination running wild with thoughts of how it would tickle and scratch if he was between my thighs eating me out.

We shared some witty banter on the way to the elevators, along with some sly innuendos when we passed an empty hospital room.

We paused in the middle of the hallway and after sharing some mischievous looks we ducked into the empty room.

Within seconds he said something which had made my blood boil—hell if I can remember what— and the look he'd given me had me tangling my hands in his hair.

My mouth has always gotten me in trouble— and, this time, my mouth found its way downward.

I'd taken one searing look at the bulge in his jeans and had figured hell, why not. Right? I figured this thing with Kitty and his brother wouldn't last, and that things would soon go back to normal. I'd never have to see this guy again.

So I'd pushed him into the squeaky plastic-leather chair beside the door, and I'd gone down on him, using every trick I knew to make him come so hard he'd gone literally cross-eyed, and had been unable to stand up right away.

Which was hot as *fuck*.

What I hadn't expected was for him to yank his jeans up, lift me bodily off the floor, and throw me onto the hospital bed.

He shoved my skirt up around my waist, discovering my little secret—I like to go commando sometimes when I wear a miniskirt, just to feel naughty.

And he'd made me scream—loudly. With nothing but a very wickedly talented tongue.

The second I was done, still whimpering, still shaking, he'd vanished.

Without a word.

An orderly had found me seconds after I'd sat up and righted my skirt—I'd made some excuse about being lost, but I don't think the orderly bought it.

I went to the ladies' room and waited for several minutes, trying to get my shit together.

But I couldn't.

It felt like he'd eaten my brain along with my pussy.

I decided right then to forget the little sightseeing trip around Seattle I had planned; I already had the best souvenir I could possibly get: an orgasm from a hot guy.

So I went back to the hospital room. I opened the door and found my hookup sitting in a visitor's chair laughing and joking with his dad and Kitty and Rome. He was also ignoring me, as if nothing had happened.

He didn't look at me, didn't even acknowledge my presence.

Later that afternoon, Kitty and Juneau and I all left Seattle together and came back to Ketchikan. I'm not normally short of words, but I have to say I was pretty quiet on the way home.

Ramsey Badd had seriously messed with my mind...and my pussy.

The whole thing became a bit weird because, somehow, people seemed to know that something had happened between the two of us, but I just kept quiet about the whole thing and eventually it all died down.

I went back to chasing bar rats and the status quo resumed.

And, as the months went on, we became experts

at ignoring one another.

But, every once in a while, I'd catch him eyeing me from across the room. Then we would both look away, and I wouldn't think any more about it.

Meantime, Kitty and Roman had become a *thing*. A serious, major thing.

And Juneau and Rem were heading in the same direction.

I truly was happy for everyone, but it left Ram and me as the last two singles standing—at least as far as our family was concerned.

I kept getting questioned by Kitty and Juneau about Ramsey, and I had a feeling he was getting the same kind of third degree from his brothers, which I think was part of the reason why he kept avoiding me.

And why I ignored him.

I refused to entertain the thoughts that flit through my head...the ones that tell me his tongue had been the best thing I'd ever felt, and that his cock had filled my hands and my mouth in a way I'd never known was possible. I vividly remembered the way he'd groaned so quietly, with such restrained power. It had been the hottest fucking thing I'd ever heard, and I'd almost squirted right then and there as he shot his thick, salty cum down my throat.

So we continue to ignore each other.

We pretend that we don't really like each other, and that we've never even had a real conversation.

That last part is actually true, though.

Except for the not-really veiled lead-up to our rendezvous in the empty hospital room, we've never spoken.

And I just can't help but wonder how long this will last.

Why?

Because of the looks he's giving me.

They give me the feeling he's having a similar problem pretending he's not thinking about me. And maybe wondering how he can get my mouth on him again.

But these kinds of weird, quasi-relationships are a terrible idea.

I can tell that neither of us are the settle-down types.

We don't date.

We don't commit.

We don't even like each other. We don't even *know* each other.

It's best to keep ignoring and avoiding each other.

Nothing good can come of this? Right?

But he *did* have a hell of a gorgeous cock, though…

BADD MEDICINE

...coming next year!

Jasinda Wilder

Visit me at my website: **www.jasindawilder.com**
Email me: **jasindawilder@gmail.com**

If you enjoyed this book, you can help others enjoy
it as well by recommending it to friends and family,
or by mentioning it in reading and discussion groups
and online forums. You can also review it on the
site from which you purchased it. But, whether
you recommend it to anyone else or not, thank you
so much for taking the time to read my book! Your
support means the world to me!

My other titles:

The Preacher's Son:
Unbound
Unleashed
Unbroken

Biker Billionaire:
Wild Ride

Big Girls Do It:
Better (#1), Wetter (#2), Wilder (#3), On Top (#4)
Married (#5)
On Christmas (#5.5)
Pregnant (#6)
Boxed Set

Rock Stars Do It:
Harder
Dirty
Forever
Boxed Set

From the world of *Big Girls* and *Rock Stars*:
Big Love Abroad

Delilah's Diary:
A Sexy Journey
La Vita Sexy
A Sexy Surrender

The Falling Series:
Falling Into You
Falling Into Us
Falling Under
Falling Away
Falling for Colton

The Ever Trilogy:
Forever & Always
After Forever
Saving Forever

The world of *Alpha*:
Alpha
Beta
Omega
Harris: Alpha One Security Book 1
Thresh: Alpha One Security Book 2
Duke: Alpha One Security Book 3
Puck: Alpha One Security Book 4

The world of Stripped:
Stripped
Trashed

The world of *Wounded*:
Wounded
Captured

The Houri Legends:
Jack and Djinn
Djinn and Tonic

The Madame X Series:

Madame X

Exposed

Exiled

The One Series

The Long Way Home

Where the Heart Is

There's No Place Like Home

Badd Brothers:

Badd Motherf*cker

Badd Ass

Badd to the Bone

Good Girl Gone Badd

Badd Luck

Badd Mojo

Big Badd Wolf

Badd Boy

Badd Kitty

Badd Business

Dad Bod Contracting

Hammered

Drilled

The Black Room
(With Jade London):
Door One
Door Two
Door Three
Door Four
Door Five
Door Six
Door Seven
Door Eight
Deleted Door

Standalone titles:
Yours

Non-Fiction titles:
You Can Do It
You Can Do It: Strength
You Can Do It: Fasting

Jack Wilder Titles:
The Missionary

To be informed of new releases and special offers,
sign up for
Jasinda's email newsletter.